TAB
THREE
D0361963

TABLE FOR THREE

RECHA G. PEAY

URBAN BOOKS

www.urbanbooks.net

This is a work of fiction. Any references or similarities to actual events, real people, living or dead, or to real locales are intended to give the novel a sense of reality. Any similarity in other names, characters, places, and incidents is entirely coincidental.

URBAN SOUL is published by

Urban Books
10 Brennan Place
Deer Park, NY 11729

ISBN-13: 978-1-59983-071-1
ISBN-10: 1-59983-071-X

First Printing: October 2009
10 9 8 7 6 5 4 3 2 1

Printed in the United States of America

To girlfriends
Ebone Corlecia Smith
Jerre Faulkner-Adams
Bernetta DeShelle Johnson
Linda Kee
Kristi Hunter-McCoy
Tonya Dionne Taylor
CJay (Risque Café)

Acknowledgments

First, I would like to thank God for His grace, which is renewed daily. Without Him, nothing is possible, but with Him, all things are possible. To Him, I owe the highest thanks and praise for the completion of this project.

Ebone Corlecia and Frederick Jermaine, thank you for making me smile during the most stressful times. The two of you always had the right things to say at the right times. I'm grateful to God for having you both in my life. To Eugene Jordan (Ruby), Jerre Adams "Lil Ma" (William, Jacques), Sam Faulkner (Barbara, Marquisa, Faith), and the entire Faulkner Clan, to you all, I owe a million thanks as you have supported me on every project. I love you all, and remember I am every one of you.

To the Urban family, thank you for another opportunity to express myself through the written word. I want to thank you for your patience and vision. Brenda Thomas, thank you for your time and talent. Kimberly Matthews (Kissed Publications, Inc.), thanks a million for being not only a great agent but an understanding friend.

Bernetta DeShelle Johnson, thanks for being a "big sister." I can't thank you enough for calling to check on me during crunch time.

Dr. Fred Howard, PhD, thank you for your prayers and encouragement during this project.

Thanks to all the book clubs and other social organizations for your support.

A special thanks to CJay @ Risque Café. Girlfriend, you had a vision for my success and hit the ground running. I can't thank you enough for all the time you've invested in marketing Recha G. Peay.

Readers, family, and friends, I love you with the love of God and know my success is directly proportional to your support!

Chapter 1

Shiquanna

Like a deck of cards, Shiquanna spread the crisp bills between her fingers, forming a fan. She arranged them from the highest to the lowest denomination, licked the tip of her thumb, and began to count. The bills snapped as she leafed through them, stacking them one on top of the other. "Twenty, forty, sixty, eighty . . . one hundred."

All clients had to agree with the terms of her cash-only, no-refund policy. The terms were nonnegotiable. Every hour was two hundred and fifty dollars. The fee was due immediately upon her arrival and had to be paid using bills no larger than a twenty. "Five hundred," she confirmed, speaking underneath her breath, then unconsciously repeated the process again. *It's all here. Now, that is music to my ears,* she thought. She made a tight roll of the bills, then lifted her right leg onto the marble-top vanity. "Shit," she spat, almost breaking an acrylic nail, as she opened the secret compartment in her wedge high-heel shoe.

She secured the payment inside the shoe, then lowered her leg to the floor. She unzipped her large black purse, which still hung on her shoulder, and peeped at her cell phone display. "Time is money." She hung the purse on one of three gold-plated door hooks, then unbuttoned her blue-jean mini shirt-dress just enough to ease it off of her shoulders and step out of it.

She looked in the ornate oval mirror above the sink, checked her heavily applied black mascara and eyeliner, then traced the outline of her lips with her index finger. Shiquanna was the epitome of beautiful and, for the first time, was held captive by her own reflection. In times past the haunting voice of her mother, Renita, had hindered her perception of her physical self. She took a step back, placed a hand on one hip, then leaned her head to one side. *Hmm . . . From this angle I look like Gabrielle Union in* Two Can Play That Game. *Some people get all the lucky breaks. I'd trade places with her on the big screen any day. My reality is hell. I go home most nights, to wake up the next morning, not always remembering how in the hell I made it there. I'm living alone, existing only in the moment, unsure who'll be used to get cash to pay my damn bills. Then, if no one calls, I go to that sleazy strip club in the hood to make ends meet. If anyone thinks I like dancing in a smoky room filled with strange men salivating with hard-ons, they're a damn fool.*

She smirked, then ran her fingers through her wig. No feature about her went unnoticed when she entered a room. Even though she was twenty-nine, her mocha skin was flawless, always giving her an ageless appearance. Many men were captivated and rendered speechless by her large brown eyes. Her natural hair, which she covered with synthetic tresses, was jet-black and hung several inches past her shoulders. It was as though God had descended from Heaven to adorn earth with one of His finest angels.

A white finger towel with WATERFORD HOTEL embroidered in gold stitching hung neatly from a holder to her left. To remove excess lipstick, she rubbed the towel between her thumb and index finger. She looked at the small stain, then rolled her eyes to the top of her head. For clients, she always wore ruby red lipstick. Their inconspicuous areas, particularly between the thighs, would be kissed aggressively, leaving lip impressions not so easily removed by soap and water. The purpose was twofold: entice the client and leave irrefutable evidence for a wife, girlfriend, or significant other. In a twisted sort of way, it was her means of retribution for a lifestyle she'd been forced into as a teenager.

Proudly, she leaned forward and adjusted her leather bra top to reveal more cleavage. The Ds she showcased were a gift from a loyal client for her nineteenth birthday. Even she loved what they did to enhance her twenty-six-inch waistline and forty-inch hips. Making sure her long, wavy black wig was still secure, she tugged one side, then readjusted a few hairpins. Wanting a more tousled look, she leaned her head forward, combed through her hair with her fingertips, then looked into the mirror. Pleased with the picture-perfect image, she blew a kiss at herself, then turned around, making sure the view looked just as good from behind.

"One for the road." Before opening the bathroom door, she reached inside her purse and pulled out a shot-sized bottle of tequila. She unscrewed the top, put the bottle to her lips, then tossed her head back. "Ahh, liquid courage. A woman's gotta do what a woman's gotta do. There's no way in hell I can look at that ugly asshole sober." Feeling light headed, she threw the top and bottle into the garbage can, then prepared to make a grand entrance. Slowly she opened the door.

Her new client, Elton Anderson, was already undressed and sitting on the foot of the plush king-size bed, which faced her direction. The married, presumably wealthy, real estate investor, with three children, a dog, and two cats, had come as a referral. Judging from the length of his legs, he stood over six feet three and weighed no more than 180 pounds soaking wet. His skin was darker than midnight and made the whites of his eyes seem translucent. He wore short dreads, had a mustache and a goatee. In no way did he appear kind on her eyes, so she swallowed hard, craving another shot of tequila.

Ready for the royal treatment, he spread his legs and lusted, looking at her five-foot-nine frame from head to toe. *Ha*, she chuckled inside as he leaned back on both elbows to emphasize what he considered an erection. *What in the hell am I going to do with that little thing? Is that an erection? I've seen raw hot dogs plumper than that,* she thought, careful not to speak or laugh aloud. She started to stroll toward him.

"Not so fast, baby doll." To stop her, he held up one hand, then rubbed himself with the other. "Stand there and let me look at you."

Time ticked in her head as she stopped, then placed one foot slightly in front of the other to pose. In her peripheral vision, she saw an armless chair to her left that could be used as a prop. Her movements seemed choreographed as she stepped to the side, placed one foot on the chair, then stood making sure he could see the golden prize between her legs. As if they were a lollipop with bubble gum inside, she licked two fingers, then allowed them to disappear between her thighs. His eyes bulged. Using her right hand, she spun the chair around, then placed a leg on each side to straddle it. With both hands, she grabbed the back of the chair, sat down slowly, then leaned backward until her head almost touched the floor.

"Damn, girl."

Using her stomach muscles, she rolled one vertebra at a time to sit erect, then stood, lifting the chair and moving it to one side. His breathing became shallow as she walked toward him, then with one hand pushed hard, making him fall backward onto the bed.

"That's what the hell I'm talking about. I love a woman who knows how to take control," he said, then let his arms fall limp to each side.

She stood between his legs, tenderly rubbed her breasts to tease him, then got down on her knees. The routine seemed rehearsed as she wrapped her fingers around the tiny projection and started to stroke it up and down. Lightly she blew.

"Oh, baby, that feels so good," he moaned, emphasizing every syllable.

She tightened her grasp, then lowered her head, covering his "shame" with her mouth. Her tongue became the bow, and his hardened manhood the strings of a violin.

"Mmm . . . ," he hummed as she maneuvered her tongue up and down, then side to side. "Yeess . . . yeess." He squirmed, gripping the sheets with his fingertips, giving her the cue to end the oral massage.

She pulled a condom out of her bra, ripped it open, and slid it on him. Like a cowgirl, she mounted him, then used her fingertips to position his manhood inside of her. Feeling nothing but the warmth from her own fingertips, she frowned. Beneath her, he'd already started to gyrate. Like a limp noodle, his manhood withered, then slipped. She reached to reposition him, but his gyrations never stopped. *Ain't this some shit?* He didn't even feel it slip out.

Shiquanna looked down, then chuckled at the Grammy Award nominee as he closed his eyes, then moved his head from side to side. *Hell, I can do this. Easy money. It's just easy money.* Not interrupting his fantasy, she leaned her body forward, eventually pressing her hands against his chest for support. A slow grind soon became aggressive thrusting up and down.

"Ride Roscoe like a cowgirl." His movements were out of sync as he gyrated beneath her, then slapped the bed with his hand. "You're making Roscoe feel so good." His eyebrows met when he grabbed her by the waist, then pulled her closer.

Roscoe? He had the nerve to name that little thing? Hell, I'm grinding against his pelvic bone, she thought, laughing inside at his antics, then rolling her eyes to the top of her head. Moving back and forward, she thrust, then used the back of her hand to wipe sweat from her forehead.

"Look into my eyes while you ride Roscoe." He

attempted to make eye contact, but she looked away. He placed his index finger on her chin, then turned her head toward him. Eye contact reminded her of a bleak adolescence, so she turned to look in the opposite direction.

"Baby, please look at Big Daddy. Nothing turns me on more than to look into a woman's eyes when she's on top of me."

Still maintaining a rhythmic thrust, Shiquanna closed her eyes, wanting to repress negative images of Renita. In silence she rode, thrusting harder and harder to force his orgasm.

"Oh, baby, this is it. I'm about to explode." He jerked uncontrollably, then fell limp beneath her.

"Time is up, cowboy," she announced after looking at the clock on the nightstand. It had been exactly two hours. With the same tenacity, she dismounted him, then got out of the bed.

"Can we cuddle for a few minutes?" he murmured, reaching out for her.

"Hell, no," she spat. "I came to make ends, not friends. It's all about finance, not romance. This is business, not pleasure, meaning body contact after sex is a no-no," she said affirmatively, snapped her neck, then moved her index finger from side to side.

Unable to move his body, he lifted his head to speak as she swished across the floor and into the bathroom. "Bitch, you're paid for."

"Your time is up." She slammed the bathroom door, then locked it, just in case he had any ideas. Shiquanna reached for her dress, then leaned back against the vanity. She closed her eyes, then lowered her head.

Shiquanna hadn't woken up one morning and

decided to become a stripper or escort. It wasn't her ideal career, but a lifestyle she'd been forced into. She'd grown up alone with Renita, her teenage mother, in a condemned housing project. Renita's own lack of parental guidance by a mother or father had led to pregnancy by fourteen. She'd been a latchkey child living in the projects, surrounded by little boys turned teenagers whose hormones raged out of control. Then one game too many of "just let me feel it" with a neighbor had led to pregnancy.

Renita's mother, who worked two full-time jobs to survive, had kicked her out, leaving her to deal with her own rebellion. Eight months later, with no prenatal care, Shiquanna was born in the emergency room of the city hospital. With nowhere to call home, Renita dropped out of school, then sought government assistance. Disgusted with life and all it didn't offer, she turned to drugs by age sixteen. It had started with the painkillers given after childbirth; these had created a desire for stronger narcotics and marijuana.

Like any impressionable single teenage mother, Renita met an older man on the streets who seemed to have it all. He had a home outside of the ghetto and several nice cars, and wore the latest fashions. He bought her a few nice outfits, took her out to dinner, and on one occasion paid her subsidized rent. Next, Renita was packing their clothes and moving in with him. Like a puppy on a leash, he led Renita into a world from which she never escaped. All in the name of love, he became her drug supplier and pimp.

His moderately sized three-bedroom, two-bathroom home was party central. Every night it was filled with strange people, alcohol, and layers of smoke. Like a sleazy motel, his bedroom was decorated in red velvet. Mood lights and a wet bar made his den look like a nightclub. For years Shiquanna's place was the back bedroom, until she developed the body of a woman. Then she was only fourteen.

One day, without knocking, Renita opened Shiquanna's bedroom door and leaned to one side. It was after school, and Shiquanna was sitting in the middle of her bed, studying for a test the next morning. For the most part, she did well in her classes and maintained a B average. She had vowed never to be like her mother and saw an education as her only way out of the jungle she lived in.

"We're going to the mall for some new clothes." Renita put the small white cigarette to her lips, inhaled, then blew the smoke to one side. She had a blank facial expression and glazed eyes.

"Thanks. I still have outfits with the tags on them hanging in the closet." Shiquanna's suspicion was aroused. Her mother never took her shopping. Mysteriously, clothes in the latest styles always appeared on the bed. Shiquanna didn't question Renita, even though the tags never matched the store names imprinted on the outside of the bags.

"I said we're going to the mall for some new clothes," her mother snapped, walked to the bed, then snatched her by the arm.

"Let go of me. You're high, and I'm not going anywhere with you." Shiquanna pulled away, threw her books to one side, and moved against the wall.

"You will do as I say." With one hand, Renita grabbed

Shiquanna's chin and pointed into her face with the other. Shiquanna moved her head from side to side, then stopped when Renita's nails dug into her skin.

"You're hurting me."

"No, you're hurting me." Finally, Renita let go, stormed out of the room, and slammed Shiquanna's door. "I'll be back in fifteen minutes," she yelled, then hit the door with her fist.

Unnerved by the unspoken implication of Renita's shopping request, Shiquanna felt her hands tremble as she rubbed her face.

Shiquanna's dreamlike state was interrupted when an old Brian McKnight tune blasted from her client's cell phone.

"Hey, babe," he answered calmly after a long pause.

Assuming it was his wife, Shiquanna moved closer to the bathroom door.

"Baby, please calm down. Your yelling is making it impossible for me to understand a word you're saying." There was another pause. "Didn't Jessica call you? Joseph called a last-minute financial meeting. I asked her to call you as soon as I found out. They sent her from a temporary service. You'd think she'd be capable of following simple instructions. I'll consult with her first thing in the morning I promise."

Financial meeting? Shiquanna thought, then folded her arms across her chest. *That lying bastard.*

"Please accept my apology. It wasn't my fault this time. Our meeting lasted longer than I anticipated. We're hashing out the final details on that multimillion-dollar land deal I talked to you about last month. I swear I'll make it up to you. Just think about the commission from that deal, baby," he said, then paused again. "Yeah, baby, I hear you. I can imagine how many hours you spent in the kitchen, preparing my favorite meal. I know it's not often that we have a babysitter. Sweetie, I'm very sorry I missed your special dinner. By the way, I'm starving. Listening to Joseph ramble for the past two hours, I've worked up an appetite."

"Ha, like hell you did," Shiquanna blurted.

"Just give me a few more minutes to make some important phone calls and wrap a few things up. In the meantime, go into the wine cellar and get that bottle of merlot I was saving for our anniversary. I want you to open it and pour yourself a glass. You really need to calm down. I don't want you upset when I get home. Remember, we still have the rest of the night to spend together alone."

Now that's why I'll never trust a man. He's in the bed, naked, with my sweat still all over him. Sorry bastard. I need another drink, she thought, ready to reach into her purse for another tequila shot. *Hell, that's right. It's girls' night out. I guess I can wait another hour.* Shiquanna slipped into her dress, grabbed her purse, then opened the bathroom door.

His back was against the headboard, and the sheet was across his legs. He winked at her, then tossed the sheet to one side. His nudeness and pathetic grin repulsed her.

"Hell, no." Not giving a damn if his wife heard, she strutted by the bed and slammed the door.

Chapter 2

India

After a stressful final exam in a world religion course titled The Names of God, India, who usually listened to motivational CDs, opted to ride home in silence. She had slept only two hours the night before and had gone past the point of exhaustion. Her head was throbbing, making her bloodshot eyes sensitive to the sun, which only peeked from behind the clouds. Even the warm air that barely blew through the vents of her 1990 Honda Civic was irritating. Deeming fresh air the better option, she turned off the AC, then rolled her windows down. Enjoying the cooler late spring breeze, she leaned her head to one side, ran her fingers through her natural locks, then rested her elbow on the door. All she wanted was to go home, shower, and relax at least an hour before meeting Yvonne and Shiquanna.

An occasional girls' night out with her friends

Yvonne Miller and Shiquanna Jenkins to socialize, momentarily forgetting life's issues, had become a weekly tradition one year ago. The Fortune 500 company to which Yvonne had devoted nine years, advancing from an entry-level accounting position to senior accounts manager, was downsizing, starting at the corporate level. India, for the twentieth time, had changed college majors and was overwhelmed by coursework. Shiquanna, whose only complaint was not being able to accommodate another millionaire client, just went along for the drinks.

India, Ms. Love, Peace, and Happiness, was the common denominator and the glue that bound the odd trio together. India had met Shiquanna in high school. They'd both been fifteen years old and in the tenth grade. She'd sat next to Shiquanna in pre-algebra, and a blind person could have seen how Shiquanna struggled. India excelled in all subjects, particularly math, and offered to tutor. India volunteered numerous times to help Shiquanna at home after school but would always get a harsh no. Finally, on the verge of failing the class, Shiquanna accepted but could only meet India thirty minutes before school started. The time restrictions seemed odd, but India wanted to help and agreed. Shiquanna passed pre-algebra, and they decided to take more classes together.

Senior year India was confronted with rumors that her friend danced nude in a sleazy strip club. The source wasn't reliable, as it was a former male graduate who had told a friend who had told another friend. From television shows and movies, India could only speculate about what strippers looked like. In her opinion, Shiquanna didn't dress or behave like a stripper, so India dismissed the rumors as such. Writing them off as child's play, India didn't confront Shiquanna with the rumors.

Three weeks before graduation, Shiquanna sped into the student parking lot, driving a slightly used red convertible Miata. A group of girls started malicious rumors about her having a pimp, and the rumors spread like a wildfire blazing out of control. Not privy to Shiquanna's true circumstances, India became more observant but didn't end their friendship.

As if overnight, Shiquanna's attitude about anything important changed drastically. Her walk changed. Even her look, which had once been beautifully innocent, changed. She started wearing heavy make-up and clothes so tight, a sneeze would break a rib. Again, she upgraded, and her designer clothes matched her shoes and her shoes matched her purse.

"To hell with this shit," Shiquanna blurted during their last study session before senior exams. They were sitting at a table together in the middle of the library. Almost instantaneously, necks snapped and heads turned to see the commotion.

"What?" India responded, with a quizzical expression, then looked around for their "no loud talking" rule–enforcing librarian. India was relieved to see her and a student in her office, with the door closed.

"I make more money in one night than some people have made in three months. I'm eighteen years old now. Legally I'm grown, and I don't need this school shit anymore. What does World War II have to do with me or my future? It for damn sure can't put no money in my pocket." Shiquanna slammed her history book closed, then jumped up from the table. She stood with her legs apart and put a hand on each hip.

"Sorry to destroy your fantasy, but you do need this," India responded, taken aback by the foul language, then grabbed her by the wrist. Shiquanna had always been withdrawn and had never used *damn* or *shit* in a sentence. "It may not seem important now, but you'll thank me later. Now sit down and finish studying." Unsure who'd taken over Shiquanna's body, India spoke aggressively while pointing at their stack of books. She leaned forward to speak into Shiquanna's ear. "Whatever you're doing to make so much money is none of my business. I've heard the rumors, and until you tell me out of your own mouth, they'll remain rumors. Hypothetically speaking, if they're true, you're not going to be eighteen years old forever. It doesn't take rocket science to conclude your income is directly proportional to your physical appearance. How long do you think your breasts will be perky and your glutei maximi firm?"

Shiquanna only stared, then leaned her head to one side as if to ponder the thought.

India went on. "Knowledge is power. A man can take your body, but he can't steal your knowledge. We graduate from high school next week."

"Whatever you say, little Ms. Gandhi. It's all peaches and cream to you. You don't know the real me or what I go through every day just to survive," Shiquanna said, then looked away. "Everybody ain't so lucky."

"You've told me nothing."

"That's how I want to keep it. If I tell you the truth, then you'll treat me like everybody else does." She pointed at a group of students who were listening to their argument intently. "What in the hell are you staring at?" Shiquanna snapped at the three female students sitting at the table next to them. "Do you like what you see?" Their necks rolled, but no one answered as they turned to look in another direction.

"My friend, have I ever treated you like everybody else does?" India asked sincerely, never taking her eyes off of Shiquanna. "Have I?" she asked again, wanting her complete attention.

"No." Shiquanna paused, looked down at the open books and notes that were spread across the table, then sat down. "India, believe me, it's a long story." She looked down, then shook her head from side to side. "I wish I had two parents at home that loved me. Hell, I'd settle for one parent that loved me."

"I can see the hurt in your eyes and feel the pain in your voice. We've been friends how long now?"

"Since the tenth grade, when I was struggling my ass off in pre-algebra class," Shiquanna said, with a half smile.

"If nothing else, you should know that you can trust me. Whenever you're ready to talk, I'm here."

"Yeah, girl, I hear you."

"Please, if you don't do anything else for yourself, at least graduate from high school," India pleaded. After a few seconds Shiquanna reopened the book and thumbed through the pages. India sighed from relief.

Shiquanna took and passed her final exams but

didn't show up for graduation. India prayed for her friend's safety, hoping she'd survive the risks of her new lifestyle. Several months later India received a phone call from Shiquanna just to say thanks for being there when no one else would. Shiquanna stayed true to her game, and India was accepted into a nearby university. They'd chosen different paths but vowed to touch bases at least once a week. It was only a matter of time before Shiquanna began to share her deepest secrets, hurt, and pain with India. Whether it was a telephone conversation or over lunch, their word remained their bond as their friendship developed over the years.

India's first interaction with Yvonne was bittersweet. Yvonne was already a senior in college when she met India, a first-semester freshman, in a philosophy class. How Yvonne passed the course was unclear, as she advocated only Jesus Christ and Christianity.

"What church do you attend?" India heard the question and knew it was the voice of the young woman behind her, but she didn't turn around to answer. Class had ended, so India started to pack her book bag. Then she felt a light tap on the shoulder.

She's sat behind me three weeks and introduces herself by asking what church I attend. Please tell me she's not one of those Holy Roller types, India thought to herself, inhaled, then turned around slowly. "I attend Bedside Baptist," she said, with a straight face.

"Excuse me?" Yvonne asked, then leaned forward because she didn't hear India's response or didn't believe how she'd responded.

"I attend Bedside Baptist," India responded confidently, then laughed inside. That candid response irritated every Sunday morning church attendee, including her mother and father. As a child, India had vowed that once she moved out of her parents' house, she'd go to church only for a wedding or a funeral.

Rain, shine, sleet, or snow, her family attended three services on Sunday and one during the week. In fact, her parents' union had begun in the children's Sunday school class. As teenagers, they'd dated secretly, then sealed their bond on a yearly church trip. Before her mother's pregnancy started to show, they were strongly advised by their pastor to marry. According to his interpretation of Scripture, it was the only way to make their act of lasciviousness right before God. Out of obedience to God and their fear of an eternity in hell, they had a private wedding ceremony. At the time her mother was eighteen and her father was twenty.

India believed in God but had never understood why she had to accept another man's interpretation of Holy Scripture. Why should she spend hours at church performing tasks that seemed unnecessary when she could read and study the Bible on her own? In her opinion, God wasn't deaf, blind, or dumb, so why did believers have to cry, scream, or run circles around the building to get His attention? She concluded that religion birthed hypocrites who would commit the sin, then hide behind the blood of Jesus.

"Oh my goodness." Yvonne put her hand on her chest. As if ashamed for India, she placed her hand over her mouth and shook her head from side to side. "My sister, everyone needs a church home," she said, then gave India that church mother rub on the shoulder, which irritated her just as much. India leaned away. "Sunday is the annual Friends and Family Day at my church. I would love for you to attend."

"Thanks, but no thanks," responded India, not wanting to get into a discussion that would undoubtedly cause a debate. She turned around. There was another tap on her shoulder. *Persistent,* India thought, then turned around slowly, ready to blurt the true reason she didn't attend a traditional church. "Yes?"

"I apologize for being rude." With a concerned facial expression, Yvonne placed a hand on her chest, then leaned forward. "My name is Yvonne Miller, and I attend Faith Believers Baptist Church, where Reverend Marion Alston is my pastor."

Following the dramatic introduction, India rolled her eyes to the top of her head.

"My sister, please let me buy your lunch. We need to talk."

Is sitting behind me and not speaking for three weeks sisterly? India thought to herself, with a slight attitude. That was the first of many invitations India refused. The crusade for Christianity continued until India finally accepted Yvonne's lunch invitation. A weekly debate during lunch became the basis of their friendship, which lasted beyond Yvonne's graduation.

The irony of it all made India smile as she turned into the driveway and parked outside the garage. She turned off the ignition, reached for her book bag, then got out of the car.

"Hello, sunshine."

India looked up. She still had the key in her hand

when the front door opened. "Tracey." There was a short pause. "Hi." Her tone was dry as she over-enunciated the one-syllable word.

"Baby, I missed you. Aren't you happy to see me?"

"You're home early." Surprised, India forced a smile at Tracey, who was standing in the middle of the doorway. She was wearing an apron and holding a wooden spoon. "I wasn't expecting to see you until after dinner tonight," she said. She readjusted her book bag, then eased by Tracey.

Tracey hunched her shoulders, then closed the front door. "A piano student canceled at the last minute, so I left the studio early, stopped by the market, then the liquor store. I remembered your final exam this morning and knew you'd be exhausted by the time you made it home."

"Really?" India said, then followed the aroma of fresh basil, garlic, and tomatoes down the hallway.

Tracey whistled a happy tune as she followed closely behind. "I prepared penne pasta with your favorite tomato-based sauce."

"Wow, it smells delicious." India stopped in the great room to rest her book bag against the couch.

"Baby, let me pour you a glass of wine." Gently, Tracey kissed her on the neck and rubbed her shoulder when she walked by.

"Did you forget I was meeting the girls for dinner tonight?" India turned around and saw the bottle of wine and two glasses already on the counter. Certain she'd told Tracey about her plans, she walked into the kitchen and leaned against the center cooking island.

Tracey walked to the stove, stirred the pasta, then

poured it into a colander placed across the sink. She placed the saucepan on the opposite side of the stove, then turned to face India. "I remembered." She sighed, picked up a wineglass, tilted it to one side, and started to pour. "I thought we could spend the evening together. It's not often I get out of the music studio before eight o'clock." She handed the filled glass to India, then poured one for herself.

India accepted her glass, then placed it on the counter. "Tracey, dinner looks great, and I'm sure it will taste just as good tomorrow evening. If you like, we can have a glass of wine together after I take my shower."

"Take your time. I'll fix your plate when you get out of the shower." Apparently ignoring India's comment, Tracey took a sip of wine, then placed her glass on the counter.

"This is my night out with the girls."

"Sunshine, that isn't a problem. We can eat my dinner tomorrow, and I'll have dinner with you and your friends tonight." As if it were a plan, Tracey picked up her glass, took a sip of wine, then toasted in the air.

"Tracey," India said to get her attention. "This is girls' night out."

"What am I?" Tracey's brows met as she stood back and pointed at herself from head to toe.

"You know what I'm talking about," India said, disappointed by Tracey's sly attempt to undermine her evening plans.

"When am I going to meet your friends? We've been living together for six months. We've been in this relationship two years. Don't you think it's time I meet someone other than your older sister?"

"I need time." Not wanting to argue, India backed toward the kitchen door, folded her arms across her chest, then took a deep breath. India remembered the last time Tracey had mentioned meeting her parents. A simple suggestion, "Let's invite your parents over for dinner," had turned into an argument that resulted in them not speaking for several days.

"How much more time do you need?"

"Tracey, I don't know," India said, then held both hands out in front of her. Being a lesbian wasn't a lifestyle that India had become totally comfortable with. Tracey was her first female lover. They were six months into the relationship before she mentioned it to her sister or Shiquanna.

"Tell me now. When will you know?"

Unable to give an honest answer, India folded both arms across her chest again, then leaned against the doorway. Tracey frowned, then placed her glass on the counter. As if mirroring India's image, Tracey folded her arms across her chest, then leaned against the counter. In silence they both stared into each other's eyes.

India had met Tracey at an outdoor summer festival that hosted live bands, food, and a variety of vendors. With a beverage in one hand and a lamb sandwich on pita bread in the other, India had paused to groove to a band. She was enjoying their rich island sound and decided to listen to the entire set. That particular day she was dressed comfortably in cut-up blue jeans and a white tank top, which were accessorized with huge loop earrings and bangle bracelets. Her natural locks were pulled back, as usual, with a head band, and she wore no make-up. What she didn't know was she'd captured the attention of the drummer from afar. Tracey rushed her last drum roll, then jumped off the stage, with sticks in hand, to introduce herself.

"What did you think?" Tracey asked, with a warm smile, then pointed toward the other band members, who were still onstage. Her breathing was labored from the mad dash she'd made toward India. She put a hand on each hip, then took a deep breath.

"It was fantastic. You made those drums talk."

"I'm glad you enjoyed it," Tracey responded, with a smile, then nodded her head up and down. "Please let me introduce myself. My name is Tracey Atkins." Still smiling, she extended her hand.

"Tracey, it's nice to meet you." Mesmerized by Tracey's large green eyes, India smiled and shook her hand. Her caramel skin tone, naturally thick, wavy hair, and unusual eye color made Tracey's ethnicity hard to determine. She was wearing a pair of loose-fitting faded blue jeans and a white T-shirt, with a printed cotton vest on top.

"What's your name?"

"My name is India."

"Wow, that's beautiful, and it suits you so well."

"Thank you." India stared into Tracey's eyes.

"If you liked the music, we'll be playing another set in thirty minutes."

"I really did, but I'm alone, and it will be getting dark very soon." India pointed toward the sun, which was already starting to hide its face behind the horizon.

"A sunset serenade will make it even better," Tracey

responded, then looked in the direction of the sun. "I would love for you to stay." She moved closer, decreasing the amount of space between them.

"It's really getting late, and I have class first thing in the morning." India stepped back, then looked around.

"Do you live nearby?"

"Maybe." Since she was unwilling to divulge personal information to a complete stranger, her answer was short.

"If you stay, I will follow you home and walk you to your front door." Tracey rubbed India gently on the top of her hand. "That is, if your boyfriend will not be offended."

"I would love to stay, but I really need to go." India hesitated, not responding to Tracey's boyfriend comment, took another step back, then looked down at her hand. Her eyes became large when a chill went down her spine. That reaction bothered her.

"I apologize if I'm making you uncomfortable." With both hands in the air, Tracey took a step back.

"I'm fine." Hugging or even touching another woman as a friendly gesture wasn't uncommon. But no woman had ever given her goose bumps. Tracey's touch was gentle, and her eyes were warm.

"I know this is crazy, and you don't know me from Adam, but I promise I'm harmless. If you decide not to stay, believe me, I understand."

"My apartment is only ten minutes away." Questioning and almost ashamed of her physical reaction to Tracey's touch, India looked away briefly.

"Is that a yes?" Tracey asked, with a huge smile.

"Yes." Confirming her response, India nodded her head up and down.

"Great." As if nervous, Tracey patted the side of her leg. "Great," she said again, still smiling at India. "I see that you've already eaten, but is there anything else I can get for you during our break?"

"Thank you very much, but I'm fine." India smiled, then nodded her head up and down slowly. She'd, in so many unspoken terms, agreed to a date with a woman.

"Are you sure?" Tracey asked, then rubbed her shoulder.

"I'm positive."

The two of them talked until Tracey heard the lead guitar player introducing the band. Again, she gently rubbed the top of India's hand, then hurried to take her place on the stage. Feeling a strong connection, India watched as Tracey took her place behind the drums and began to play.

"India, I love you and will do anything for you. But at some point you'll have to make a decision about our relationship. I can't be your little secret forever." Tracey leaned against the counter and finished her glass of wine.

Still daydreaming about their first encounter, India rubbed the top of her hand, then looked across the kitchen at Tracey. India saw the sincerity in her eyes. Without responding, she went into the bedroom to shower and change.

Chapter 3

Yvonne

"Hola. Cómo está, usted?" the dark-haired, medium-built Hispanic gentleman said loudly once Yvonne opened the door and stepped inside the lobby area. With one hand, he gestured toward the main dining entryway, then moved to one side.

Feeling uncomfortable with the location of Shiquanna's restaurant choice, Yvonne clutched her purse to secure it underneath her arm. "Hola," she said tentatively. Instead of returning the friendly smile with which she was greeted, she curled the corners of her mouth.

Ethnic music blared from hidden speakers, and loud voices competed with it. Out front, the white wooden sign with peeling paint and hand-painted letters said EL REYES AUTHENTIC MEXICAN DINING. Yvonne begged to differ, as the restaurant was located in the heart of the ghetto and was surrounded on each side by housing projects. In

Yvonne's opinion, Shiquanna's interpretation of fine dining was a number two combo at a twenty-four-hour establishment that looked like your great-grandmother's kitchen.

"Bienvenido a El Reyes," said the Hispanic host. He took a few steps forward, then looked around the room.

"I'm sorry, but hello is the extent of my Spanish vocabulary," Yvonne responded while observing the bright, multicolored decor. The eccentric color combination of red, yellow, orange, and green made her eyes dance. The already small Mexican restaurant was divided into three sections, and a large bar overwhelmed the far rear corner. Each section was painted a different primary color, and an assortment of ceramic sunburst plaques, world maps, and sombreros covered the walls. Excluding the makeshift lobby in which she stood, with one wooden bench and two chairs, the restaurant already seemed filled to capacity.

"No habla español? I'm so sorry." He moved his head from side to side, then chuckled. "Welcome to El Reyes. Will anyone else be joining the beautiful lady?" Wearing a smirk, he turned to look over her shoulder.

"Yes," she responded firmly, not impressed with his flirtatious comment. She inched forward, then noticed the unframed health department certificate posted with thumbtacks on a corkboard behind the cash register. The certificate was wrinkled, but the numbers nine and four were written boldly with a black Sharpie. *Impossible*, she thought to herself when a gentleman with a long ponytail used a tray filled with plates to force his way through two swinging doors. *Oh my goodness. This place is a madhouse.* She cringed when she got a glimpse of two male employees tossing a plastic bag of something back and forth across a counter. She leaned back to see more of the kitchen, but the swinging doors obstructed her view.

"Would you like to wait in the lobby, or should I find you a seat now?" asked the host. As if his behavior was normal in this establishment, the host moved to one side when the waiter with the ponytail rushed by. Even though the waiter wore a dingy white apron, Yvonne couldn't help but notice his faded blue jeans, which were torn on both knees. No other patrons seemed to care as he held the tray high above his head, then weaved through the aisles, finally stopping at a table in the rear. Yvonne held her breath as he placed the plates on the table, then hurried back through the same set of swinging doors.

This place is insane. The kitchen looks like a three-ring circus. I'm a thirty-four-year-old professional African American woman with a master's in business administration. A woman of my status shouldn't be caught dead in this atmosphere, not to mention this neighborhood. With a notion to leave, she scanned the restaurant, then exhaled when she didn't see India or Shiquanna already seated. Looking for them was only a stubborn habit as Yvonne was the first to arrive every week. Impatiently, she tapped the ball of her foot against the floor, then turned toward the door.

"Would you like to wait for your friends in the lobby?" the waiter asked, sensing her urgency.

"I need a table for three," Yvonne responded when three giggling women and two outspoken men entered. She looked at the group, then entertained a devious thought. *If I let them go first and wait in the lobby, maybe all the seats will be taken when Shiquanna and India arrive.*

The waiter grabbed a stack of spiral-bound menus and silverware wrapped in paper napkins off of the counter. "Senorita, please follow me." He waved his hand to get Yvonne's attention.

Just then her cell phone started to vibrate. As she expected, it was India. "You're running late, and you will be here in about fifteen minutes," Yvonne said sarcastically as she followed the gentleman down the short and narrow aisle. She nodded her head up and down when he pointed at a booth next to a window overlooking the patio.

"Not this time. I'm turning into the parking lot now," said India.

"Sure you are." Not wanting to ruin her new silk skirt ensemble, Yvonne frowned after looking down at the worn wooden seats. She rolled her eyes, looked around for an empty table, then blew after seeing a small square table in the middle of the room. "This will be fine," she said softly to the waiter. Using her free hand, she tucked her skirt tightly beneath her, slid between the table and a seat, then sat down carefully. To shield her eyes from the sun, she placed a hand over her eyebrows, then looked out the window for a Honda Civic with four shades of red paint. "I thought you were driving into the parking lot?" she asked, not seeing India's car, which they kindly referred to as Betsy.

"I'm parking now. I'll see you in a couple of minutes."

"What in the world was that horrible noise?"

Yvonne asked, startled by the clunking noise she heard in the background.

"I just turned off the ignition. All Betsy needs is a tune-up."

"It sounds like Betsy needs more than a tune-up. It's been how many years? I'm sure you could use a new car." Knowing India could care less about the car she drove, Yvonne smiled, then shook her head from side to side.

"Is Shiquanna there yet?"

"No," Yvonne said, then frowned, knowing she wouldn't be disappointed if Shiquanna didn't show up. In Yvonne's opinion, Shiquanna was the poster child for ghetto fabulous. She was loud, she drank like a sailor, and every other word that came out of her mouth was profane.

"May I get you anything to drink while you wait on your guests?" the waiter asked after detecting a pause in her conversation.

"We'll have bottled spring water and a bowl of fresh cut lemons," India said, then leaned down to hug Yvonne around the neck. Yvonne looked at her cell phone, then smiled as she reached up to hug India.

"Excuse me?" the waiter asked, with a look of confusion.

"That would be two bottles of spring water and a bowl with a freshly cut lemon in it." As though he couldn't comprehend English, India spoke slowly and gestured with her hands.

Unsure what India expected from Shiquanna's poor restaurant choice, Yvonne shook her head.

"Sorry, senorita, but we only have bottled drinking water. Nothing fancy," said the waiter.

"That will be fine," Yvonne responded as India parted her lips and lifted her hand to say more.

"Senorita, may I get anything else for you?" He looked at Yvonne, then leaned his head slightly to one side.

"Thank you, but that's it for now," Yvonne responded.

"Be back with your waters." He smiled, turned his eyes toward India, then walked away.

"Would you please sit down? This is El Reyes, not one of your all-natural specialty food cafés." Yvonne motioned with her hand for India to be seated. "Not to mention Shiquanna chose this place, so be glad they have tap water."

"You know how I am about drinking from the tap. Do you know how many harmful chemicals are present in an eight-ounce glass of tap water?"

"No, I don't," Yvonne answered sternly, not wanting to hear a ten-minute environmental infomercial, then folded her arms on the table. "When did this health-food-craze phase start, anyway? When we met in college, you'd eat whatever you could afford."

"Knowledge is power." India shook her head, removed her large purse from around her neck, then sat down. "Where is Shiquanna?" She looked toward the door, then slid one of the laminated menus across the table and picked it up.

"When has Shiquanna ever been on time?" Yvonne asked, then rolled her eyes toward the door.

"Just thought I would ask," India said, then frowned as she glanced at the menu. "Guess she had another late night."

"Jesus, please don't go there. Her lifestyle is an abomination in the sight of the Lord, and you know it." To discourage any details, Yvonne held up her hand. The thought of Shiquanna squirming up and down a silver pole in front of strange men repulsed her.

Yvonne was an only child and grew up in a very strict Southern Baptist household. Her mother was forty-one and her father was forty-five when she was born. They'd married during her mother's sophomore year in college but decided to put their education and careers first. Yvonne's father was a tax attorney, and her mother was an assistant hospital administrator. Her parents were the only African Americans in their gated community and were registered Republicans.

Both parents were workaholics, but they made sure Yvonne's daily routine wasn't interrupted. Instead of sending her to preschool, her parents hired a tutor to work with her at home. Miss Rosita, the nanny, cooked, cleaned, and drove Yvonne to all her dance and piano classes. Yvonne attended the best private schools, where she became well versed in Scripture and graduated in the top 10 percent of her high school class. Ninety percent of her classmates were Caucasian, so growing up, she never befriended an African American. At times she questioned her own race.

Before high school graduation, Yvonne decided to attend the local university. She confided in her parents, letting them know she wanted to be around a more diverse group of students. They despised the idea and threatened to withhold the funds set aside for her education. A day didn't go by when she wasn't reminded by either parent of how hard they'd worked to get out of the ghetto. Their own parents were uneducated, and both of their pasts were filled with struggle and hardship. Their objections only increased Yvonne's determination to attend the local university. She applied and was granted a full scholarship.

Yvonne accepted the scholarship, but she wasn't prepared for the school's social, ethnic, or economic diversity. She didn't like the atmosphere, the student-to-teacher ratio was large, the counselors were impersonal, and her dorm room felt like a prison. Befriending African Americans became a priority, but she never fit in. They all accused her of acting like a white girl. She was out of her element but wouldn't admit her mistake to either parent. She learned a tough lesson in social-class division, managed to graduate with honors, and obtained her master's degree from a private college.

"What does Jesus have to do with it?" India placed her menu on the table, positioned one hand on top of the other, then looked at Yvonne.

"He has everything to do with it. You need to pray for your friend."

"*I* need to pray for her? She's your friend, too."

"Not exactly. I met her through you. Never in a million years would I have associated myself with a who—" Yvonne's lips were formed to complete her sentence.

"Oh, hello, girlfriend. We were just talking about you," India said, with a huge smile, then looked toward the aisle.

Yvonne heard the sound of stiletto heels against

the hardwood floors and turned her head to look over her shoulder.

"What's up?" Shiquanna asked once she got closer to the table.

"We've been here twenty minutes already," Yvonne said, looking at her from head to toe, unsure why she was stunned by her outfit or lack of one. Shiquanna wore a black micro-mini shirt-dress, with a slit on each side and unbuttoned to the bottom of her breast.

"Damn, girl, loosen up a little. It is only dinner, not an IRS audit," Shiquanna said sharply, snapping her neck, then putting a hand on her hip. "Honey, move over." She motioned with her hand for India to move closer to the window. As if campaigning for potential clients, she arched her back, tossed her hair over one shoulder, then sat down.

Yvonne's eyes rolled. Just then the waiter returned with two glasses of water.

"Hola, senorita," he said sensually, emphasizing every syllable. "Can I get your usual for you today?"

"Jose, you know me so well. Let me have my Grand Margarita with an extra shot of Patrón." Shiquanna arched her back to reveal cleavage, then waved her hand at him.

"A Grand Margarita with a shot of Patrón," he repeated as his eyes were drawn to her breasts. "Are you ladies ready to order, or do you need a few more minutes to look at the menu?" he asked, never taking his eyes off of Shiquanna's cleavage.

"I'm ready," Shiquanna volunteered. "I'll have the usual."

"That will be one enchilada combo with rice coming up for my beautiful queen." He smiled.

"I would like a few more minutes to look over the menu," Yvonne interjected. She placed her index finger on her chin, then stared at Shiquanna, who seemed to be a frequenter.

"So what the hell you been doing for the past twenty minutes?" Shiquanna blurted.

"We've been discussing your salvation," Yvonne offered, then leaned her head to one side.

"Ha! Well, who in the hell is going to save you, Ms. Goody Two-shoes? So don't start that shit with me today, because I'm not in the damn mood, and I'm tired as hell."

"Sir, please give us a few more minutes," India said ever so calmly, then waved her hand in front of Shiquanna's face to change the topic.

"My queen, I'll be back with your drink. Maybe your friends will be ready to order," said Jose.

"Thank you," India said. "Do the two of you have to disagree every time we're together?"

"Hell, yes!" Shiquanna exclaimed, then frowned.

India and Yvonne laughed at the same time; then each picked up a menu. They glanced over it, then placed their orders when the waiter returned with Shiquanna's drink.

"How was your day?" India asked Yvonne calmly.

"It was fantastic. I volunteered at the church four hours today."

"Volunteered?" Shiquanna interjected. "So that means you spent four hours at the church doing something for free."

"Yes, I did. I'm helping the financial secretary create a database," Yvonne explained.

"Uh-huh. Baby, ain't nobody doing nothing for free," remarked Shiquanna.

"Well, of course, nothing is free in your line of work," Yvonne retorted, remembering the shock from their first encounter. She was meeting India, then her former colleague, for lunch and knew only that one of India's good friends from high school was going to join them. Yvonne had agreed to the get-together but had never imagined the woman that walked through the door, wearing three-inch heels, black leather hot pants, and a bra top, as that friend. Yvonne's lips had fallen apart when Shiquanna sat down and India made the introduction. Yvonne had been speechless but had extended her hand as she stared at the woman, who looked like she had just left a strip club. Shiquanna had seemed restless, had eaten her meal in a hurry, then had made a mad dash toward the door when she received a phone call. "Is she a stripper?" Yvonne had asked India discreetly once her friend left. Yvonne had interpreted India's silence as a yes.

"Naw, girlfriend, let's be real about the situation." Shiquanna leaned her head to one side, then pointed at Yvonne. "You haven't worked in how many months now?"

Wanting to ignore Shiquanna, Yvonne looked at India.

"Well, I will answer for you. I know it's been at least three months," said Shiquanna. "Now let's do the math. You have that fancy-ass condo, and you driving that cute little convertible BMW."

"Shiquanna," India sang.

"Aw, hell naw, I'm not done yet," Shiquanna declared. "Not to mention every time I see you, you got on a new pair of shoes or you're carrying a new purse. So tell me, little Miss Executive, how can a woman without a job still afford your lifestyle?"

Yvonne shook her head. "For your information, unlike you, I have a career that comes with benefits. Do you know what those are? For example, a four-oh-one (k) plan, health insurance, a checking account or savings account?"

"Ladies, I'd like to have a conversation," India interjected. Wanting to hear Yvonne's news, India waved her hand at Shiquanna. "Yvonne, please tell me about your project at the church."

"Over the past year the church membership has doubled, making it impossible to do accounting tasks the old-fashioned way. So I'm creating a database that will be multifunctional and make their jobs ten times easier," Yvonne reported.

"Yvonne, it's impressive that you're doing it for free. Anyone else would charge them by the hour," said India.

"I'm more than blessed, not to mention I have a job interview in the morning. It's for a position I applied for only three weeks ago. But I must admit, volunteering at the church three days a week has been the answer to the first of several prayers." Yvonne smiled when she visualized her pastor.

"I still think you're crazy. There's no way in hell I would have turned down that last job offer with the city. Hell, you'd have been working with the mayor, right?" Shiquanna asked, then poured the extra shot of Patrón into her margarita.

"Yes, I would have been working closely with the mayor and his staff," Yvonne confirmed.

"How much did they offer you? With all of those damn letters behind your name, I know it was at least eighty thousand," Shiquanna blurted. She swirled her straw, then took a huge sip of her jumbo margarita.

"I'm sorry, but for some of us, it isn't always about the money. Is it, India?" Yvonne asked, then looked at India, who hadn't worked at a real job since she'd known her.

"Hell, you know she's going to agree. Other than summer camp or tutoring students, she's never worked at a real job," said Shiquanna.

"I beg to differ," India said slowly. "All my jobs have been real jobs."

"Ha." Shiquanna took another drink. "Let's be real. You call tutoring a bunch of bad-ass teenagers a few days a week real employment?"

"We all have a divine purpose in this universe. Being in constant search of wealth and material gain is a selfish desire," India said, then leaned back when two waiters returned with their food and placed it on the table.

"Yeah, sure. I can't survive off of air. Baby, I need money and a hell of a lot of it to survive," Shiquanna said, then reached for her silverware.

"So is that the reason why you're willing to break every commandment in the Bible for it? Your body is your temple and should be preserved for the one man God has ordained for you to spend your life with. It should be kept holy and undefiled. Ten years ago I rededicated my life to God, and I've been celibate ever since." Yvonne closed her eyes for a moment of prayer, then reached for a napking and silverware.

"Oh, hell. You mean to tell me you ain't had none in ten years?" Shiquanna all but shouted across the table. "Well, that explains it all, then. That's why you stay all up in the church. You can't fool me, sister girl. Your uptight ass needs some—"

"Shiquanna, don't you dare," India interjected.

"Seducing men, especially those sex-craved married men, has to be an abomination in the sight of God." With a look of concern, Yvonne unfolded her paper napkin and wiped each piece of silverware before placing it on the edge of her plate.

"You really don't want to go there with me." Shiquanna waved her index finger in the air. "You may go to church every Sunday, but you don't want to go to war with me. I know the Bible, girlfriend."

"Knowing the word of God and living it are two totally different things. A lot of people, including Satan himself, know the Scripture." Ready to put on the whole armor of God, Yvonne opened her purse and placed a hand on the small Bible.

"All right, Ms. Perfect, you mean to tell me you follow it to the letter?" With her fork, Shiquanna cut a piece of enchilada, put it into her mouth, then started to chew aggressively.

"Ladies, please let's not ruin our dinner talking about the mental strongholds of religion," India said, finally easing her way back into the conversation.

"No, India, she started it, and I'm for damn sure going to finish it. This is our girls' night out, right?" Shiquanna asked.

"Yes, but not the way I ever intended it to be. We're here to unwind and relax." India looked at Yvonne, then leaned her head to one side.

"We're three adults. Let's finish the conversation like adults." Shiquanna took another bite of food, then twirled her fork in the air. "Now back to you, girlfriend. So you mean to tell me you follow every commandment in the Bible?"

"God sent His only son to die for our sins. Everyone, from the least to the greatest, falls short of the glory of God." Meticulously, Yvonne lifted her knife and fork, then cut into her grilled salmon. She examined the small piece, then put it into her mouth. Slowly she chewed, then swallowed.

"Would you answer my damn question?" Shiquanna asked, then tapped her fork on the side of the plate. "Do you follow every commandment in the Bible?"

Yvonne shook her head. "Only one perfect man walked the face of the earth, and his name was . . ."

"You're just like the other Bible toters I've ever met in my life. So don't get mad at me for pleasing the husband of a woman who will not go down, because it isn't in the Bible." Shiquanna cut off another piece of enchilada and tossed it into her mouth. She chewed, swallowed, then used both hands to pick up her jumbo margarita glass. She toasted the air.

"I rebuke Satan right now in the name of Jesus." In total disbelief, Yvonne removed the small Bible from her purse and fanned it in Shiquanna's face.

India rolled her eyes to the top of her head, then looked around the room.

"You can rebuke him all you want to. The truth is the truth. You churchwomen get on my last nerve. You're so proper and ethically correct. If you ask me, I think you all are just a bunch of damn hypocrites with a shitload of skeletons in your closet," Shiquanna blurted, so loud that the couple seated in front of them turned to look. Then there was dead silence.

"May the Lord have mercy on your soul. Shiquanna Jenkins, you need Jesus, and I mean right now." As if she was feeling the Holy Ghost, Yvonne leaned her head back and waved both hands in the air.

As though watching a tennis match, India folded her arms across her chest, then looked at Shiquanna.

"Girlfriend, I got all the Jesus I need. My clients call him several times before I'm done riding them." Shiquanna rolled her hips in her seat, then moistened her lips with her tongue.

"Shiquanna." India's eyes got large. She placed one arm across Shiquanna's chest and held her hand up at Yvonne.

"Well, it's the truth," Shiquanna said, leaning forward, then moving her neck from side to side.

"Excuse me." Yvonne waved her hand to get Jose's attention. Her plate was still full, and India hadn't taken a bite of her meal. "May I have the check please?" she called. To check the time, she reached inside of her purse for the cell phone. "If I leave now, I'll make it to Bible study ten minutes early."

"Bible study?" Shiquanna asked, with raised eyebrows.

"Why are you acting brand new? You know I go to Bible study every week," Yvonne returned.

"That's the problem. You go to Sunday school, morning service, and everything in between. Hell, you should have the Bible memorized by now," Shiquanna quipped.

Yvonne nodded. "I'm working on it. You should join me this evening. Everyone needs prayer."

"Girls . . . girls, enough is enough," India said calmly to ease the tension between them.

"Don't worry, India. I'm going to the house of the Lord. In the name of Jesus, I rebuke Satan right now." Yvonne snatched the paper napkin off of her lap, then snapped it at Shiquanna.

"There she goes. I rebuke Satan this . . . I rebuke Satan that," Shiquanna said. She looked at India, then snapped her neck at Yvonne. "While you're rebuking, throw one in for yourself." Playfully, Shiquanna made the same snapping motion in the air with her hand.

"Ticket please," Yvonne said, louder this time, to Jose, who was standing on the other side of the room. He smiled, then walked toward their table.

"Will these be paid together or separately?" he asked.

"They'll be together. I'm in a hurry." Before anyone could respond, Yvonne had taken the ticket out of his hand. She glanced at it, looked through her wallet, then removed three twenty-dollar bills. She placed them on top of the ticket, then handed everything to him. "Keep the change," she said, then waved him away from the table.

"Thank you, my sister," India said poetically.

"Humph," Shiquanna said below her breath but loud enough for Yvonne to hear.

"My sister, please take care of yourself." India blew Yvonne a friendly kiss, then stared at Shiquanna.

"Next time," Shiquanna grunted, then looked out of the window.

"You're welcome, India. It was my pleasure. Next

week we're meeting downtown, at Chez Lorenz. I'll call you with the details." Yvonne stood, rolled her eyes to the top of her head, but couldn't resist an outburst of laughter.

India looked as Shiquanna fought not to turn her head toward Yvonne, then laughed.

"I love you, too, girlfriend." Yvonne blew a kiss at them both, exited the restaurant, and hurried to her car.

Chapter 4

Shiquanna

"That's your damn friend," Shiquanna said loudly, rolling her eyes at Yvonne as she walked toward the door. She wanted Yvonne to hear her comment as theirs quickly became a love-hate relationship.

"No, she's *our* friend," India said, then touched her bean burrito with a fingertip, making sure it wasn't too cold to eat. She removed her silverware from the napkin, then placed it across her lap.

"She's full of shit. I told you that after the first time I met her at the coffee shop on campus. I will never forget how she looked at me from head to toe, turned up her nose, then extended her hand like a princess. I guess she thought I was going to kiss the damn thing. Ha." Shiquanna laughed aloud, then rolled her neck. "After I sat down, what was the first thing she asked me? I know you remember." Each corner of her mouth turned up.

"Hell, she didn't even give me a chance to pick up the damn menu."

India laughed, cut into her burrito, then took a bite.

"Ha . . . ha," said Shiquanna. "She asked me the name of my church. Could you believe that shit?" India opened her mouth to speak, but Shiquanna interrupted with the wave of her hand. "Oh, hell, never mind. There's something about her that's not right. Dealing with all these low-down-ass men has taught me a lot about character. She tries too hard to make everyone think she's so damn perfect. She's hiding her real flaws from you. I can feel it in my gut."

"No one, including me, is perfect. I think I'm in love with a woman," India said, pointed at herself, then shook her head from side to side. "All this time, just to avoid her sermons of salvation and redemption, I've allowed her to think Tracey is a man."

"Damn that. What gives her the right to criticize either of us whenever we're together?" Shiquanna asked, then used her fork to combine the last bit of rice left on her plate.

"We've been friends for how many years now? So you know how she is when it comes to dealing with moral or religious issues. She can't see past what her preacher, who's human like you and I, tells her is in the Bible."

"Yeah, she's a hypocrite, just like half of my clients. They're married, and they take their little wifey and runny-nosed children to church every Sunday morning. They praise God, pay penance for their sins, then eat family dinner at a restaurant afterwards. To their neighbors, friends, and church members, they're the picture perfect little family." To emphasize her point, Shiquanna used her fingers to make quotation marks in the air. "Well, let me tell you the low-down and dirty truth. No sooner than that man can get everyone out of the car and into the house, he's blowing up my cell phone. Now, go figure that shit out."

"Shiquanna, I love you, but why are you so bitter toward her?"

"Just like today. You'll never admit it, but I know she had a problem with this restaurant," Shiquanna said, then looked around the room, which was still filled to capacity and bursting with conversation and laughter.

"Why would you say that? She didn't say anything negative to me about it."

"You're so naive. Girlfriend, due to the nature of my business, I'm always on guard. I see and hear everything."

"You didn't see or hear anything," India responded, certain there was no way she had heard Yvonne's comments about her.

"The hell I didn't. Girlfriend, a blind man could have seen how tense she was when I walked in. She was clenching her damn purse so tight underneath her arm, I thought it was going to rip at the seams. Plus, the heffa doesn't know how to whisper. I heard her little nasty-ass comment. It was something about me needing prayer. Your recovery was nice, just a little too late. Plus, she wiped off all her damn silverware with a napkin, then looked at her meal like it had legs."

"That's just how she is." India hunched her shoulders and nodded her head up and down. "I'm sure her concern for you is genuine. I've always worried about you and your safety."

"Genuine, my ass. Does she honestly think I enjoy sliding up and down that cold-ass pole three or four nights a week? Well, I don't. I never have and never will. That lifestyle found me. I wasn't looking for it. Watching married men drool over me and throw an occasional wrinkled-ass one-dollar bill they've saved from lunch money my way disgusts me. For that reason, I will never trust a man, let alone fall in love. If you ask me, ain't none of them about shit. My real daddy, whoever or wherever he is, may be included. So I'm sure she has some damn skeletons in her closet. Hell, probably more than she has designer pumps and matching purses. I'm willing to bet a whole night's pay on that one."

"Chill out, girl." India held up both hands.

"Why is she volunteering at the church so much when she needs to find a damn job? The state offered her more money and better benefits than the job she lost. Go figure that shit out. She ain't telling the whole truth, and you know it." Shiquanna waved her fork at India.

"It's not always about the money," India added, even though she, too, questioned Yvonne's decision.

"The hell it ain't. All right, little Miss Buddha. Tell me, what is it about?" Shiquanna let her fork fall down on her empty plate.

"It's about personal fulfillment."

"Personal fulfillment? Speaking of personal fulfillment, excuse me." Shiquanna felt her cell phone vibrate, so she reached into her purse to remove it.

She looked at the caller ID, then cleared her throat. It happened to be her most frequent yet disgusting client, Judge Ronald Haskins. Using a sensual bedroom voice, she answered generically. "Hello, sexy." Even though she knew for certain who it was, she'd learned never to use a name. A few years ago name confusion cost her one valuable client. Every client knew the nature of her business but wanted to believe he was the only one.

"Thirty minutes," he whispered, letting her know he was sneaking a phone call from his home. Familiar with his sly character, she guessed his wife of fifteen years was in the kitchen, decorating cookies for their three children.

"Boo, I got you. Do you have any special requests?"

"The usual is all I need," he answered in a hurry, then ended the call.

"Duty calls." Shiquanna looked at India, then leaned her head to one side. *Duty calls,* she thought to herself, feeling wrinkles form across her forehead. She picked up her glass, then swirled it to mix up the last bit of margarita. She moved the straw to one side, lifted the glass, then placed it to her lips. In one swallow, the last of her drink was gone. She leaned her head to one side, looked at the empty glass, then placed it on the table.

"Will I see you next week?" India asked, with a look of concern.

"Maybe."

"Peace, my sister."

Shiquanna grabbed her oversize purse, stood, then walked toward the door. Before exiting, she paused, placing her hand on the door, but never looked back.

Chapter 5

India

Be careful, my friend, India thought to herself when Shiquanna pushed the door open and walked through it. She stared across the room for a second, then looked down at her half-eaten meal. All she could really think about was the argument she'd had with Tracey. In deep thought, she picked up her fork and moved the rice around her plate with it. *Is Tracey still upset? How long will she deal with my uncertainty? She truly loves me and goes out of her way on a daily basis to prove it. Now I have to ask myself, what has kept me in the relationship for so long, and do I love her back?* Without taking one bite of food, she gently placed her fork on the side of her plate. She wiped her mouth, placed the napkin on her plate, then inhaled deeply. Unsure what mood to expect from Tracey, she wasn't in a hurry to leave. But in Tracey's defense, she had every right to be upset.

With a look of disappointment, India looked to

her right, then straight ahead. The seats her best girlfriends—only girlfriends, for that matter—had occupied were empty. This was one time she'd wanted to pour her heart out to them, ask questions, and get feedback about her own situation. But both of them had seemed caught up in the throes of their own madness, leaving her to deal with her own privately. Knowing she'd soon be faced with the reality of her situation, she got her purse, then stood to leave. She took a few steps, looked over her shoulder at the empty plates her friends had left behind, then walked toward the door.

"Have a good evening, senorita," their waiter, Jose, said, with a huge smile. "Please come back to see us again." He waved good-bye as she walked through the door.

"Come on, Betsy, and start for me," India pleaded with her old car when she turned the key and the engine only sputtered. To release any negative energy she might have harbored throughout the day, she inhaled, then exhaled. She closed her eyes, gently rubbed the steering wheel, then meditated for the car to start. Feeling calmer, she held the steering wheel with her left hand, then turned the key with the other. "Creator, what lesson do I have to learn from this experience?" she asked aloud once the engine barely coughed when she turned the key. Discouraged, she rested her head on top of her hands. She lifted her head, loosened the grip on the steering wheel, then looked inside her purse for her cell phone.

Maybe Shiquanna isn't too far away and can turn

around, she thought as she dialed her friend's number. It rang, but there was no answer. She dialed again. Still Shiquanna didn't answer. She looked at the time, then dialed Yvonne's number. It went straight to voice mail. "Inhale, then exhale," she reminded herself, fighting to stay calm, then tried to start the car again. Silence. "Friends, where are they when you really need them?" After their disagreement, Tracey was the last person she wanted to call for help.

Hoping to see a friendly face, she looked around the parking lot. A few minutes later the front door opened. She perked up but was soon disappointed when three men tumbled, one behind the other, down the steps. Again, she called Yvonne. Again, it went straight to voice mail.

Reese, she thought to herself, snapped her fingers, then scrolled through her list of contacts. Professor Reese Jones was her religion and philosophy instructor. Her final term paper titled, "The Mental Strongholds of Religion in the African American Community—Is That What God Intended?" had got his attention. Wanting to delve deeper into the subject matter, he'd requested a meeting with her after class. They had a common interest in the topic, and he wanted to develop their ideas into a nonfiction manuscript. They both knew the research would be arduous and would require hours of their time.

Initially, their interactions were innocent, but conversations about religion led to other topics. Other topics led to more intense conversations, which started to occur in places other than his office and the school library. On beautiful days the school lawn became their meeting place. Sometimes they met at the nearby coffee shop.

Nine months later their project was complete and ready to send to the publisher. To celebrate the accomplishment, they went to their favorite coffee shop, where they'd spent hours working.

"Can you believe we finished in nine months?" Reese asked India, with a look of surprise.

"No, I can't. I've heard it takes some people years to finish their first manuscript."

"To the dynamic duo." He held up his cup of coffee for a toast.

"To the dynamic duo." Together they celebrated with a toast. For a moment their eyes met, but India looked away.

"India," he said in a mellow tone to get her attention. She looked at him and, for the first time, saw a hint of passion in his eyes. "I know this is unethical, but I'd really like to take you out on a date," he said sincerely.

"Reese," she said, as he preferred to be called by his first name outside of the classroom, "I'm flattered, but I'm currently in a relationship." Actually, it had only been a few months before that she'd met Tracey. To India, Reese was very attractive. He was only six years older than her, but he was her college professor. So anything other than a professional relationship was out of the question.

"I'm sorry, but you've never mentioned anyone. Normally, people in a relationship make references to their significant other."

"You never asked."

"You have a point. I didn't ask. Please tell him I think he's a very lucky man."

"By the way, that's the other thing. I'm in a relationship with a woman," India replied bluntly.

"You're in a relationship with a woman?" he asked, with wide eyes, then pointed at her. "Please forgive me if I appear dumbfounded, but I never assumed you were a lesbian."

Unsure how to respond, India stared blankly, as she'd never considered herself a lesbian. Tracey was her first female lover. She'd never been attracted to women before or associated with anyone that lived an alternative lifestyle. Until Tracey, she'd dated men, and she had been in more than two committed relationships.

"Does she have a name?"

"Yes, her name is Tracey."

"I must admit that wasn't the response I'd expected, but Tracey is a lucky woman to have you in her life." After his initial shock, her limitations were respected, and they remained friends.

"Hello, gorgeous," he answered after the second ring.

"Reese, this is India." Certain he was confused, she reminded him who she was. She expected that a single man with his qualities would have several female friends.

"I know who this is," he said, then laughed. "What's going on?"

"If you're busy, please let me apologize for interrupting."

"Please stop being so paranoid. I was only grading a class assignment. When have I ever been too busy to talk to you?"

"Never." She smiled, thinking again about the long conversations they'd shared over coffee. "I need a huge favor." Hoping he was available, she crossed her fingers.

"What is it?"

"I'm stranded in the parking lot of El Reyes, on the corner of Fourth and Prescott. What's so funny?" she asked when he started to laugh.

"You mean to tell me Betsy finally let you down? How many times did we discuss your purchasing a newer car?"

"That's not funny. But, yeah, she has," she said, then laughed herself.

"Don't worry. I'll be there in a few minutes. As a matter of fact, I know exactly where Fourth and Prescott is. I will talk to you until I get there. I'm walking out my front door now."

India smiled when she heard the sound of a door closing in the background.

"Where have you been? I haven't seen you around campus lately. You used to stop by my office at least once a week."

"Yes, I did," she answered, thinking about how many female students were jealous of their friendship. "I've been extremely busy. I've changed majors again, so my course load has been heavier than usual. I've set another goal. I want to graduate within a year."

"That's great. I want a personal invitation to your graduation."

"Reese," she said, laughing, "you're a professor. You're at every graduation."

"Of course, I am, but only one of them will be yours."

"On that note, when the time comes, I'll be sure to bring an invitation by your office."

"You know, I miss our conversations about world religion and politics, which always turned into debates. You are the only student that has made me feel like the student and not the professor."

"If you saw things my way, they would have never been debates." India laughed, then relaxed her head on the headrest.

"That's my girl."

"Do you remember I predicted years ago we would have a black man run for president?" she spat into the phone. "And you thought it was going to be Reverend Jesse Jackson."

"Okay . . . okay. I must admit you were right about that one."

"Of course, I was right. I told you then he didn't have the . . ." She almost jumped out of her skin when someone tapped on her window. "Oh my God, Reese, you almost gave me a heart attack," she said, with wide eyes.

"If I had, that would have been the perfect opportunity for me to save your life using mouth-to-mouth resuscitation," he said, with a huge smile. "Now, get out and let me see what you're dealing with." He opened her door, she got out of the car, and he got in. He turned the key in the ignition, then shook his head from side to side. Dead silence. He looked at India, waited a few minutes, then tried again. "Maybe it's your battery. Do you have a set of jumper cables in your car?"

She looked at him, then placed a hand on each hip.

"Never mind. I have a set in my trunk." He got out and found the cables. He reached inside her car to open the hood, then walked around front.

"I'm going to need your help." He looked around the hood at her. "Get inside your car, and turn the key when I tell you to."

"I can do that." India got inside the car and waited for his cue.

"All right, give it a try."

India turned the key and shook her head when the car didn't start.

He removed the cables, then lowered her hood. "Silence is beyond my expertise. I'm a religion professor, not a miracle worker." He wiped his hands on his jeans, then opened her door so she could get out of the car. Carefully, she closed it. "My recommendation is a tow truck. Do you have a mechanic?"

"Look at this thing. Does it look like I have a mechanic?" She pointed at her car, then laughed.

"I guess you have a point. I know a really good mechanic. Let's give him a call." He pressed a few buttons on his cell phone.

"Reese, I really appreciate it."

He whispered "No problem," when someone answered on the other end. After a brief conversation, he ended the call. "Fortunately, he is in the neighborhood and can be here in five minutes."

"Reese, you're great." Ready to give him a big hug, she extended both arms.

"But there's good news and bad news." He held up his hand to stop her. "Which would you like to hear first?"

"At this rate, it really doesn't matter. Let's hear the bad news." She held both hands in the air.

"This has been a really busy week for him, so it may be two or three days before he can look at your car. If that's too long for you to wait, he doesn't mind towing it to a dealership."

"For Heaven's sake, no. A dealership will charge me an arm and a leg for repairs on that old thing." She put her hands in her front pants pockets and shook her head from side to side.

"Well, those were his words exactly."

"So tell me the good news."

"Because I've sent him so many customers and you're my friend, he's willing to waive your storage fee."

"Anything will help."

"That's him turning into the parking lot now." Reese pointed toward the bright red tow truck, then waved his hand to get the driver's attention.

"Wow, that was fast," India commented, then opened the passenger door to get her purse out of the car.

"Is there anything I can get for you?" he asked.

"Sure, you can get my book bag off the backseat." She stood to one side while he got her things and turned to place them on the backseat of his own car. Together they greeted the mechanic, then watched with folded arms as he worked to secure her car. He gave her a business card and told her to call the shop in three days.

"Man, I appreciate you coming through for me on short notice," Reese said, then shook his hand.

"Not a problem," replied the mechanic. He hopped into the large truck, slammed the door, and drove away.

"Now that that's taken care of, let me take you home," Reese told her.

"Reese, thanks, but you've done enough already. I can call a cab," said India.

He looked at her, then touched her forehead with the back of his hand.

"What's wrong?"

"I had to make sure you weren't running a fever. India, that's the most insane thing I've ever heard you say. I'm here and I'll take you home."

"Reese, I live on the east side of town, and that's about a thirty-five-minute drive." That was only an excuse to deter him, as she preferred taking a cab. She imagined Tracey standing in the front door as she got out of Reese's car and her initial reaction. How could she leave home for girls' night out after a heated discussion, then return with a man?

"Honestly, I don't mind. Plus, that's enough time for us to catch up on religion and politics."

"Yeah, just enough time for you to start a debate," she said jokingly when he led her around to the passenger's side of the car and opened the door. She looked at him, then got in. He walked around to the driver's side, then got in.

"Which way do I go to get to your place?" He put the key into the ignition, turned it to start the car, then looked at her as he prepared to back out.

"Let's go east on Interstate Fifteen."

"Are you a single woman now?"

India's neck snapped. His question shocked her. "Where did that come from?"

"Honestly, I was shocked when you called me for help. I don't mean any disrespect, but I expected your partner to be with you. But, for all I know, she could be at work, right?" he asked, hoping they'd broken up and that this would be an opportunity to prove that good men still existed.

"No, I'm not single," she said slowly, then sighed. Her car trouble had briefly taken her mind off of her disagreement with Tracey.

"India, if I crossed the line, please accept my apology. A man can only hope, right?" He looked at her then smiled.

"Believe me, you're okay." She frowned, then shook her head from side to side.

"Is everything okay between the two of you?"

"I guess we're experiencing growing pains. I don't know why I assumed dating a woman wouldn't be as emotionally challenging as dating a man."

"I'm here if you want to talk."

"Thanks," she said, then stared blankly out of the window. "Please accept my apology for being so negative."

"Don't be ridiculous." Gently, he rubbed her leg. "How much time do you have?" he asked after a few minutes of silence between them. "If you're not in a hurry, let's stop by our favorite coffee shop."

"That will be fine."

He got off the interstate and drove in the opposite direction. India smiled.

Chapter 6

Yvonne

The enormous white cross on the steeple was well within view once Yvonne turned right onto Hestler Street. Instantaneously, her heart started to race. She arched her back to look into the rearview mirror, used her fingers to smooth a few untamed hairs, then checked her lipstick. *This lip liner is too dark,* she thought to herself, opened her console, then felt blindly for a napkin. What was I thinking? She questioned her color choice, then blotted her lips with the napkin. *He stares at my lips when I wear the red lipstick.*

With only a few minutes to spare, she sped by the church and made a right onto the next street. *Looking good for my future husband is a priority.* She pulled over to the side, put the car into park, then got her purse off the seat. In a hurry, she snatched it open, pulled out her make-up bag, and searched for her crimson red liner and matching lip gloss. She pulled the top off the liner, lined her lips, then filled them in with gloss. She checked her face in the rearview mirror, then blew a kiss. *Perfect,* she thought. She put her liner and gloss into the make-up bag, tossed the make-up bag into her purse, then put the car into drive.

"Dammit, brother, please watch where you're going," she fussed after almost sideswiping a red pickup truck being driven by an innocent man. She threw up a hand, pulled out in front of him when he slammed on his brakes to avoid hitting her, then sped around the corner.

Again, her heart raced, so she placed her hand over her chest and took a deep breath. *I've got to calm down,* she thought, turned onto Hestler Street, then drove into the parking lot. She took her foot off the gas and cruised by a few empty spaces. Parking by the front door wasn't her intention. Unsure how much time was left, she looked at the clock in her car. "Not one minute too late. It's now fifteen minutes before Bible study." Finally, she found a space that could be viewed from Reverend Marion Alston's office window.

"Like clockwork, he should be standing at his office window facing the parking lot to meditate and pray. Well, that is, until I get out of my car, leg first to emphasize the long slit in my skirt. Any man, even an ordained man of God, would be distracted by my beautiful legs." She turned off the ignition, then took another look at herself in the rearview mirror as she leaned over to get her purse. She opened the door, then exposed her leg. Pretending to look for something, she leaned over again before getting out of the car. *I'm so good,* she thought, using her peripheral vision to observe the window as she started to strut across the parking lot.

He was standing in the middle of the window, with one arm folded across his chest and a hand below his chin. She couldn't see his eyes clearly but knew he was looking. Wanting him to enjoy every moment, she slowed down her pace. "Good evening, Sister Mayfield. Good evening, Mother Haywood," she sang, addressing the infamous church gossipers individually as she walked by them in the parking lot. The two women's shoulders touched as they stood side by side, with their backs facing the church. Sister Mayfield's lips were moving ninety to nothing, and Mother Haywood had a hand over her mouth.

"Evening, Sister Miller," Sister Mayfield mumbled, then rolled her eyes at the slit in Yvonne's skirt, which Yvonne accentuated with her long strides.

"Evening," Mother Haywood said, then nudged Sister Mayfield on the shoulder. No sooner than she spoke, she covered her mouth with a white handkerchief, and Sister Mayfield leaned over to listen.

"Humph," they both said together, then continued their gossip session.

Proud of her saunter across the parking lot, Yvonne opened the door to the church and entered the lobby, wearing a smile. "Good evening," she called to one of the ushers. Her warm greetings and sultry saunter continued as she walked through the lobby and entered the sanctuary. *Oh no, she isn't,* she thought to herself and paused when she noticed a female church member sitting in her usual seat. From disapproval, her eyebrows met. *Everyone, I mean everyone, knows that's my damn seat.* No, the seats weren't assigned, but some rules were unwritten. Everyone, the ushers included, knew that Yvonne Miller sat on the left side of the second row.

With every intention of asking the young woman to move, Yvonne inhaled deeply, then strutted down the aisle. Her stride was long as she stepped, placing each foot firmly on the carpeted floor. *How dare she sit in my seat? Everyone knows this is my seat,* she thought, walking faster and harder. Beside the pew, she stopped. No sooner than Yvonne reached out to tap the woman on the shoulder, she stood and waved at someone on the other side. "Good evening," she called. Wearing a fake smile, Yvonne stepped back as the young woman got her purse, then moved. *Humph, you're too young for him, anyway. He's only into real women,* Yvonne thought to herself after looking at the twenty-something-year-old from head to toe. *You definitely do not have first lady potential.* Yvonne frowned at the young lady's faded blue jeans, yellow Gap T-shirt, and brown flip-flops. Inside she laughed. Yvonne used a hand to smooth her skirt around her hips, sat down then crossed her legs. She put her purse down beside her, then got out the same Bible she'd waved at Shiquanna.

"Let all the people of God say amen," Deacon Johnston said as he walked to the podium, which was on a lower level, directly in front of the pulpit. Amens echoed throughout the congregation. He turned his head, covered his mouth to cough, then cleared his throat. "It's prayer time," he said, licked his thumb, then flipped through the pages of the large Bible in front of him. "It's prayer time," he said louder after pulling the microphone down to readjust it and leaning into it. Again, amens echoed throughout the congregation, and a few talking teenagers in the rear were shushed by ushers. "If you have your Bibles, please go with me to the twenty-third number of Psalms."

Deacon Johnston paused, took a pair of reading glasses out of his shirt pocket, and wiped them with a handkerchief. "This is Bible study." Making sure the glasses were clean, he held them toward the light, squinted, then put them on. He shook the handkerchief, then put it back into his pocket. "If you don't have your Bibles, raise your hand and an usher will assist you." He waited as ushers assisted those without Bibles. Ready to proceed with the formalities, Yvonne looked around the congregation, hoping everyone would hurry with the menial task. "Once you've found the Scripture, please stand to your feet in reverence for the mighty word of God," he said deeply, then placed a hand on each side of the podium. On the tip of his toes, he rocked back and forth.

With her Bible open to the correct passage of Scripture, Yvonne stood to her feet. Wanting to look her best for Reverend Alston's entrance, she glanced down at her outfit, then posed.

"Let's read together," Deacon Johnston said, then recited the entire passage aloud. "Please bow your heads and close your eyes for a word of prayer." He removed his reading glasses, put them into his shirt pocket, then looked down.

Yvonne closed her Bible, leaned her head down, but kept her eyes open. Expecting Reverend Alston to be standing in the doorway, she moved her eyes to the left. When she didn't see him, she tapped her fingers on the pew in front of her and closed her eyes. Certain of his weekly routine, she opened her eyes, then, without moving her head, looked again. He wasn't there. She closed her eyes, then supported herself by placing both hands on the pew in front of her. *I know he's here, because I saw him in the window. Did he get sick or have an emergency and have to leave? I hope he's okay.* Suddenly she felt nauseated. *Dear God, please watch over the husband you've sent me. Please protect him and allow him to make it back to me safely,* she prayed silently, not listening to Deacon Johnston.

"In the precious name of Jesus, we pray. Amen," said Deacon Johnston. "Y'all may be seated." He made a downward motion with his hands toward the congregation. Yvonne sat down but couldn't take her eyes off of the door Reverend Alston usually entered. "Before we go into the study of the word, Sister Eula Jenkins is going to review our discussion from last week."

Now, this is a first, Yvonne thought, then looked over her shoulder as Sister Jenkins stood, then walked toward the front. With a legal pad in hand, she greeted the congregation, then started her review. Becoming restless, Yvonne watched the door, still expecting Reverend Alston to enter any second. Sister Jenkins concluded her review, which had seemed to never end, and Deacon Johnston stood. From disappointment, Yvonne folded her arms across her chest and tapped her right foot.

"God is good," Deacon Johnston said, with excitement, as he walked toward the podium.

"All the time," the congregation responded. Not responding, Yvonne sat still and allowed her eyes to move from one entrance to the other. By the second, she was becoming more impatient.

"All the time," Deacon Johnston responded, lifting both hands into the air as high as his suit coat would allow.

"God is good," the congregation concluded loudly, with applause.

"God is good," Yvonne muttered after the congregation.

"It's study time. Everyone should still have their Bibles in their hand," said Deacon Johnston. In one hand, he lifted the large black Bible. "The title of our sermon for the evening is 'Financial Success, How to Apply the Word of God.'"

Oh my God, he isn't coming, Yvonne thought, turning her attention away from Deacon Johnston and the large Bible he still held in the air. *Why didn't he inform me when I saw him earlier? Even if we are separated by the pulpit, spending time together is crucial to our relationship.* Almost in a panic, Yvonne looked at the door Reverend Alston normally entered. Nervously, she tapped her right foot, then looked at another entrance, on the opposite side of the church. *Where is Reverend Alston?* she asked herself as Deacon Johnston started to read a passage of Scripture from the Bible. Yvonne didn't reopen her Bible and continued to look from one side to the other. *No need to waste my time. I have a million and one things to do at home.* Preparing to leave, she looked down to put her Bible into her purse.

"Amen. I want to thank Deacon Johnston for starting our study this evening."

Yvonne's heart skipped a beat when she heard his smooth tenor voice. Reverend Alston, the man of her dreams, her future husband, and the father of her three children, had arrived. *Thank you, God, for answering another prayer. Thank you for allowing my future husband to arrive safely, without any harm or danger,* she thought, trying to hold back a smile as she rocked gently from side to side.

"The word of God tells us to 'be ye also ready.' I'd like to take this time to thank Deacon Johnston for standing in for me at the last minute."

"Amen," Yvonne said softly, then looked up, eased her Bible from her purse, and placed it on her lap. "Praise the Lord." She quietly turned to the passage of Scripture Deacon Johnston had previously quoted and gave Reverend Alston her full attention. With authority, he stood tall behind the pulpit. Even though he was wearing the same black suit, crisp white shirt, and red tie from that morning, Yvonne was enamored by his stance. In awe, she contemplated his moves as he placed his personal Bible on the pulpit, turned to the Scripture, then removed his notes.

"Because I want it embedded in your spirit, I'd like to repeat our sermon title for this evening," he said. While looking around the audience, he placed his finger behind the knot on his tie, then twisted it until it was loose. He cleared his throat, then took a drink of water from the crystal glass he always kept on his pulpit. "'Financial Success, How to Apply the Word of God.'"

His voice alone sent a cool chill down her spine. "Praise God," Yvonne said, with a wave of the hand, thanking him for allowing her to be the luckiest woman in the world.

Two years prior, the founding pastor of their

church had announced his retirement but had assured the membership they'd be left in good hands. In keeping with his own recommendation, he preselected three ministers and allowed them one month to conduct services on his behalf. Reverend Alston was one of those three who came to the congregation, presenting himself as a natural leader and a man of God. Not only was his deliverance of the word of God articulate, but he proved to have excellent teaching and administration skills. The vote among the board members was unanimous. Two months later their founding pastor retired, and Reverend Alston was ordained as their new pastor.

The title of his first sermon as pastor of their church was "Name It and Claim It, The Abrahamic Promise." Yvonne thanked God for the sign and did just that. She named him and claimed him as her godsend.

For years she'd asked God for a husband. Her requests had seemed simple as she'd prayed for a God-fearing man who would love her unconditionally, who was successful, and who was open to having at least three children, and good looks would be a bonus. In her opinion, Reverend Alston was all that she'd asked for and more. He was an ordained man of God, was successful in his mission as minister, and loved children. Not to mention he was tall, slim, and extremely handsome.

"Being poor isn't God's divine plan for his people," Reverend Alston said sternly, bringing Yvonne out of her trance.

"Amen." With a wave of the hand, she continued watching as he stepped from behind the pulpit.

"My God," she said out of context when he rested one hand on the side of the pulpit and unbuttoned the top button of his shirt with the other. Back and forth he started to pace, motioning with his hands to emphasize important points. Her thoughts became lustful. Then everything around her became silent as his lips moved but she didn't hear one word. Through his white cotton shirt, she visualized a firm chest and bulging biceps. Her mouth watered as she only imagined the fullness concealed in his pants. With her eyes affixed on his every movement, Yvonne said an occasional amen or praise God.

Yvonne's head turned slightly when the person seated next to her stood. Her Bible slid off her lap and onto the pew as Yvonne stood to repeat the benediction. She picked up her Bible and purse, stepped into the aisle, and maneuvered to the front of the crowd to greet Reverend Alston.

"Sister Miller." He smiled, then extended his hand.

"Reverend Alston," she said, careful not to call him by his first name. "I really enjoyed Bible study. I'll start applying those principles you taught immediately." She extended her hand, then posed, exposing her leg through the slit.

"Thank you, Sister Miller." He rubbed the top of her hand, then patted it.

"You should do more just like it," she replied, not caring who stood behind her.

"Only if the spirit of God leads me to do so." He patted the top of her hand again, then smiled at the couple standing behind her. "Have a blessed evening." Slowly, he let her hand go, then reached for the couple behind her.

"I'm already blessed," Yvonne said softly. She smiled, then strutted toward the door only a few feet away. *I know he's watching me.* She paused momentarily before exiting the sanctuary. This time she ignored Sister Mayfield as she glided down the steps and out the front door.

Even though Reverend Alston was inside, she performed that same sultry glide across the parking lot to her car. She turned the ignition then tuned in to a local gospel station. She increased the volume when she heard her favorite gospel song playing. In sync with the beat, she bobbed her head as she drove out of the parking lot and turned onto the street.

Chapter 7

Shiquanna

Forty minutes later Shiquanna pulled up to the iron security gate and entered Ronald's code. Slowly, the gate screeched open, allowing her entrance into the secluded community, which hid only one of his private getaways. The two-story, three-bedroom condo was an hour away from his home. Using an alias, he'd purchased it from a colleague who was also a real estate investor. Knowing those secrets only added to her distrust of men.

As she drove past the lake, she shook her head at a couple seated on its banks. They were on a blanket, and beside them was a picnic basket. From the street she could see two wineglasses and what might be a bottle of wine or champagne. His arm was around her shoulder, and he was nibbling on her earlobe. The woman's shoulders bounced from laughter. Judging by first impressions, they seemed so in love. From Shiquanna's perspective, real love didn't exist, so she concluded that the woman was his mistress, not his spouse.

Quickly letting go of that image, she drove about a quarter of a mile past the lake, which could be seen from Ronald's master bedroom, then turned right onto his street. She turned into the stone driveway and followed it to the back side of the property, all the way to his garage. His wife's shiny new candy-apple red Cadillac SLR had been backed in. After his wife found a condom in his pants pocket, Ronald had given her the car as a "please don't divorce me and sue me for alimony and child support" present. Shiquanna drove inside the garage, parked, then watched through her rearview mirror as the garage door lowered. She inhaled, opened her glove compartment, then removed the shot-sized bottle of Jose Cuervo. She unscrewed the cap, and in two swallows, the tequila was gone. She looked at the empty bottle, tossed it on the seat, then got out of her black convertible Corvette.

In no hurry, she walked around the front of his wife's car, wiping her index finger across the hood. Scratching the paint with her acrylic nail, or at least leaving a traceable fingerprint, was her intention. She looked over her shoulder at the noticeable scar embedded in the paint, then smiled. In her opinion, the low-down, dirty bastard deserved to get caught. Knowing the kitchen door was unlocked, she turned the knob, then eased it open.

Wearing no shirt, a pair of white cotton boxers, and long black nylon dress socks, he was leaning against the kitchen counter. The sight of his saggy breasts and huge stomach repulsed her, so she swallowed hard and closed the door behind her. He reminded her of a high school jock whose physique eventually went from muscles to flab. Even though his face was round and his cheeks were chubby, she could tell he might have been a handsome young man. His complexion was flawless, and he had a million-dollar smile.

To appease her highest-paying client, she forced a smile, then swished toward him.

"I've already fixed you a glass of wine." Inside, she giggled at his soft tenor voice, which didn't fit his huge body. He handed her a glass of white wine with sliced strawberries, pomegranate, and grapes in it.

Wondering if his wife performed the same romantic gestures for him, she looked at him, then at the beautiful crystal glass. It was a thought, as very few men were that romantic.

Before she could lift the glass to take a drink, he kissed her on the lips. It was wet and sloppy. She fought not to frown. "Baby, I've missed you like hell." He put both arms around her waist as she turned her head to take a sip of wine and wash away his kiss. "My days at the courthouse are long and stressful. What female in her right mind would have several children with the same unemployed individual? If he didn't pay child support for the first child, what makes her believe he'll pay for two or even three? Dealing with hundreds of deadbeat dads and frustrated baby mamas on a daily basis is more than the average man can handle."

"Humph," she sputtered, almost choking on her wine. In her opinion, any man that spent hours away from home and cheated on his wife was a deadbeat dad.

"Not to mention, when I get home in the evening, Alana starts to bitch before I can open the door." He got a strawberry out of the bowl on the counter, bit into it, and started to chew.

Preparing for his gripe session, she looked into his dark brown eyes, which were hidden behind a pair of wire-rimmed glasses. As if paying attention, she leaned her head to one side.

"Today she was complaining about me not spending enough time with Junior. Sure we can afford it, but no one told her to sign him up for so many activities. I'm a great man, but not a magician," he said, then extended his chest. "That means I can only be in one place at a time."

Already bored with his arrogant comments, Shiquanna took another sip of wine and stared blankly into his eyes.

"What does she expect from a man that's away from home at least twelve hours every day? I work hard so she doesn't have to."

Still not responding, Shiqaunna looked at him intently.

"How many women do you know that would love to walk a quarter of a mile in her shoes? I know several. A day doesn't go by that someone in the courthouse doesn't flirt with me. If one clerk becomes any more aggressive, I may have to file sexual harassment charges. Getting back to Alana." He took another bite of strawberry, then pressed it to Shiquanna's lips. She bit off a tiny piece and tried not to frown. "She doesn't have to work, has a maid and a part-time nanny to help with the new baby. Who wouldn't love to be with a man that took care of her like that?" he asked, then tapped Shiquanna in the center of her chest when she didn't respond.

"Oh, baby, a million women would love to be her right now," Shiquanna answered, thinking she'd rather die alone than live with a jerk like him all her life.

"Thank you," he said, then nodded his head up and down in agreement. "She doesn't see that."

"No, baby, she doesn't see that," Shiquanna repeated, then finished her wine. Already exhausted from his complaints about his wife, she looked toward the bottle of wine that was sitting on the counter.

"When God created me, He broke the mold." He took the glass out of Shiquanna's hand, placed it on the counter, then pulled her into him. To avoid another kiss, she turned her head to one side, then frowned. All she could feel was stomach. "That's enough about me and my problems." He embraced her tighter. "Baby, I really need some of your good loving right now."

He broke the embrace, then led her by the hand through the family room and into the bedroom. Except for the recessed light above the fireplace, which cast a shadow onto the floor, the room was dark. But it wasn't so dark that she didn't see the spread of one-hundred-dollar bills placed on the nightstand beside the bed. *One, two, three, four, five, and six,* she counted to herself as he pulled her closer to the bed.

"You're so beautiful," he said, then plopped down on the end of the bed.

"Umm . . ." She suddenly craved another shot of

tequila when his breasts drooped onto his stomach, then jiggled back and forth.

"Where are you going, baby?" he asked when she pulled away and took a step toward the door.

"My purse . . . ," she responded, then pointed toward the kitchen. "Your favorite outfit is in it."

"Baby, please hurry, because I'm ready for the royal treatment," he said, then looked down at his bulging underwear.

"One minute," she said just above a whisper, held up her index finger, then backed out of the room. Not concerned with his erection, she sauntered through the family room and into the kitchen. Searching for another shot bottle of tequila, she rustled through her purse, then emptied the contents onto the kitchen counter. Impatiently, she ran her hand over loose papers, then tossed tubes of lipstick and a make-up compact to one side. "Nothing," she panted. She used both hands to scoop up the contents, then threw them back into her purse. Desperate for a more intense high, she picked up the bottle of wine and drank.

"Found it yet?" he asked from the bedroom.

She removed the bottle from her lips just enough to speak. "Yeah, I got it, baby."

"Big Daddy is ready for you."

"Coming." She looked over her shoulder, then took another drink. Satisfied, she sat the bottle on the counter, then walked away. "Shit." Remembering the lie she'd told, she turned sharply on her tiptoes and hurried to grab her purse. Pretending to have changed in the guest bathroom, she unbuttoned her shirt-dress as she walked across the great room. She looked down, adjusted her bra to reveal more cleavage, then rubbed her fingers through her hair. For his viewing pleasure, she stopped in the bedroom doorway and allowed her large purse to fall to the floor. To remove her dress, she moved her shoulders from side to side, then allowed it to fall.

"Please don't tease me," he said, then rubbed himself as she leaned against the doorway to pose. "I've waited all day for this. I want you now." He grabbed himself, then closed his legs.

Wanting him to ejaculate prematurely, she spread her legs apart and allowed her head to fall back. Knowing that made her breasts appear larger, she rubbed one with her hand. "Mmm . . . ," she moaned, then eased her hand inside her bra. Gently she rubbed.

"Shiquanna," he called, then crossed his legs at the ankles, pressing his thighs tighter together.

"Mmm . . ." Seeing how close he was, she removed a breast, then fondled her nipple. Her movements were slow and sensual. *Come on, you shit. I'm not in the mood to deal with your fat ass all evening. I've got shit to do,* she thought to herself while continuing the erotic show.

"Shiquanna, please. I want you now," he begged.

Damn, you're good, she thought to herself when his right leg started to tremble. Able to skip the oral massage, she walked toward him, then stopped. Knowing what he'd do next, she stared into his eyes. Like a dog in heat, he panted, then allowed his legs to fall apart. She tucked her fingertips inside his elastic waistband, slid his underwear down his legs until it was around his ankles. With his foot, he tossed it to one side. She straddled his lap, then, with one hand, pushed him back onto the bed. Without thinking, she removed a condom from her bra, tore the wrapper with her teeth, then slid it onto him. She mounted him, then closed her eyes. Her right hand slid underneath a disgusting lump of fat, but she never lost momentum.

"You look so good riding me," he said, then grabbed her waist so tight, she could hardly breathe. "Is it good to you?" he asked.

Not responding, she placed a hand on each of his breasts and rode harder.

"Ohh, Shiquanna, this is it," he moaned, breathing hard between syllables. He jerked uncontrollably, then fell limp beneath her.

Focusing on her payment, she lifted one leg, then turned her body sideways to get off of him. She looked down, then smiled when she heard a deep snore. His sweat dripped from her palms, so she rubbed her hands on the sheets. Deciding against her usual shower, she gathered the six one-hundred-dollar bills, found her dress, and draped it over her arm. Without a second thought, she grabbed her purse and headed toward the kitchen door, letting it close hard behind her.

Anxious to leave, she let her purse fall from her shoulder onto the ground, then put on her dress. Leaving it totally unbuttoned, she snatched her purse up by the strap, pressed the remote to open the garage, and walked to her car as the garage door lifted. She opened the car door, tossed her purse onto the passenger's seat, then started her car. Feeling nauseated from the scent of his sweat, which permeated her pores, she backed out, sped down the driveway, and turned onto the street.

Lying down on the banks of the lake, with their arms folded behind their heads, was the same couple she'd passed two hours ago. Envious of their apparent connection, she couldn't help but stare. Suddenly the wells of her eyes filled with tears as she became overwhelmed by emotion. *What the hell?* she thought to herself, then wiped her face with the back of her hand. Another tear fell. Again she wiped. *I don't cry.* Before she could wipe again, her crying was out of control. Barely able to see, she drove alongside the lake and parked. *Somebody please help me. God, if you're out there, like Yvonne says, I need your help. I can't keep living like this,* she pleaded as her stomach contracted from the pressure. She placed both hands on the steering wheel and leaned her head back. Warm tears continued to flow down her cheeks as she was unable to suppress thoughts of Renita.

"Let's go," Renita shouted at Shiquanna after she shoved the door open and entered her bedroom. Shiquanna hadn't moved. "You'll do as I say, dammit. It's time for you to earn your keep up in this house." Renita grabbed her by the arm and pulled her out of the bed.

"Mama, please! Why are you doing this to me?" With tear-filled eyes, Shiquanna pleaded, pulling in the opposite direction.

With glossy eyes, Renita tightened her grasp on Shiquanna's arm and tugged her out of the room and down the hallway. Shiquanna fell to her knees, but Renita never stopped as she grabbed her purse and keys. Suddenly Renita stopped, then pulled Shiquanna to her feet.

"You listen to me, and I mean listen to me good," Renita said sternly, pressing her index finger against Shiquanna's nose. "I didn't ask for this shit, either. Be-

lieve me, you weren't supposed to be here. If I had had enough money, I would have aborted your ass. But I didn't, so here we are, standing face-to-face. I had to do what I had to do. Now it's your turn. Now let's go. The party starts in two hours." Renita grabbed Shiquanna in the same tender spot on her arm and shoved her toward the door. "Wipe away those damn tears. I mean it. Crying never did shit for me, and it ain't gonna do shit for you."

Patiently she waited until the last tears appeared, then rolled down her cheeks. She lifted her head, which was heavy, admired the couple in front of her, then drove away.

Chapter 8

India

It had been months since they'd last eaten there, and India smiled when Reese turned into the parking lot of their favorite twenty-four-hour coffee shop. Only half of the sign with broken glass was illuminated, and the red and white striped awning was torn around the edges. The inside was small and extremely clean, and booths lined each wall. A long countertop extended the length of the coffee shop, with the grill on the other side.

He parked near the front entrance, and they both got out. Again, India smiled when he opened the door to the coffee shop and the silver bell, dangling from a piece of red yarn, chimed. She had a flashback of times past. They'd spent countless hours seated at the booth in the far left corner, organizing notes and querying on the Internet. Amazingly, the booth was available.

"Hey, where have the two of you been?" Gail, the

waitress, yelled from behind the counter. She turned away from the grill and took off her disposable gloves to receive a payment from another customer. "I ain't seen the two of you in months."

"Hello, Gail," they said in unison and waved.

"Want your usual?"

"Yes, ma'am," India said, then smiled as she and Reese sat down across from each other.

"Two black coffees coming up," called Gail.

"Thanks," India said, then rubbed her index finger across the small packets of sugar in a tiny ceramic container.

"Here you go. Be careful. That pot is hot." Gail placed a silver coffeepot and two cups on the table. "Can I get you anything to eat this evening?" She pointed at the laminated menus that had been placed behind the mustard and ketchup containers.

"India, would you like anything?" Reese asked.

"No thank you. The coffee is fine," said India.

"Gail, we're both good," Reese responded.

"Yell if you need me." Gail wiped her hands on the front of her apron, then walked away.

"Thank you." India stared blankly across the room as Reese poured their coffee.

"You're in deep thought," he said, then placed a cup in front of her.

"If you'd like to call it that," she said, then wrapped both hands around the warm cup. Gently, she blew as the steam appeared, forming small circles, then dissipated. India blew again, then lifted the cup to her lips.

Reese took a drink of his coffee, then looked into her eyes.

"Tracey." As if to say "Never mind," India shook her head from side to side.

"Tracey?" Reese asked, then leaned his head to one side. "Your partner?" He'd concluded that their relationship was going well.

"Before I left to have dinner with my girls, we had a disagreement."

"Would you like to talk about it?" Gently, he placed one hand on top of hers.

"Reese, I don't want to bore you with the issues in my relationship." She slid her hands from beneath his and took another sip of coffee.

"What makes you think you're boring me?" he asked, remembering the first time he put his foot in his mouth with her by asking her on a date. After the letdown, becoming her best friend was the only option left.

"Let's be realistic. We're not talking about a normal heterosexual relationship."

Reese smiled.

"What's so funny?" she asked, then leaned her head to one side.

"You forget I have been a college professor for years and have seen and heard it all."

India looked at him, then laughed. "I guess you have a point."

"Do you think all my sessions after class are about class?" he asked, then hunched his shoulders. "Well, if that's what you believe, you're sadly mistaken. I spend fifty percent of my time counseling students about personal issues that may have affected their grade. Like I said, I've seen and heard it all. I promise you can't offend me or hurt my feelings."

India looked at him, then inhaled. "I don't know where to start."

Reese looked at his watch, then smiled. "My first class doesn't start until eight in the morning. Let's start with the disagreement."

"One year ago, meeting my girls for dinner once a week became a ritual. We get together to eat and talk about whatever. Today was our day to meet. I wasn't expecting Tracey to be home after class. My plan was to take a shower, then rest, before getting with my two girls. Tracey surprised me when she opened the front door. She never gets home before eight o'clock. If she does, it's rare. Not only did she get home early, but she had a nice dinner prepared for me in the kitchen."

Reese listened intently, then nodded his head up and down.

"Meeting my girls once a week is nothing new. It's been a year now."

"Okay."

"To make a long story short, Tracey wanted me to have dinner with her at home. I reminded her it was girls' night out and told her we could eat her meal tomorrow. Then she invited herself and reminded me that she was also a female." India held both hands in the air.

"Ouch," Reese interjected, knowing if he only listened, she might resolve her own situation.

"Reese, of course, I know she's a female. I go to bed beside her every night and wake up with her every morning. But in our situation, it's different."

"Different? How?"

"Yes, she's a female, but not so in our relationship."

"In so many words, she was offended that you may not consider her one of the girls."

"Possibly. But think about it. That's like you inviting your girlfriend to hang out with the boys on boys' night out."

"You do have a point, but you're in a same-sex relationship. Even though she may function as the male, she's still a female. She's a female just like you, with feelings and emotions. Think about it this way. How do you think she's able to relate to you so well? Who better knows how to please a woman than another woman?"

India nodded her head up and down.

"With that being said, any relationship involves compromise." Reese took a drink of coffee, and India inhaled. "Have you ever considered inviting her to one of your girls' nights out?"

India's eyes widened as she rubbed the rim of her cup with her fingertips, then pushed it away.

"Did I say something wrong?" Reese held both hands in the air. "If so, please let me apologize."

"No, you didn't say anything wrong. Yvonne, my girlfriend that's saved and sanctified, thinks Tracey is a man."

"Now that puts a different spin on the scenario." He folded his arms in front of him and leaned back against his seat. "If you're best friends, why doesn't she know?"

"Reese, it's a long story. Tracey is the first and only woman I've ever dated. I know it may sound unusual, but I've never had feelings for a woman before. Honestly, I'm still dealing with it myself. I've been with Tracey a few years now. I love her, and I know she loves me, but I'm still uncomfortable with the term *lesbian.* My best friend Yvonne lives and breathes the Bible and is the last person I want damning me to the pit of hell."

"If she's truly your best friend, she'll love you no matter who you decide to date. She'll support you either way. Tracey, on the other hand, has a point. You have to deal with the reality of your situation. At some point, she's going to give you an ultimatum. When the time comes, what are you going to do?"

"Reese, that's the problem. I don't know."

Reese nodded his head up and down, then waved his hand for their ticket. At a loss for words, India placed her elbows on the table, clasped her fingers together, and rested her chin on top. Reese paid Gail and gave her a tip.

"Let me take you home." Reese tapped the table to get India's attention.

Together they stood, waved good-bye to Gail, and exited the coffee shop.

"Reese, thank you for everything. I hope you understand why I didn't want to call Tracey for help," India said thirty minutes later, when he turned into her driveway.

"You're welcome. I'm glad I was available. Helping you was a pleasure. Besides, we got a chance to visit our old hangout."

India looked at him, then smiled.

"Remember what I said . . . compromise." He reached across the console and placed his hand on hers. Gently he rubbed.

"I'll remember."

"It's dark outside. Let me walk you to the front door." He reached for his door handle.

"I appreciate it, but no thank you." With a frown, she looked toward the condo. There were no lights on outside.

"Are you sure?"

"I'm positive." She waited as he got out and walked around the front of the car to open her door. "Again, thanks for everything." She got out, hugged him, and waved as she walked to the front door. Unsure what to expect, she looked through the small window in the door while searching for her key. The entryway was dark, and she could see a hint of light coming from the family room. Knowing she couldn't stay outside all night, she opened the door and eased it shut. Tracey was sitting on the couch, with a drum machine on her lap and headphones on. India stopped and stood in the doorway.

Tracey undoubtedly saw India's shadow in the television and turned her head to look over her shoulder. She turned off the drum machine, then removed her headphones. "Can we talk?" she asked in a normal tone of voice.

India folded her arms across her chest, then leaned against the doorway.

"Baby, I think we should talk," Tracey said, using a softer tone, then patted the cushion on the couch beside her.

India unfolded her arms, entered the room, and sat in a chair across from the couch. Against the dim light, Tracey's eyes, which usually sparkled, seemed sad and dull.

"About earlier . . . ," Tracey began, then ran her

hands through her hair. "I must admit, I did know you were going out with the girls. I'm woman enough to say there was motive behind my meal."

India folded her arms across her chest again, then leaned her head to one side.

"You go out with your friends once a week. This was one week I thought you could stay at home and have a romantic meal with me. I didn't think that was too much to ask for."

"You didn't ask. You plotted."

"Okay, maybe I did," Tracey said, then hunched her shoulders. "All I'm saying is I wanted us to spend the evening together. It didn't matter if it was here or with your friends, which brings us to another point. When am I going to meet your friends?"

"Tracey," India mumbled, "you'll meet them when the time comes."

"The time *has* come. When are you going to include me in your life? You know all my family and friends. You can't hide me forever."

"I'm not hiding you."

"You most certainly are hiding me. Well, let me rephrase that. How long are you going to hide?"

"I'm not hiding, either." Tracey's comment had struck a nerve, causing India to change positions in the chair.

"Friday I'll cancel my evening classes, come home early, and cook dinner for your family and girlfriends. You can call everyone tomorrow to share our plans and invite them over."

"Tracey, no," India stated firmly, sliding her body to the edge of the chair.

"Why not? I think it's a great idea. It will be an

opportunity for me to meet your mother and get to know her better. I am in a relationship with her daughter." Looking India in the eye, Tracey picked up her drumsticks and tapped them on the couch.

"Why are you being sarcastic?"

"This isn't sarcasm. It's time for people other than the two of us to know we're a couple. Wouldn't you agree?"

"No, I don't agree."

"How long are you going to deceive yourself, or those around you, for that matter? I'm a lesbian and you're my partner, so that makes you a lesbian." She tapped hard, then placed the drumsticks down beside her.

"I'm not a lesbian," India insisted.

"Is there another term in the dictionary for a woman who likes other women? You're the scholar in this relationship. Educate me."

"Tracey, I didn't ask for this, and you know it. You came on to me."

"Point taken. I did come on to you, but you didn't have to respond, did you? The first time I rubbed your hand in the park was your opportunity to resist. That was your time to curse me out, doom me to hell, and walk away. But you didn't."

"Tracey, you knew what you were doing. Your advances were subtle."

"I didn't take advantage of you. We were two consenting adults."

"Please. I don't want to argue with you." India threw up both hands, then stood.

"You didn't refuse my first kiss, and you didn't stop me the first time we made love. I didn't rip off your clothes, throw you onto the bed, and force you to make love to me. At any point you could have said no, but you didn't." Tracey looked at India, put on her headphones, then turned on her drum machine.

India went into the bedroom and closed the door behind her. Wanting to embrace Tracey, she held onto the doorknob, then leaned her head against the door. *I really love her, and I know she loves me. Why is expressing my love for Tracey to my friends and family so difficult?* She attempted to twist the knob but froze, knowing she couldn't confront Tracey unless she was sure. Sure about her own sexuality, emotions, and commitment to their relationship. She let go of the doorknob, then ran her fingers back and forth through her hair. Wishing Tracey would walk through the door, she turned and walked into the bathroom to shower.

Not wanting to look at her reflection in the large vanity mirror to her left, she turned her head. Growing up in a home with religious parents had made her feelings difficult to deal with. Whether it was in Sunday school or at morning service, the carnal sins were reiterated. According to everything she'd learned about her parents' God, there was a place in hell for gays and lesbians. India, on the other hand, viewed God as universal love. If God was indeed love, how could He destroy two people that loved each other?

One article at a time, she removed her clothes, opened the shower door, then turned on the water. Expecting Tracey to enter any second, she reached inside to feel the temperature, then looked over her shoulder. They showered together every night Tracey was at home. Uncertain of the fate of her relationship, she stepped inside, stood beneath the spray, and allowed it to saturate her body. Still giving Tracey time to join her, she lathered her body slowly. Minutes later she was done, and Tracey still hadn't entered the bathroom.

Desiring Tracey's presence, she removed her dark blue terry-cloth robe from the hook and inhaled her favorite Kenneth Cole scent. For comfort, she put the robe on, tied the belt around her waist, and went into the bedroom. She walked toward the door, then stopped. Still with no answers or solutions, she flicked the light switch off, then turned around. In love with Tracey but questioning this seemingly unethical ideal, she crawled into bed, then extended her arms above her head to stretch. She turned onto her back, tucked Tracey's pillow beneath her head, then listened for the door to open. With only the scent of Tracey for comfort, she finally fell asleep.

Chapter 9

Yvonne

In love with the idea of being in love, Yvonne's mini gospel concert continued from the church's parking lot to her home. One by one she counted her blessings, with Reverend Marion Alston ranking number one, as she turned into her driveway. Her words turned into a hum as she drove into her garage. From the garage to her door, she hummed. In a state of elation, she entered her home, closed the door, then leaned her head back against it. Giving thanks for every material possession she considered a blessing, she closed her eyes and rocked her head from side to side with the song still echoing in her ears. She began singing as she opened her eyes, strolled toward the kitchen island, and rubbed the marble top with her index finger. She stopped to place a hand on her hip. Mentally evaluating her many accomplishments she glanced upward.

From her custom-designed kitchen, with maple

cabinets, marble countertops, and hardwood floors, she went into her family room. She allowed her eyes to move fluidly from one wall to the other, appreciating the authentic art pieces collected from exotic vacations taken in Africa, Japan, and Italy. She placed her hand on the white Italian leather couch and followed the outline of the plush pillows with her fingertips. She stopped to rub. Her assessment continued as she entered her bedroom, then touched the light switch one time. Simultaneously, the lights in her master bedroom, its separate sitting area, were illuminated. The dim light enhanced her romantic theme, which was inspired by her favorite Jamaican resort. Gold walls served as a backdrop for her king-size whitewashed canopy bed, which dominated an entire wall. The bedposts were draped with red handwoven silk. The comforter and accent pillows were coordinated to match. The same color scheme flowed into her master bathroom. It was her sanctuary. As if floating on a cloud, her song of praise and adoration continued as she removed her shoes, then leaned down to pick them up.

Holding them by the straps, she sauntered across the room and into her closet, which was filled from top to bottom with designer clothes, shoes, and purses. She opened a drawer of her lingerie chest, chose her most seductive gown, then draped it over her shoulder. Her assessment didn't stop but was heightened by the vision of Reverend Marion Alston standing by her bed, waiting. Wearing a smile, she walked toward that image, shedding her clothes one article at a time. Imagining his warm smile as a sign of approval, she turned around in a circle, stopped to pose, then went to shower.

Her fantasy continued as he followed her, stopping her just before she stepped beneath the warm flow of water. She leaned her head to one side, welcoming his string of kisses, which started at her earlobe and continued down her neck. "Marion, stop. I need to take a shower. We've got the rest of the night to make love," she cooed as she entered the shower, then stood beneath the spray.

He undressed and took his place behind her, rubbing his body against hers. Pressed against her hips, he started to swell. Her desire for him increased as he moved from side to side. Unable to withstand it a second longer, she reached behind her and held him with her hand. Slowly, she stroked the shaft. He moaned from pleasure. To intensify his level of pleasure, her strokes became faster, and her grip tightened. "Oh my God," he blurted, letting himself go in her hand.

"Marion, I love every inch of you," she moaned. She leaned into his embrace and allowed her natural juices to mix with the water that streamed down her legs. For her, it was a sweet release. Content, she showered, then put on her sexy nightgown, with Marion still on her mind.

Preparing to turn in, she moved her purse, which was on her bed. Out of habit, she checked her cell phone. There were four missed calls. Hoping Marion hadn't called while she was in the shower, she hurried to check them. It was India. She looked at the time, then realized India had made the calls while she was in church. Her phone was set to vibrate, so how she'd missed them was unclear, as her purse was beside her. She pressed the button to redial India's number. It rang, then went straight to voice mail. After a few minutes, she tried again. The response was the same, as it went straight to voice mail. She hunched her shoulders, then went into the kitchen for a glass of sparkling apple cider. Her heart still raced from her climax.

She opened the cabinet, then smiled at her trembling hands as they reminded her of the experience. She got her sparkling apple cider, then poured a glass. *To my love.* She toasted, grabbed her newspaper off the counter, and went into the family room. Against a plush sofa pillow, she relaxed to read her paper and drink. She took a few sips, sat her glass on the table, and started to read her paper. Soon she could feel her eyelids become heavy.

Yvonne's eyes opened when she heard the doorbell ring. Her glass was on her glass-top table, and the newspaper was spread across her lap, with a few pages on the floor. *Marion.* Her heart raced as she stood and grabbed the remaining newspaper sections as they slid down her lap. "One second," she sang, then walked to the door, stopping in front of the mirror to check her appearance. With her fingers, she wiped each corner of her mouth, removed a spot of mucus from her eyes, then checked her hair. Her complexion glowed, so she looked down at her long black satin gown with a side slit. Quickly, she adjusted the neckline to show all but the nipples of her breasts. "I'm coming, dear."

Even though her heart pounded, she opened the door slowly, then posed to accent the slit in her gown. Without speaking, he snatched her to him with one arm, then placed his hand on the back of her head. He kissed her aggressively, moving her head from side to side. Her heart rate increased as his tongue went deeper and deeper. She took a step back to enter the house, but he lifted her body with one arm and closed the door behind him. She wrapped her legs around his waist. With her in one arm, he wiggled the opposite shoulder, causing his jacket to slide down. Taking large steps toward the bedroom, he yanked off his tie, which was already unfastened, and threw it on the floor.

"I don't know how much longer we can live apart," he gasped, still struggling with his jacket, which was only half on. "I know I'm a man of God, but that doesn't stop my flesh from getting weak."

"Oh, baby, I want you beside me every night. There's only one way to make that happen." She was referring to their union by marriage.

"Please get undressed." He tapped her in the center of her back, then rubbed her legs, which were still around his waist. She allowed her legs to fall until they touched the floor.

"You're all I've been thinking about." His hands and feet were coordinated as he stepped out of his shoes and unbuttoned his pants almost simultaneously.

With a sexual appetite larger than his, Yvonne watched as he let his pants fall to the floor. "Oh my God," she panted when his erection revealed more than she'd ever imagined. She'd had countless fantasies about making love to him but never imagined it happening before their honeymoon. Looking at him and his facial expression made her nipples harden. Before she could slide her fingers underneath her spaghetti straps to remove her gown, he'd grabbed her around the waist. He kissed her aggressively on the lips, then stopped suddenly to step back.

"I want you right now," he said, then used his fingertips to reach through the small slit in his boxer briefs to expose himself. His girth alone as he placed a hand around himself made her gasp. He leaned forward, raised her gown around her waist, then pressed her body into his, allowing her to feel his full erection.

Oh my God. Her head fell back when he reached inside of her gown and fondled her nipple. She gasped when he covered it with his lips and flicked his tongue. She moaned from pleasure, then fell back onto the bed. Wanting him more, she spread her legs and watched as he found his place between them. Receiving him was easy, as her warm juices saturated every wall, then overflowed onto the bed. His long strokes stimulated every nerve. Unable to withstand the sensation, Yvonne wrapped her legs around his body and pulled him closer. The strokes became shorter, heightening the internal stimulation. "Marion," she barely called.

"Please cum with me." He lifted his body and used his arms for support. Again, his strokes became long and hard. "Yvonne," he called. "I'm about to . . ."

Buzzz . . . Yvonne's eyes opened. Falling asleep on the couch was her last memory. Frantically, she patted the covers around her, then felt the wet spot beneath her body. The combination of sweat and cum had penetrated through her gown, saturating her sheets. From disappointment, she smacked the empty space beside her with her hands then turned off her alarm clock. It was six o'clock the next morning, and she was still alone.

"My word as bond, sooner than later my name is going to be Mrs. Marion Alston." She spoke affirmatively, emphasizing every syllable, then repeated the statement again. She threw the covers off of her body, sat erect, then used her feet to kick them away. "Every being has a purpose. My purpose became clear the moment I laid eyes on Reverend Marion Alston. I am Mrs. Marion Alston. God created me for that purpose and that purpose only."

With conviction, she placed her feet on the floor, then looked over her shoulder at the remnants of her wet fantasy. "Soon, Marion, soon," she declared as she used her hands to push herself off the bed. She reached down to remove the gown by the hemline, which was glued to her body. Like peeling a banana, she removed it, went into her closet, then tossed it into the wicker hamper. "You will be mine." The sweat that glistened on her body served only as a reminder of what she hadn't yet accomplished. Yvonne was driven and wouldn't be defeated.

The hangers scraped against the rack as she pushed her suits to the side one by one. Looking but not seeing the black Armani that she wore on all of her job interviews, she started to tear through the racks of neatly arranged clothes. Frustrated, one by one she lifted them off the rack and tossed them on the floor. In minutes, clothes were piled around her feet. "Whatever it takes, Marion, I'll be with you. As a formality, I'm going on this interview, but I will work with you every day at the church. You don't have to say it. I know that's what you want. Actions speak louder than words. Your face lights up every time I enter your office. I understand, baby. We need to keep our love for each other a secret. I'm patient enough to wait. One day you'll want the world to know."

After minutes of tearing through her closet, she found the black Armani that she was looking for, stepped over her mess, then went into her bedroom. She tossed the suit on her chaise, fell onto the bed, and covered the wetness with her bare body. Pretending he was there, she closed her eyes, then inhaled to create another fantasy. In that very same spot, her pores filled with sweat, and her secret place secreted juices. With a temporary sense of satisfaction, she used her hands to get off of the bed, then hurried to take a shower. Her interview with another Fortune 500 company was in one hour, and it was a thirty-minute drive.

Defining herself as a professional African American woman, she dressed, grabbed her clutch purse and briefcase. Assuming another personality type, she pulled her shoulders back and walked through the family room and into the kitchen. She opened the door leading to the garage, then turned to access her accomplishments. With confidence she smiled, then closed the door, with only one mission in mind, becoming Mrs. Marion Alston.

Chapter 10

Shiquanna

Exhausted from the day before, Shiquanna fought to open her eyes, which were sealed from conjunctivitis. She placed both hands over them, then rubbed her temples, which throbbed from excessive alcohol consumption. Again, she tried to separate her eyelids. Like a zombie, she sat up in bed, lowered her feet to the floor, and used her hands to feel her way into the bathroom. Along the way, she stubbed her toe on a chair and stumbled over the pile of clothes she'd left in the middle of the floor. Once she felt the entry to her bathroom she held on to the door and exhaled. Her big toe was throbbing from the bump and competed with her head. *Oh, God,* she pleaded silently, then leaned her head against her hand. Then she heard a horrible rumble as her stomach began to churn. With so many aches, she didn't know where to place her hands for comfort. Should she place them over her eyes, which were glued shut, or on her aching head, her throbbing toe, or her upset stomach? *This is fucked up,* she thought, stepped into her bathroom, then fell forward onto her sink.

Blindly, she felt for a face towel. After knocking over who knows what and listening to it fall into her sink, she found a towel. She grabbed it, felt for the faucet, then turned on the water. "Shit," she swore when she held her hand beneath the flow of steaming hot water. Again, she felt for the faucet, this time to adjust the water temperature to a level her aching head could tolerate. She wet the face towel, then pressed it against her eyes. Eventually, she could feel her eyelids loosen. She rewet the towel, then pressed it against her eyes again. Gently, she rubbed until the matter that served as glue softened. She rotated her eyeballs, then opened her eyes. The sunlight glared through her bathroom window, forcing her to shut her eyes and look away. "Jesus," she exclaimed, enduring yet another discomfort, light sensitivity.

She let the towel fall into the sink and placed both hands on the basin for support. Her head was heavy as she leaned it forward. In sync with the beat of her heart, it throbbed, becoming more intense by the second. She inhaled, opened her eyes, and picked up the face towel, which had the outline of her lips in dark brown lipstick and her false eyelashes stuck on it. She shook her head from side to side, then laughed at the impression on the towel. It looked like a funny face laughing at her ass for being so damn stupid. She lifted her head and ran her fingers through her matted wig. With one hand, she yanked it off and tossed it on the vanity.

Black hairpins flew in every direction as the wig landed.

Barely able to stand erect, she wobbled to the shower, opened the door, and stepped inside. She turned on the water and leaned against the back wall. The splatters of cold water gave her chills. She rubbed the chill bumps on her arms and waited until the spray was warm enough to stand beneath it. When the water became warm around her toes, she stepped forward and just stood beneath the spray. From her natural hair, which was tucked beneath a stocking cap with a knot in top, to the soles of her feet, the water flowed. At that point she didn't care about a towel, or soap, for that matter. Giving in to the comfort the shower provided, she placed a hand on each side wall and leaned forward. The warm water hit the back of her neck and followed her natural curves, streaming down her body. Wanting to forget the day before and the day before that, she stood with her eyes pressed together tightly. They were so tight they hurt, but not worse than her throbbing head and aching big toe.

When the warm water started to run cooler, she reached for a towel and body wash. Slowly she washed, then started to scrub. "Ugh," she yelled as she scrubbed her stomach, then looked down at herself. Like a madwoman, she scrubbed, then filled her towel with more body wash. Using a circular motion, she washed her vagina, then spread her legs apart. As if she could wash away all her previous sexual encounters, she made circular motions with the towel, then scrubbed up and down. Faster and harder, she rubbed until it stung. *God, if you're out there, please help me. What did I ever do to deserve this? I didn't ask for it.* Feeling weak, she dropped the towel and leaned back against the shower wall. Her eyes filled with tears as Renita haunted her thoughts.

"We don't cry," Renita yelled, spitting in Shiquanna's face as she threw the shopping bags onto her bed. One bag opened, and nothing but hot pants, miniskirts, and halter tops spilled out.

With tear-filled eyes, Shiquanna looked at the contents, then looked at her mother. Renita placed the long brown cigarette she held between two fingers against her lips, inhaled, then blew the smoke in Shiquanna's face. Shiquanna coughed uncontrollably. With a menacing look, Renita took a few steps back and leaned against the door. Renita folded her arms tightly across her chest, then rolled her eyes at Shiquanna.

Shiquanna leaned back on her hands, then looked around her mother. Her first thought was to jump out of bed, knock the hell out of Renita, and run away, never looking back again. With that vision in mind, Shiquanna searched for the nerve. She inched forward, but Renita put her cigarette in her mouth, placed her hands on her hips, and spread her legs across the threshold. She stood only five feet two inches tall and didn't weigh over 110 pounds, but Shiquanna was afraid to run by her.

"Get yo' ass dressed. The party starts in twenty minutes. Yo' ass better be on time. Don't make me come in here and get you. If I do, it ain't gonna be pretty." She inhaled, removed the cigarette from her mouth, and thumped the ashes onto the dresser. "Wipe dem damn tears right now," Renita said, then pointed toward the floor.

Hearing those words reverberate in her mind like a broken record, Shiquanna wiped her face with the back of her wet hands. "We don't cry," she repeated sternly. She stepped into the water spray and stood only long enough to rinse off the lather. Soaking wet, she stepped out of the shower, wrapped a towel around her body, and got back into bed. Afraid to close her eyes, she stared at the ceiling. No sooner than she got the nerve to close her eyes, her cell phone started to vibrate. She turned her head toward the nightstand it was on and looked at it. Momentarily, it stopped, then started to vibrate again.

She reached over to pick it up and looked at the caller ID display. "Hell, I got enough for my car note now," she said when she saw the judge's cell phone number in black. "I'm not in the mood to hear about your damn wife today." Wanting to turn it off but leaving it on for another client, she placed the phone facedown on her nightstand. "To hell with his ass," she said as her cell phone started to vibrate again. She picked it up, looked at the caller ID display, and, yes, it was him. No longer wanting to hear the buzz, she opened the top nightstand drawer and tossed the cell phone inside. It stopped vibrating, then started again before she could close the drawer. She turned up the corners of her mouth, then slammed the drawer shut.

Yes, her car note was paid, but her rent and utilities were due the following week. Working as a stripper came with no benefits. She didn't have a checking account, a savings account, health insurance, or a 401(k) for retirement. What extra cash she had was in a silver fireproof box, which she kept hidden in an upper kitchen cabinet. Fortunately, she'd been able to maintain her clientele, but she knew one day, when Mother Nature took over her body, all that would end. Who wanted to see an old-ass woman sliding up and down that silver pole? She knew one day her lips—not the ones on her face—would lose their elasticity and droop. Her breast implants would eventually sag, and she'd need another surgical lift. Yeah, she'd seen some girls stay in the business until their late thirties, but for them to maintain themselves physically was a lot of work. In the business they were considered old asses and had to work ten times as hard to compete with the fresh sixteen-year-olds that came in off the streets.

Repeating her yesterday for the next five years was physically and mentally impossible. To fight back more tears, she grabbed the pillow off of her bed and placed it over her face. *God, one day I hope you will hear me. I know I haven't been the best damn . . . Please excuse my mouth. I know I haven't been the best person, but you made me. This I know for a fact. If you made me, then I know one day you will listen to me. I didn't want to be a whore like my mother. I didn't want to be like her, and you know I didn't. She made me do it. Some nights I stayed up all night just to pass my tests the next day. You were there and you saw me do it. Hey, God, I really need you to listen to me.*

Like a jack-in-the-box, she sat up straight in her bed and looked out of her window. The sun was shining and the skies were clear. *Hey, God. Hey, God, you're supposed to hear and see everything. If you're out there, and I know you are, please listen to me.* She beat on her bed with her fists. *From now on, dammit . . . Oh, please forgive me for cursing so much. From now on . . . I'm going to bug you every day, until you help me. I've never been to church, and I wouldn't know what to do if I went to one. But if you're as big as Yvonne says you are, I don't have to go to church. You can hear me from right here. You made me, and you know how I roll. I'm persistent and I don't stop until my money is on the table.* She pointed at her nightstand. *I'm going to call on you the same way every day, until you respond. Are you listening to me? If you hear me, give me a sign.*

She almost jumped out of her skin when her cell phone started to vibrate in her drawer. Its hollowness made the buzzing sound echo even louder. She placed her hand against her chest, then looked out of the window. *That shit ain't funny, God. Please excuse me again. Scaring me like that ain't funny.* Thinking it was the judge, she decided not to look, but something told her to look, anyway. She opened the drawer, then reached inside. "What the hell?" she muttered when she saw Yvonne's name on the caller ID display. "Her stuck-up ass never calls me," she said, holding the phone in her hand as it vibrated, then stopped. *Humph,* she thought, still staring at the phone in total disbelief. Then she dialed Yvonne. Defensively, she placed her hand on her hip.

"Shiquanna."

Shiquanna removed the cell phone from her ear and looked at it. She couldn't see her face, but it sounded like Yvonne was smiling. "Yvonne," Shiquanna said slowly, shocked that she had called. As a matter of fact, it was the first time she'd ever called. All their communication, except at the weekly dinners, was done through India.

"I was on my way to my job interview."

"Yeeaah," Shiquanna responded slowly, wondering why this information was important enough for her to call. Yvonne didn't call her when she was on her way to volunteer at the church.

"I was driving, and the spirit of God placed it on my heart to call you," Yvonne said tenderly.

Shiquanna frowned and turned up the corners of her mouth. "Oh, really?" she asked, always thinking Yvonne was full of shit.

"I'm running late, but I knew I had to be obedient."

"Uh-huh," Shiquanna responded, not relating Yvonne's phone call to her plea for help. In her opinion, Yvonne would be the last person on the list of Christians whom God would send to help her out.

"He wants you to know that He loves you and salvation is free. Well, I'm turning into the parking lot now. If you ever need someone to talk to or pray with, you remember I'm here."

"Sure," Shiquanna responded hesitantly.

"I have to go and nail this interview. See you next week at dinner. If I don't hear from you before then, have a blessed week."

Just that fast the conversation was over, leaving Shiquanna to ponder Yvonne's sincerity. "God loves me," Shiquanna repeated, then looked out of the window again. Almost instantly the sun beamed brighter through her window and cast the reflection of a rainbow on her wall. In awe, she stared, fluffed a pillow behind her, then leaned back to rest her head, which was still throbbing.

Chapter 11

India

Creator, I would like to thank you for another day. Please help me to remain centered as I'm used as a vessel to complete your tasks on earth. With her eyes closed, India silently repeated the affirmation three times, then used her hand to feel beside her. The covers weren't turned back, so she opened her eyes and turned her head. From the looks of it, Tracey had never come to bed. India folded her arms across her chest and closed her eyes again. It was the first night since they'd moved in that they'd slept separately. Yes, they'd had the occasional lovers' spat, but one of them would relent and make up before the night was over. Most times it was Tracey. Realizing they'd fallen asleep in separate rooms, with unresolved issues, saddened her.

Ready to talk but uncertain what she'd say, India rolled over and sat up. To loosen the tension in her neck, she leaned her head forward, then moved it from side to side. Slowly, she rotated her shoulders in a circular motion, then stood. Wanting their bedroom to be a place of total rest and solitude, India refused to have a television or alarm clock in it. Initially, Tracey had misunderstood her preference but soon appreciated not waking up to a startling buzz.

Barefoot, she walked across the carpeted floor, contemplating how to greet Tracey in the other room. *Good morning. Did you rest well on the couch last night? Are you too upset to talk?* Unsure what to expect, she inhaled, then opened the door. The blinds were open, allowing natural sunlight to illuminate the great room. In her opinion, that alone was a good sign. If Tracey was still upset, the blinds would have been closed, as she preferred to sit in the dark to think. Tracey wasn't on the couch.

"Trace," India called, then listened to her voice echo. There was no response, so she walked down the short hallway and opened the door to their extra bedroom. There were no signs of Tracey having slept there, either. *Humph,* India thought, closed the door, then went back into the family room. She looked at the time on the DVD player. It was only eight o'clock, and Tracey normally left home at eight thirty. Because of her late nights at the jazz club, she never scheduled a lesson before nine o'clock. Disappointed but confident all things worked together for good, India hunched her shoulders, then went into the kitchen.

"Tracey," India said, then smiled when she looked down and saw a clear glass plate with fresh strawberries and pieces of pineapple on it. Underneath it was a note. India took a piece of pineapple, bit into it, then picked up the note to read it.

My dearest India,

For us, eating breakfast together every morning is customary. This morning I felt differently. I love you with all my heart, but I need to know you love me back. Writing this seemed easier than saying it, but at some point, you have to make a decision. I have. Enjoy your breakfast.

Love always,
Tracey

P.S. I didn't see Betsy parked in the driveway and assumed you had car trouble. I left the spare key to the Jetta in the top kitchen drawer next to the stove.

India put the remainder of the piece of pineapple back on the plate, then tried to chew and swallow the bite in her mouth. Suddenly her appetite disappeared. From the note, India sensed Tracey's disappointment, but she knew Tracey loved her enough to look out for her needs. India leaned back against the kitchen counter and stared at the fruit, which was neatly arranged on the plate. Tracey's love was deeper than India had ever imagined. She turned around, opened the top drawer, and got out the cellophane wrap. She tore off a piece, covered the fruit, and placed it in the refrigerator. Deep in thought, she tapped the box of wrap against her fingertips, then put it back into the drawer. She took a step forward, stopped, then leaned back against the counter to reflect.

How long will Tracey deal with my uncertainty? Is the note an apology or an ultimatum? India pushed herself away from the counter and reached for the telephone. It didn't matter that she had class in an hour, because talking to Tracey had become more important. She dialed Tracey's cell phone and waited as it rang. Three rings, no answer. Four rings, no answer. Then the call went to her voice mail. India waited a few seconds, then dialed the number again. The outcome was the same. "Tracey, we really need to talk," was all she could think to say after the beep. Then she thought to call the studio, which she'd only done one time, for an emergency. She dialed the number and listened as the phone rang and rang. Really wanting to talk but accepting the missed calls as divine intervention, she went into the bedroom to get ready for class.

"Hello," she answered, gasping for breath, when she made a mad dash back into the kitchen to answer the telephone.

"Hello. May I speak to the owner of the home?" A gentleman with a foreign accent asked.

"She isn't here," India said, disappointed it wasn't Tracey returning her call. "This is . . ." Without a second thought, India ended the call, went into the bedroom, and shut the door.

All things work together for good. She repeated the affirmation to herself as she walked through the bedroom and into the bathroom. She turned on the water at the sink, put both hands together, and allowed them to fill with water. She closed her eyes, lowered her face, and splashed it with water. With a face towel, she patted it dry, then brushed her teeth. *All things work together for good.* She looked in the mirror, trying to convince herself it was true in every situation.

Her first class started at ten o'clock, so she went into the closet, got a pair of faded jeans off of a hanger, an Obama T-shirt, and her favorite worn sneakers. She dressed, got her things, then left.

"Need a ride?" Reese asked, getting straight to the point when India answered her cell phone. Hearing his voice made her smile, even though she'd hoped it was Tracey.

"Good morning, Reese," she responded, impressed he'd called to check on her after everything he'd already done the night before. "Thanks for looking out, but Tracey left me the keys to her car. Actually, I'm on my way to class now." By then she was only five minutes away from campus.

"Great," he said. "What time does your class start?"

"Ten o'clock. I'm running a little late, but it's not the first time. It's my aerobics class, and you know how I feel about exercising for a college credit," she said, then laughed. "But I need it to graduate, and I've avoided it as long as I can. You know I've been a senior forever." Together they laughed.

"I know you'd rather take a class that stimulates you intellectually."

"Definitely. How will toned biceps and taut abdominal muscles help me serve as an ambassador in a Third World country?"

"I guess you'll be able to lift four ten-pound bags

of rice instead of two," he said, then burst out into laughter again.

"Reese, only you would find humor in my observation. That's what I miss about you the most." She paused.

"Yeah, we did laugh a lot when we had only three hours left to finish the final edits on our manuscript and FedEx it to New York."

"No, I beg to differ. *You* laughed a lot." She remembered how warm his smile really was.

"Maybe so, but together we got it done. I really miss those long hours we spent together. Even though we were working, I'll admit I enjoyed every second."

"Yeah," India said, sensing the conversation had taken on a more serious tone.

"What are you doing after class? I wanted to know if you'd like to meet again at the coffee shop."

"After class I'm going to the library to finish a research paper I'm working on."

"Then after that?"

"After that I was going home." She really hoped Tracey would return her call and want to talk.

"Please don't take this the wrong way, but I really enjoyed being with you last night. I know you're in a relationship, but I would love to be your friend. Everyone needs someone to confide in."

"Of course, we do." She turned into the parking lot and drove around until she found an empty space in the back row. She parked, grabbed her book bag, then got out of the car.

"Contrary to popular belief, every black man isn't interested in women for sex only. For me, good conversation is far more stimulating and can last forever. I'd rather have a best friend."

"Now that's peace." India adjusted her book bag on her shoulder and prepared to walk across campus.

"I know you're on your way to class, but remember, I'm here if you need me. It doesn't matter what time of day or night it is. Call me."

"Reese, friends like you are rare. Thanks a million."

"No, India. Thank you."

India traipsed across campus, with a smile, after she ended the call.

Chapter 12

Shiquanna

Grrrr . . . The gruesome roar of her stomach stirred Shiquanna out of a deep sleep. She placed her hand on her midsection, then rubbed, hoping the sound would go away. The more she rubbed, the louder her stomach growled back at her. *Grrr* . . . It roared again.

Like a child, she kicked her feet, then yanked the covers over her head. It was the first night in weeks she didn't work at the club, and she didn't have any lunch-hour commitments. Her client who preferred to meet during lunch twice a week was out of town, at a convention. With the covers over her face, she opened her eyes, then turned onto her side. Unable to ignore her hunger pangs, she threw the covers back, sat up, then placed her feet on the floor.

She looked at her reflection in the dresser mirror directly in front of her. *I look like shit.* Sometime during the night, her stocking cap had come off of her head and the elastic band that held her hair back in a ponytail had broken. Her shoulder-length hair was everywhere. She used her fingers to pull it back, then wrapped it in a bun. "Jesus," she called, rocked back and forth, then used her hands to stand. Her long days and late nights were obviously starting to catch up with her, as she heard every bone in her body snap. It was a first, as far as she could remember.

She couldn't account for previous mornings, as she always woke up to a shot of the tequila that she kept on her nightstand. Most days she was absent from her own reality. Her toes popped with every step as she shuffled across the floor. From disbelief, she stopped for a second, then looked down at her short toes, which seemed to be fine. When she started to walk, the noise reoccurred. All she could do was frown.

She bent down to grab a pair of hot pants and a T-shirt off of the pile on the floor, then held her back as she stood erect. *I ain't believing this shit.* She rubbed the spot that ached the worst. Only two nights before she'd performed before a standing-room-only crowd at the club. Why didn't she ache then? she wondered, then credited her flexibility to endless tequila shots and vodka from the bar. She stepped into her hot pants, slid the T-shirt on over her head, then put on a pair of high-heeled sandals. A short blond wig was on her dresser, so she grabbed it and went into the bathroom.

The impression of her face was still on the towel from earlier, so she picked it up and laughed. "Ouch!" she exclaimed when the laughter made her head ache. She held her forehead, then got a clean towel. She looked in the mirror, then frowned at her swollen eyes, which had black rings of mascara around them. Veins popped in her eyes, making them look red as fire. For that, she was prepared: she picked up the eyedrop bottle, leaned her head back, and let a couple of drops fall into each eye. She looked in the mirror, then batted her eyes. *Damn, I look forty-nine instead of twenty-nine. Are those crow's-feet? I'll be damned if I have wrinkles around my eyes.* She leaned forward and turned her head to one side to take a closer look.

She wet her towel, filled it with soap, then washed. She put on the blond wig and adjusted it as she walked back into the bedroom. Looking at it in the mirror wasn't necessary, as she'd had to change many times in gas stations with fewer amenities. For a final adjustment, she rubbed her fingers around her ears. She grabbed her purse and the darkest pair of shades off of her dresser. *Oh shit, my cell phone.* She walked to the nightstand, opened the drawer, and removed her only means of communication. Still not wanting to leave her apartment, she walked into the kitchen and opened the refrigerator. The blast of cold air created condensation on her shades. She took them off and wiped them on the bottom of her T-shirt. There was nothing but a liter of tequila on the bottom shelf. She stared a second longer, then closed the refrigerator door.

She opened the front door and was blinded by the sun's beaming rays, which filtered through her shades. She squinted, then placed her hands over her eyes to shield them as she walked to her car and got inside. The radio blared when she started the ignition, reawakening the headache, which she thought was gone. It was more than she could tolerate, so she turned off the radio and massaged her temples. The pain increased, so she dumped the contents of her large purse onto the passenger's seat to find anything to assuage it. She shook an old prescription bottle whose label was worn from being in her purse so long.

It was a painkiller prescribed by a dentist over six months ago, after an extraction. Something rattled inside. She twisted the top and let two medium-sized white pills fall into her hand. She leaned her head back, placed one in the center of her tongue, and washed it down with saliva. She did the second pill the same way, almost choking when it didn't go down as easily as the first. She looked around but didn't have anything in her car or purse to drink. Not even a shot-sized bottle of tequila. She swallowed again, then backed out of her driveway.

C.J.'s, her favorite twenty-four-hour eatery, was only four blocks away. After a strenuous show at the strip club, she would often stuff herself there, then go home and drink herbal laxative teas. Her body was her only source of income. Whether it was dancing at the club, doing a private party or her personal clients, her body had to look perfect at all times. She was on call twenty-four hours a day.

She turned into the parking lot of C.J.'s, parked, then got out. She strutted toward the door, ignoring the stares and whistles of two men standing by an old black pickup truck. She adjusted her purse on her shoulder, threw her head back, and looked in the opposite direction. The fact that her firm buttocks were exposed could have been a factor, but she knew right off neither of them could afford her services. They both had on cheap two-piece linen outfits and too-shiny man-made shoes. She was a whore but not a desperate one. Even she had standards. She swung the glass door open and found her place at the bar.

"Hey, girlfriend. What can I do for you this morning?" asked Portia, the heavyset cook, with an assortment of clip-on ponytails, which she kept tucked inside a hairnet. She was blue black, weighed at least two hundred pounds, and sang when she cooked. She wore heavy make-up and kept her full lips lined with brown liner. To Shiquanna, none of that mattered, because Portia had the personality of an angel. Plus, Portia fixed a mean Philly cheese-steak sandwich, and Shiquanna loved it when she was there.

"I'd like two of your award-winning Philly cheese-steak sandwiches, hash browns with cheese and onions, and sweet tea." Shiquanna sat her purse in her lap and rested her head against her hand.

"You a'ight, girlfriend?" Knowing Shiquanna worked late nights at the strip club, Portia patted the counter to get her attention. She got a large plastic cup, filled it to the rim with sweet tea, then sat it in front of Shiquanna.

"Ain't nothing a good meal can't cure," Shiquanna said, then barely smiled. She lifted the cup to her mouth and drank half of the tea before putting it back down.

Portia put a hand on her hip and looked at Shiquanna sideways. "Thirsty, girlfriend?" she asked, then refilled Shiquanna's cup with tea.

Shiquanna lifted her right hand and shook her head from side to side.

"I got you, boo. Two of my famous Philly cheese-steak sandwiches coming up." Portia turned her back to Shiquanna and went to work.

For the next few minutes, all Shiquanna heard was the noise of utensils against the hot grill and Portia singing the new Rihhana hit. Shiquanna drank more tea and waited.

"Would you like some mayo to go with those sandwiches, sweetie?" Portia asked, sounding like somebody's grandmother when she turned around and put the plate in front of Shiquanna.

"Yes, girl, you already know," Shiquanna said. She took a bite out of a sandwich, then chewed a couple of times before swallowing.

"Let me know if you need any more tea." Portia pointed at Shiquanna's cup, which was almost empty again.

Shiquanna's mouth was full, so she lifted her hand to respond. Her ice cubes rattled when Portia refilled her cup. The next time she looked up, her plate was empty. She drank the rest of her tea, then wiped her mouth with a napkin. "You did it again. If I ever hit the lotto, I want you to be my personal cook."

"Girlfriend, I clean, too." Portia laughed, then threw up both hands. "Beggars can't be choosers I'll even do windows." Together they laughed.

"Pretty lady, I'll do your windows for free," said an older gentleman with a bald head, who was sitting next to Shiquanna.

Shiquanna looked at him and all his wrinkles, then rolled her eyes. None of her potential clients would be caught dead in this place. Plus, the thought of going down on an old man really disgusted her.

"Girl, he don't even know." Portia looked at the old man, then laughed.

"No, he doesn't," replied Shiquanna. She'd done fat, but old was out of the question.

"Here's your check, girlfriend." Portia removed the yellow pad from her pocket and tore off the top sheet. She placed it on the counter, in front of Shiquanna.

Shiquanna's total was nine dollars and some change, but she complimented Portia by putting a twenty-dollar bill on top of the check. "Keep the change."

From years of late-night conversations, Shiquanna knew Portia had three girls at home. She was a high school dropout but could cook her ass off. Her dream was to get her GED and go to culinary school to become a real chef. In so many ways, Shiquanna tried to help by leaving a large tip. One night Portia had cried secretly and then had shared with Shiquanna how her middle daughter needed a new pair of basketball shoes, which she just couldn't afford. That night Shiquanna had pulled out her stack of tips and counted out fifty-one dollar bills. Portia had thanked Shiquanna through tears and promised to pay her back the next week. Shiquanna had assured her she didn't want the money back, but Portia tried to repay her the next week, anyway. Shiquanna had refused because her donation was genuine. She admired a mother who would slave over a hot grill to provide for her daughters. Renita had made her sell her body.

Fighting another flashback, Shiquanna leaned her head down and closed her eyes. "I'll see you later." She lifted her large purse, then stood to leave.

"Love ya, girlfriend. Be careful out there." Portia placed a hand on each hip and smiled from ear to ear as she lifted the check and the twenty-dollar bill in the air.

"I will," Shiquanna said, looking over her shoulder as she exited the restaurant. She walked to her car. She got into her car, then watched Portia through the large window as she turned around to face the grill. Her coordination was perfect as she listened to orders and cooked all at the same time. With that visual of a hardworking single mother, Shiquanna started her car, then drove away. Her first destination before going to the club was the liquor store, to restock her tequila shot bottles.

Chapter 13

Yvonne

With her shoulders back, her clutch purse underneath her arm, and her leather briefcase in hand, Yvonne stood in front of the clear double automatic doors and waited. She smiled, then winked at her own reflection. The doors separated, and with an air of confidence, she strutted through. Immediately her eyes were drawn upward as she admired the seven- or eight-story crystal fountain with a water display in the lobby. To her left, a male security guard in a dark blue suit, with a bald spot he'd covered with a few long strands of hair, was seated at the front desk.

"Yes, ma'am? How may I help you this morning?" he asked, with a head nod, momentarily taking his eyes off the small television screens in front of him.

"I'm looking for the Henry, Johnson, and McClerkin accounting firm."

"Take the set of elevators on your right to the

tenth floor. It's suite ten-twelve." He pointed, then gave the television screens his full attention.

"Thank you very much." She smiled at him, then started to walk in that direction.

She opened her purse to look at the time on her cell phone and saw that she had only twenty minutes to spare. Her heels made a click-clack sound against the marble floors as she took longer steps toward the elevators. Just as she got closer, one opened up. She saw that it was going up, stepped inside, and pressed the number ten. A bell chimed as the elevator passed the first three floors, then stopped on the fourth. Yvonne watched, then blew, as two ladies and a gentleman took their time getting on. Their conversation seemed more important than the delay for the other passengers already on the elevator. The silver doors closed, and the bell chimed as the elevator ascended. All was well, until it seemed to stop on every floor thereafter, either for someone to get on or get off.

Yvonne's patience was being tested, and she looked at her cell phone, then started to tap her feet against the floor. "Finally," she grunted through clenched teeth. She "pardoned" her way from the back of the elevator, where she'd been forced to stand as people got on, and stepped off. She stood in front of the elevator, then looked from left to right as the doors closed behind her. Not only did the hallway seem endless, but there were hallways off of it. She looked ahead, but there were no signs to indicate which way she should go. *Suite 1012.*

With very little time left, she had to make a decision. She decided to walk to the right. The first office door on her left read SUITE 1050, and she hadn't a clue if she was indeed going in the right direction. She walked faster, and the next door read SUITE 1054. Seeing that the numbers were increasing, she turned and walked in the opposite direction. She passed the elevators, finally seeing a silver plaque displayed at eye level on the right side of the wall. At that point she was running late and didn't criticize herself for not seeing it to begin with. Her steps were long as she hurried, not wanting to make a negative first impression.

"Suite ten-twelve." She inhaled, then opened her purse to remove a powder sponge. Her cheeks felt warm from perspiration. She blotted her face a few times, then put the sponge back into her purse. Before opening the door, she fanned herself with her jacket to cool off. Then she entered.

"Good morning," said a young woman with perky boobs, proudly displayed in her low-cut blouse. She was sitting behind an oval cherrywood desk, with the partners' names in gold letters across the front, in an office that had an elegant design. A beautiful black art print hung behind her. "Welcome to the Henry, Johnson, and McClerkin accounting firm. How may I assist you?" Trying to mask what Yvonne thought was a hint of ghetto, she spoke slowly, overenunciating her words. She was very attractive, but her multicolored eye shadow and black eyeliner were a bit much for an office setting. Her blond hair was short, and long bangs covered her left eye.

"Yes, you may," Yvonne said sternly, trying not to judge the partners by their representative at the front desk as she leaned forward and saw the young woman's black miniskirt. "I have a nine o'clock interview."

The receptionist forced a smile, batted her eyelashes at Yvonne, then made a few keystrokes in the computer. Her long acrylic—a different design had been airbrushed on each nail—tapped against the keys. "You may be seated. I'll let them know you're here." She pushed a button, then spoke into her headset.

Just as Yvonne turned to find a seat either on the plush leather sofa or in the row of office chairs placed against the wall, a tall gentleman opened a door. "Ms. Miller," he called smoothly.

"Yes, sir." Yvonne gasped when the Boris Kodjoe look-alike stepped forward and extended his hand. She loved Reverend Alston to death but was stunned by this gentleman's exceptionally good looks. She played it cool by allowing her right hand to brush the side of her skirt before shaking his.

"My name is Gerald Johnson. I'm one of the partners of this organization."

Yvonne looked at the man, who didn't look a day over thirty. She'd done hours of research on the accounting firm, which had been founded thirty years ago by three gentlemen named Henry, Johnson, and McClerkin. This man's young looks didn't equate, but she didn't want to question the firm's credibility prematurely. "Good morning, Mr. Johnson. It's a pleasure to meet you."

"Very well, Ms. Miller. We're already set up for you in the conference room." He pointed to another door. He tapped on the receptionist's desk to get her attention. "Please hold all calls."

She stopped her conversation long enough to move her head up and down. "Yes, sir," she responded, then crossed her long legs at the knee.

"Ms. Miller, if you would please follow me," said Gerald Johnson.

Yvonne followed him down the short hallway to the conference room. He opened the door and interrupted what appeared to be a very heated discussion, as evidenced by the frowns and body movements. No sooner than she entered the room, the atmosphere changed and all conversation ended. An older version of Gerald Johnson was seated at the head of the table. The slim, bald-headed man with a thick gray mustache was leaning back in a large leather chair, with his hands clasped across his stomach. Two gentlemen sat on either side of him.

"Dad, this is Ms. Yvonne Miller," Gerald said as they entered the room. All five gentlemen stood and shook her hand as Gerald introduced them individually.

"Ms. Miller, please be seated," Mr. Gerald Johnson Sr. said, then motioned with his hand at an empty seat next to him. Gerald took his place by a chair opposite her. Together they sat down and the interview began, with Mr. Gerald Johnson Sr. asking the first question. Yvonne sat erect, looked him in the eyes, then answered. He encouraged input from the other board members. For the next hour, Yvonne was engrossed in the conversation. Then, suddenly, she stopped talking, almost choking on her words when she became delusional. Each board member, young and old alike, looked like Reverend Marion Alston.

"Ms. Miller, are you okay?" Mr. Gerald Johnson Sr. asked as he tapped the table with his fingertips to get her attention.

She looked at the person who she thought was Gerald Johnson Jr., then patted her chest to end a cough. All she saw was Reverend Alston's face as Gerald stood to pour her a glass of water, then handed it to her. She held up one finger, then took a couple of sips of water. Before responding, she took the time to swallow and clear her throat.

"Gentlemen, please excuse me. I swallowed incorrectly," she exclaimed, then closed her eyes tightly for one second to erase any images of Reverend Alston.

"Ms. Miller, we're a tough crew, and we have been drilling you nonstop for the past hour. If you have to step outside for a few minutes, believe me, we will not be offended," Mr. Gerald Johnson Sr. exclaimed as he looked at his partners, who all shared a look of concern. Together they nodded as Mr. Gerald Johnson Sr. gestured toward the door.

"No, sir, that will not be necessary. I'm even tougher," Yvonne said through a smile, then took another sip of water. Uncertain about what had caused her panic attack, she inhaled to slow her heart rate, then refocused. In her opinion, it was only an opportunity to prove how she'd respond in the most stressful environment. As if nothing had happened, she welcomed another question with a smile and a head nod.

With no additional interruptions, thirty minutes later the interview ended. Everyone stood, shook hands, and Yvonne walked toward the door, with her shoulders back and her head held high. *Oh my God! Please allow me to get out of here without passing out in front of them.* Even though she'd experienced the most embarrassing moment of her life, her posture exuded the same air of confidence she'd entered with. She held her breath as she exited the conference room and walked by the receptionist, who said something, which she completely ignored.

Her stride length was long as she walked to the elevators and pressed the button repeatedly. The doors of one of the elevators started to separate, and she turned her body sideways to step through the narrow opening. She "pardoned" her way by four people to find a spot in the back. Embarrassed, she let her head rest against the back wall and closed her eyes. *Oh my God. What happened in there? Yvonne, you made a complete idiot out of yourself. You absolutely blew it. A firm with that reputation will give you only one shot, and you blew it.*

She heard the elevator chime as the doors opened and closed. After a few more stops, she opened her eyes and saw they were on the second floor. Then she became anxious, patting her right foot as the elevator stopped on the first floor and the doors opened. She followed a group of people off the elevator and into the lobby. In her opinion, they moved too slowly. Panting for fresh air, she walked around them and stopped directly in front of the double glass doors. They barely separated before she started to walk through.

Your savings are down to almost nothing. You can pay your bills only for another three months. Her criticism continued as she walked out the front door and to her car. *Don't worry, girlfriend. This is only a test of your faith.* She changed the tone of her internal monologue from one of critique to consolation as she got into her car. *God is an on-time God. Just when you've exhausted all your resources and all else has failed, God will deliver your husband.* She thought of an old gospel song, then searched her console. She found the CD, inserted it into her player, then started her car. Certain her God would deliver her husband, she sang with the artist as she drove out of the parking lot and toward the church.

Yvonne's heart raced when she turned onto Hestler Street. It was eleven thirty, and she had taken her chances, not knowing whether Reverend Alston would be at the church or not. If nothing else, making edits to the database, which she'd completed last week, could be her excuse. She turned into the parking lot and smiled when she saw Reverend Alston's white Mercedes parked in its usual spot by the side entrance.

Parking with his office window in view was easy as there were only a few cars in the parking lot and they belonged to staff. She parked, then used her rearview mirror to look toward Reverend Alston's office window. She couldn't see him, but that didn't mean he wouldn't look out while she was getting out of her car to go inside. With that in mind, she leaned forward to check her make-up in the rearview mirror. Other than a little touching up, which could be done with her make-up sponge, nothing was needed. She was pleased. Her lip liner and gloss were darker than usual, but they coordinated perfectly with her natural eye shadow. She opened her car door, placed one foot on the ground, then stole a look, hoping to see him in the window. He wasn't in the window, but she knew he was on the premises. Before leaving, she would see her one true love. Knowing that, she walked across the parking lot and entered the church, with a smile. The entryway was empty, but she could hear laughter and conversation coming from downstairs. She paused but didn't hear the reverend's voice, so she went upstairs and into the main office.

"Good afternoon. How may I help you?" asked a light-skinned woman with the facial features of a supermodel and large brown eyes. She was seated behind the secretary's desk.

Who in the hell is this bitch sitting behind Sister Hathaway's desk? Yvonne asked herself before speaking aloud. "Where is Sister Hathaway?" Yvonne asked, with wide eyes, looking around the office for the church secretary. For as long as Yvonne could remember, Sister Hathaway had been the church's secretary. The fifty-something-year-old, with three children and five grandchildren, had never been a threat to her relationship with the reverend. Sister Hathaway weighed at least two hundred pounds, wore loose floral dresses, and hadn't seen a perm in years.

"Sister Hathaway will be out of the office for at least three weeks," said the woman, then stood.

"Three weeks?" Yvonne asked as the tall, perfectly proportioned woman stepped from behind the desk. She was wearing a beautiful red silk blouse, which fit snugly around her bust, and a long skirt with a slit. Yvonne gasped at her sexy ankle-strap shoes with peep toes when she walked to the printer on the other side of the room. *This is the house of God, not a damn nightclub,* Yvonne thought as she continued to size up her competition.

"Yes, ma'am. Her daughter from out of state called yesterday with a family emergency. Sister Hathaway called the pastor and said she was catching the first thing smoking this morning."

"So does that mean you're going to be filling in as secretary for the next three weeks?" Yvonne asked, then pointed at her while looking toward the reverend's office door.

"Yes, ma'am, it does." The woman tapped the papers she was holding against her hand, then looked toward the reverend's office door, with a smile.

"My name is Sister Yvonne Miller." Yvonne's stance became defensive as she placed a hand on her hip. "From first impressions, it seems like we may be the same age, so please don't call me ma'am," Yvonne said sternly, then looked at her from head to toe.

"Ma'am, I'm so sorry. It's an old habit," she said, returning the look and hunching her shoulders.

"Well, some old habits are meant to be broken. Addressing me as ma'am will be a good place for you to start." Yes, she might look like a supermodel, but Yvonne let her know that she was nothing to be played with. Seeing Jesus at the pearly gates was of utmost importance, but she had no problem laying her religion down to fight for her man.

"Yes, ma'am." She grinned mischievously, then walked to her desk. "Did you have an appointment?" She placed the papers on her desk, then carefully tucked her skirt underneath her before sitting down. Yvonne watched as she crossed her legs, tucked one foot behind her ankle, then rested her legs against the desk.

"No, I didn't." Yvonne placed her clutch purse underneath her arm and swished toward the extra office, which she'd been using to complete her project. She opened the door and caught herself before slamming it shut. *Yvonne,* she thought, addressing herself. *Yvonne, what if Reverend Alston is in his office and overheard the tone of voice you used with his new secretary? Is your insecure attitude appropriate for the future first lady of this congregation? No, it is not. Just in case Marion is in his office and overheard the conversation, you have to fix it immediately. You can't let a pretty face and fine figure discourage you or make you feel insecure. Plus, you have so much more to offer. Look at her. She's a peasant with a perfect face. Who wants to marry a secretary when he can have a woman with degrees and a career?*

Yvonne placed her purse by the computer and opened the door. The main computer was off and a note that read "Out to lunch" was on the desk.

Good, Yvonne thought and closed the door. *I don't want to talk to that slut, anyway. How dare she think she's going to steal my man? I really like her nerve, coming up in here dressed like that. Reverend Marion Alston is my man, and nobody, I mean no damn body, will ever come between us.* Instead of turning on the computer and pretending to edit the new database, Yvonne sat down behind the small desk and contemplated her game plan. There was no way she was going to let some new secretary come between her and her future husband. She leaned back in the chair, placed a hand over her mouth, and rocked back and forth.

Chapter 14

India

Tracey's back was turned when India opened the door and entered the kitchen. Except for the sound of water running into the sink, the house was quiet. The television wasn't on, and no music was playing. Tracey hated complete silence when she was home alone and always had some type of background noise. Interpreting the silence as a negative sign, India inhaled, then hoped today wouldn't be a repeat of the day before.

"You're home early," India said calmly, then looked at the time on the microwave. It was only four o'clock. Again, that was unusual, as Tracey never made it home before eight o'clock.

"Yeah," was all Tracey said. She never turned to look at India and appeared busy doing something in the sink.

Stumped by her short answer, India walked around to the opposite side of the kitchen and leaned her book bag against a cabinet. Tracey never looked up, which shocked India after the note and fresh fruit she'd taken the time to prepare earlier. "Thanks for breakfast this morning." India only hoped to start a conversation that would lead to their making up. She didn't want them to sleep apart another night.

"No problem."

"How were things at the studio?" India asked, then leaned against the counter.

"I canceled all my classes."

"Wow. Are you feeling okay?" India asked, with a look of concern, then placed a finger over her lip. The studio Tracey had opened in her old neighborhood five years ago was her dream. Teaching music, especially to underprivileged children, was her passion. The studio was open six days a week, and India remembered only one time Tracey didn't go in. Even with a severe case of gastrointestinal distress, Tracey had done everything to make it to the studio that day but couldn't.

"I'm fine." Tracey blew, then splashed the water with her hands.

"I'm only concerned. Unless you're falling over and almost half dead, you never cancel classes."

"If I were falling over dead, would you even notice?" She rinsed off a plate, then slammed it into the dish rack. The other dishes rattled against each other.

"Where did that comment come from?" India had never seen Tracey so temperamental. "I thought after breakfast and the note you left this morning, we were okay."

"You know what?" Tracey rinsed off her hands,

then turned around. "Never mind where it came from. Did you read the note?" she asked, then held both hands up in the air.

"Yes, I read the note." India was surprised by Tracey's bad attitude. How could she have taken the time to prepare breakfast, leave the keys to her extra car, and write a note if she was so upset?

"India, how did you read the note?" Tracey leaned against the sink and folded her arms across her chest.

"What do you mean?"

"How did you read the note? Did you read it literally, or were you wearing those cute little rose-colored glasses?"

"I read the note, and I'm ready to talk about our relationship."

"I'll admit I fell in love with you the first time I saw you, standing alone at the music festival. There was something about your smile. You had a unique glow, and there was a warm aura all around you." For a moment Tracey looked away. "I only hoped that you were there alone. Then I hoped you weren't dating anyone. I watched closely, and no one, male or female, showed up. I assumed even if you were in a relationship, you were there alone. I got up the nerve and promised myself I would not leave without an introduction."

India watched as Tracey recapped their meeting for the first time, without smiling. That hurt India.

Tracey went on. "I dealt with my sexuality in high school. Being attracted to girls wasn't an easy issue to deal with as a teenager. I had my first real relationship with another woman in college. And believe me, I know a lesbian when I see one. But with you, I was willing to take my chances. Yeah, maybe I was wrong for coming on to you. But I didn't think it was strong, and you had every opportunity to stop me or walk away. India, you didn't. You accepted my invitation to stay for our last set. I followed you home that night. You didn't stop me when I touched you or rubbed the top of your hand. You didn't turn your head when I leaned in for a kiss good night. You welcomed my embrace."

India closed her eyes and remembered that touch again.

"Come on now. You're not that naive. At some point early on in the conversation, I'm sure you figured out I was a lesbian and was making a pass at you."

India parted her lips to speak.

"No, let me finish my thought. For months after we met, knowing you were straight, I questioned my approach. I'll admit I even talked to one of the fellas in the band about it. You know what he asked me? How did you respond? I admitted you never told me no. For me, your willingness was a cue that you were open to me and this relationship."

"Tracey, listen to me please." India tried to speak again.

"No, this time I have the floor." Her brows touched when she pointed toward the floor. "I want you to listen to me. You knew the more time we spent together, the deeper our—no, let me rephrase that—my feelings would become. You knew the more we made love, the more intense my feelings for you would become. But you've proven to be selfish, in that you've considered no one but yourself in this situation. I've dealt with your secrecy for two years, and no matter how much it hurts me to say this, you have to make a decision."

"Tracey, I love you," India said, then took a step toward Tracey, with outstretched arms. No, she'd never considered herself a lesbian, but her love for Tracey was undeniable. With Tracey's help, she knew she could overcome her fears.

"You've said that to me for how long now? It's time for you to show it," Tracey said sternly, then turned around to face the sink.

India stood speechless, hoping she would turn around to finish their conversation.

Tracey got a dish towel, wet it, and started to wipe around the sink.

India got the message, picked up her book bag, and walked toward the door. "I don't have a car. May I borrow yours again?"

Tracey didn't answer and never turned her head, so India left.

Perplexed, India got into the car. Again, it was a time she could have used the shoulder of a girlfriend to lean on. Shiquanna knew about Tracey but was the last person she'd call for advice on relationships. Yvonne's input, even if India told the story from someone else's perspective, was out of the question. All she'd do was damn the person, who happened to be India, to hell. With that in mind, India started the car and pulled out of the driveway. Going nowhere in particular, she started to drive.

Minutes later she turned into the parking lot of her and Reese's favorite coffee shop. She looked inside and noticed their favorite booth was empty. Fortunately, Reese had become the one person she could talk to about her relationship with Tracey. She reached into her bag and got her cell phone. She rested her head against her left hand, then dialed his number.

"What's up, India?"

"Reese, did I catch you at a bad time?"

"India, no time that you call me is ever a bad time."

"I'm inclined to believe you'd tell me that even if you were busy." She looked at the empty booth inside, then laughed.

"Honestly, you're probably right. I'd put down everything for you."

"I really hope this isn't a bad time. I'm sitting in front of the coffee shop, and our booth is empty. Would you like to join me?"

"Your timing couldn't have been better. I just finished my last class a few minutes ago and was getting ready to leave. I can be there in a few minutes."

"Great. You know where to find me." India turned off the car, got out, and went inside.

"Hello, ma'am," said a tall, thin white man that India had never seen before. He gave her a huge smile. He wore a paper cap, a uniform shirt, and blue jeans. "The regular cook walked out on us today. That leaves only me cooking and one waitress, so you can have a seat anywhere you like." He looked toward the waitress, who was on the other side of the coffee shop and was busy taking orders. Her face was new to India.

"Thank you," India said, then walked toward their usual booth in the far corner.

"We'll be with you in a minute," replied the man. He went to work preparing another order that the waitress had called out from the end of the counter. India took a journal and pen out of her bag, turned to a blank page, and started to write.

"Hey, my name is Lisa, and I'll be your waitress until someone else comes in," said the waitress, a fragile lady who looked like she didn't weigh even one hundred pounds. Suddenly she looked over her shoulder at the door.

"I'll have a cup of coffee." India looked up from her journal and saw Reese's car turn into the parking lot. "Make that two cups of coffee," she said, knowing that was what he would ask for.

"All right. I'll be back in a second with your coffee."

"Hello, India," Reese said, then leaned down to hug her.

"I thought you were on campus," India said after hugging him back.

"Campus is only a few minutes away."

"It seemed like I just ended our conversation."

"Yeah, you ended it about twenty minutes ago."

"Wow," India said, then looked down at her journal, not realizing she'd filled three pages with thoughts and lines of poetry. "I guess I lost track of time." She put her ink pen in between the pages and closed her journal.

"That's fine. I was glad you decided to accept my invitation from earlier."

"Yeah." India looked at him, then remembered he'd called during her drive to school. "But that's not why I'm here."

"Here's your coffee. Can I get the two of you anything to eat?" asked Lisa.

"Are you hungry?" Reese asked India.

"As a matter of fact, I am." She hadn't eaten since that morning. "I'd like egg salad on rye bread."

"And for you, sir?" asked Lisa. She scribbled on her little white spiral notebook, then turned to look at Reese.

"Let me have a double cheeseburger with everything on it and a small order of fries," Reese replied.

With wide eyes, India looked across the table. "Are you hungry?" she asked jokingly, having never seen him eat more than a patty melt and chips.

"Yeah, I don't know what's come over me the past few days. My appetite has gone through the roof." He laughed, then rubbed his stomach.

"Young man, it sounds like you got the appetite of someone who just fell in love."

Both of their necks snapped when they turned to look at Lisa as she scribbled Reese's order in her notebook.

"Can I get anything else for you?" Lisa asked Reese, as though her previous comment had never escaped her thin lips.

"A sweet tea," said Reese.

"If that's it, I'll be back with your order when it's ready," said Lisa.

"Humph. What was *that* about?" India asked Reese when the waitress walked back to the grill. "Are you holding back on me? Have you met someone spectacular and not told me? I thought we were closer than that." India smiled, then leaned her head to one side.

"Humph. Never mind me. How are things between you and Tracey?"

Just that fast India's smile turned upside down into a frown.

"Did I ask the wrong question?" asked Reese.

"Hey, you know me well, but no one can read my mind."

"We're here, so let's talk about it." He leaned forward and placed both hands on the table, with his palms up. India looked down at his hands, then took a sip of coffee. He pulled them back slowly.

"When I woke up this morning, Tracey was gone, but she'd left breakfast, with a note and the keys to her car. I read the note, which I originally understood to be an ultimatum. But why would she have taken the time to leave breakfast and spare keys if she was that upset?" she asked, then looked at Reese.

"Because she genuinely cares about you?" he asked, then leaned back when the waitress returned and placed their food on the table.

"Before leaving this morning, I tried to call her. She never answered her phone, so I went to class not really knowing what to think. When I got home from class, she was already there."

"Did the two of you talk?"

"If that's what you'd like to call it." India picked up her sandwich and attempted to take a bite. Frustrated, she put it back on her plate. "It's the first time she's ever been this upset with me. When I left, she didn't look at me."

"India, have you ever evaluated the relationship from her perspective?" he asked, reaching across the table and placing one hand on top of hers.

"No, I haven't really thought about it from her perspective. Honestly, I've been selfish and only considered my feelings in the matter."

"Just think about it. It may resolve a lot of your issues with her. Being a male, I can only imagine how she feels. Being in love with someone and not knowing for certain if they love you back is difficult."

"I tell her that I love her several times a day every day."

"Sometimes saying the words just isn't enough. Love is an action word. I can tell you that I love you one hundred times a day and not really mean it. Remember, actions speak louder than words."

"It's more than just words. We have a great physical connection."

"If you're referring to intimacy, let me ask you the million-dollar question. Are you making love to her or just having sex? There's a profound difference between the two."

She thought about his comment, picked up her sandwich, then bit into it. The tone of the conversation changed when they decided to eat. After another hour of laughing and talking about nothing in general, they decided it was time to go. Reese paid their ticket at the register, and they exited the coffee shop together.

"If you need to talk, remember I'm available anytime of the day or night." He opened her car door, then waited as she got inside.

"Thank you. I'll remember that." Ready to resolve her issues with Tracey, she drove out of the parking lot.

Chapter 15

Yvonne

Yvonne entered the classroom reserved for their bimonthly women's fellowship meeting with one thing on her mind, becoming the first lady of Faith Believers. The attendees had already formed a semicircle with their chairs and were chatting among themselves. A few of them were standing around a table in the far corner, nibbling on cookies and drinking punch prepared by a church mother. Yvonne sneered when she looked and saw the new secretary already seated on the opposite side. She was wearing the same outfit and the too-sexy-for-church ankle-strap shoes. *Humph,* Yvonne thought. She'd at least taken the time to go home, shower, and change into something far more attractive. Reverend Alston loved her in red, so she'd put on a red swing dress with a V neckline and black ankle-strap shoes. Becoming first lady wasn't a task she'd ever taken lightly.

Yvonne wanted to roll her eyes at the interim secretary but caught herself, knowing jealous behavior wasn't appropriate for the first lady of their congregation. Unsure who might be watching, she smiled, then waved her hand instead. The secretary forced a smile, then started a conversation with the lady seated next to her. *Whatever, heffa, because I know you want my man,* Yvonne thought to herself, feeling the corners of her mouth turn up. *You can wear all the short skirts and sexy shoes you want. I'm going to get my man. Even if it means volunteering to be secretary for the next three weeks.* Yvonne never once blinked or took her eyes off the secretary.

"Let all the women of God say, 'Praise the Lord,'" Evangelist Angelina said after she took her place behind the white podium that had been placed in the middle of the semicircle.

The praises echoed around the room as Yvonne lifted her finger and tiptoed to a seat on the opposite side of the new secretary. "Praise the Lord," she responded energetically after sitting down. She reached inside of her purse for her Bible, notepad, and ink pen.

"Praise the Lord," Evangelist Angelina said.

Yvonne looked at the woman, who was plainly dressed in a long-sleeved white blouse and long black skirt, then smiled. She had a beautiful face with strong facial features, which she did nothing to accent. Her long hair was always pulled back in a bun. A pair of gold hoop earrings was her only accessory. At one point Yvonne had felt threatened by her knowledge of the word of God. After many hours of reading and studying the Bible like Reverend Alston had recommended, Yvonne soon felt confident in Bible study class. Evangelist Angelina had two children, a six-year-old son and a four-year-old daughter. Yvonne had never been married and had no children, making her ideal for Reverend Alston.

"As is customary, we're going to start our meeting with a word of prayer. Sisters, would you please bow your heads." Together they bowed their heads as the evangelist started to pray. "Amen," she concluded after praying so eloquently that her prayer seemed written and rehearsed. Yvonne applauded her efforts every week, confident even she didn't have what it took to be first lady. "Before we start, I'd like to ask for a volunteer to teach our next class in two weeks."

Yvonne saw it as a perfect opportunity to further impress Reverend Alston and raised her hand, along with three other women.

"Praise the Lord," Evangelist Angelina said, then raised both hands into the air. "Seeing so many women ready to serve and help build the kingdom is a blessing. To make it fair, each of you can teach a class for the next four sessions." She looked down, then recorded their names on her legal pad. "This evening we're going to discuss the virtuous woman as defined by the word of God. Does everyone have a Bible?" she asked, then looked around the room. "If not, we have one you may borrow." She paused, then started to speak again.

Intently, Yvonne listened to her ever-so-dramatic presentation, making mental notes from the discussion, as it all applied to her future marriage. An hour later the meeting ended with prayer. Some ladies left immediately, while others formed small groups to gossip. Yvonne looked around the room, said her farewells, then decided to leave hoping to see Reverend Alston on her way out.

She exited the room, then looked up and down the hallway. Reverend Alston wasn't in sight, so she decided to walk by the classroom where the men were holding their meeting. The door was open, and they, too, had been dismissed. Her heart skipped a beat when she saw Reverend Alston standing in the middle of a group, having a conversation. Wanting to be heard, if not seen, she walked harder, making her heels sound against the floor. She passed the door and used her peripheral vision to watch his response. He was engrossed in conversation and didn't even look her way. Determined to get his attention, she reached inside her purse, then let her keys fall to the floor.

"Sister Miller," Deacon Harris said as he exited the room and entered the hallway. "Please let me get those for you." He bent down in front of her, then picked up the keys.

"Thank you, Deacon Harris. They slipped right through my fingers." She accepted her keys, still using her peripheral vision to look at Reverend Alston. "Finally," she said, thinking aloud.

"Excuse me?" Deacon Harris asked.

"Please forgive me for thinking aloud." To stall a few seconds longer, she patted the deacon on the shoulder when she noticed the reverend end his conversation and walk toward the door. Not wanting to be so obvious, she thanked the deacon again and took a step forward, planning it meticulously and never intending to leave.

"Sister Miller," Reverend Alston said, then extended his hand.

"Reverend Alston." She wiped her tongue across her teeth before smiling at him. She arched her shoulders, then turned slightly to one side. She wanted him to have a glimpse of all she had to offer. Just when she heard the voice of the new secretary in the hallway, she shook his hand, then hugged him. He responded hesitantly, his arms remaining glued to his sides. His stance didn't matter as much as the fact that she had her arms wrapped around him when the new secretary entered the hallway.

"Is everything okay, Sister Miller?" He ended the embrace, then placed his hands on her arms. His response wasn't important; all that mattered was the secretary seeing them interact.

Yvonne paused long enough for the secretary to walk by and see the body contact. "Reverend Alston, everything is fine. If you would include me in your prayers, I would be grateful as I had another job interview today."

"Did you? I'm certain with all things, the will of God will be done. He said it in His word. Not to mention, you're a highly intelligent woman, with the anointing of God on her life. I love how you've allowed God to use you in the area of finance for the ministry. You'd be a valuable asset to any corporation. Don't doubt God, as the time you've devoted to the ministry will be rewarded. Keep the faith, Sister Miller." With a look of concern, he leaned his head to one side, then rubbed up and down her shoulders with his hands. His gesture alone gave her the satisfaction she needed as the new secretary approached the end of the hallway and disappeared around the corner.

"Reverend Alston, thank you for your prayers, and have a blessed evening." She smiled, rubbed the top of his hand when she shook it, then walked away.

Chapter 16

Shiquanna

"Well, well, look who decided to show up." Ecstacy folded one arm across her double Ds, then licked her red lollipop.

Shiquanna looked her up and down and rolled her eyes. Ecstacy wiggled her body to make her tassels spin, then placed a hand on her hip. Her cottage-cheese thighs made Shiquanna nauseated, so she pretended to gag.

It had been several weeks since Shiquanna had danced at the Pink Palace, but from the looks of the dressing room, nothing had changed. There was the new girl seated in the corner, with the baby face, which she'd tried to cover with layers of make-up. She was fighting to be brave, but the stark look in her eyes said it all as she trembled inside. Shiquanna knew because one night not too many years ago, that girl was her. Even though the newcomer was too young to drink, someone would give her tequila shots, hoping to turn her out before the night was over. Lesbian couples were making out wherever there was enough space. The local drug dealer made his nightly round, making sure everyone had what they needed for a ruthless performance. And then there was Ecstacy.

"Humph. Thought you'd gotten too good to work with us locals. Word on the street, you ain't pulling nothing but dem big shot millionaires." Ecstacy tilted her head to one side, then leaned back, pressing her bare bottom against the mirrored glass.

"Hello to you, too, asshole," Shiquanna spat, then turned up the corners of her mouth. She'd had only one shot of tequila, and she wasn't in the mood for sarcasm, especially from the lips of the oldest dancer in the room. Ecstacy was who Shiquanna was fighting not to become. She was thirty-eight years old, her bloodshot eyes had permanent dark rings from so many late nights, and her implants were droopy. "You damn right it cost to play hide-and-seek on these playgrounds." She looked down at herself, then rolled her eyes at Ecstacy.

"I heard dat shit," another dancer piped, with an attitude, from the other side of the room.

"You better recognize," Shiquanna said, then swished to a vacant dressing area. She hung her purse up on the hook to her left, which could barely support the weight, sat down, then looked at her face in the mirror. It was bare. "Damn, girl, do you like what you see?" she asked Ecstacy, who was still staring at her. With a hard stare, Shiquanna dared her to say or do anything.

Ecstacy licked her lollipop, rolled her eyes, then turned her back.

"That's what I thought." Shiquanna turned up the corners of her lips, then reached inside her purse.

"Oh, shit! This heffa got a gun," the dancer standing next to her shouted, then covered her head with both hands.

Shiquanna looked at her, then pulled out a metallic gold make-up bag. "Now, who the hell am I going to kill with a tube of lipstick? Take your crazy ass somewhere, and sit down. You need to get off of that cheap shit." Making sure Ecstacy didn't try to show out in front of her girls, Shiquanna watched her from the corner of her eye. Never letting Ecstacy out of her sight, she leaned into her mirror, applied her make-up, then got dressed.

"Da house is packed, and dey tippin', too," Sinsations said when she entered the dressing room, waving a stack of bills.

Shiquanna looked up because she was the next to perform. She stood to look at her black see-through bodysuit with a piece of material that barely covered each nipple and her precious garden. She lifted each breast for maximum exposure, then turned to look at herself from behind. The spaghetti straps hit each shoulder blade perfectly, tapering down to wrap around her waist. She looked at Ecstacy, snapped her thong, then swished across the room and out the door. She followed the dark hallway a few feet and went up the wooden steps, which were desperately in need of repair. "Shit," she cursed when she almost scratched her metallic gold stilettos.

The crowd roared when the DJ called her name and started his introduction. The energy from the other side of the curtain made her heart pound. Taking it all in, she leaned her head back, then moved it from side to side. She lifted her left leg, held it by the ankle, and stretched until it reached her ear. She held the pose, then lowered her leg to the floor. Ready to make every man empty his pocket, she walked closer to the black curtain when it started to open. Suddenly she froze.

"Fantasia! Fantasia!" From every corner of the room, her stage name was being yelled. "We missed you, baby," someone shouted from a far corner. "Come on, baby. Show us what you're working with," someone else yelled after the curtain was completely open.

Blinded by the glare of the stage lights, Shiquanna stood motionless.

"All right, baby. You can't tease us all night," someone said, then threw a tip onto the stage.

She watched as the bill seemed to float in slow motion, finally landing on the stage. After it was another one, then another one, and they all seemed to float toward her like feathers.

"Fantasia! Fantasia!" The chant continued.

I can't do this anymore. Her eyes scanned the smoke-filled room, and she took a couple of steps back. Out there was somebody's husband. Definitely, somebody's boyfriend sat in the crowd. *How would I feel if the shoe was on the other foot and I was the woman waiting at home for her man? Oh my God, where did that come from? It sounds like a conscience,* she thought, then looked down at her perfect figure, which hadn't been ruined by childbirth.

"Shiquanna Alize Jenkins, put that damn dress on now," Renita said, then threw a red minidress across the room. The large silver buckle hit Shiquanna in the

mouth, making her lips throb. "Our first guest is in there, and he's expecting us to deliver."

Shiquanna placed her hand over her throbbing lips, then lowered it. There was a drop of blood on her fingertip.

"What the hell! It's just a little blood. What in the hell are you crying for? What did I tell you? No matter what, we don't cry. So wipe your face and get your ass out there."

Remembering Renita's words, Shiquanna felt faint. She shook her head from side to side to suppress yet another memory. *There has to be a better way. God, it's me again. If you're really up there, I need your help. You know if I walk away tonight, I'll never be able to show my face in this club again.* As if an angelic image were in the main spotlight, she stared into it as a million thoughts ran through her mind. *Dancing and selling my body for money are all I know. I barely finished high school, and you know I'm too damn old to go to college now.*

The DJ called her name with more enthusiasm than before, but she took another step back. She wasn't drunk and was completely aware of her surroundings. Still staring into the main spotlight, she backed off the stage, turned, and hurried into the dressing room.

"Excuse you, bitch," one of the other dancers said when Shiquanna bumped into her, almost knocking her over.

Shiquanna didn't respond as she slipped into her jeans and put on her T-shirt. She looked down at her hands, which were shaking uncontrollably. She grabbed her purse, then headed for the rear exit. She opened the door, then paused to take a deep breath. A black limousine was parked outside the door. She watched as one of its black-tinted windows started to lower. Just in case shit was about to happen, she reached inside her purse and felt for her pepper spray. Dancing in the hood didn't come with security. Making sure the pepper spray was in view, she took it out, then tightened her grip on her purse strap. She started to walk in front of the limousine.

"Excuse me." She didn't stop but looked over her shoulder. She watched as the black-tinted window lowered completely.

"May I speak to you for a second?" asked an extremely handsome gentleman, then waved her to the limousine.

"No thanks." Gasping for breath, she looked toward her car, which was parked on the other side of the parking lot.

"I'm in town all week for a tournament. I don't know anyone here and was looking for a beautiful lady like you to accompany me for dinner and a few drinks. No strings attached." He held up both hands, then smiled.

"If that's the case, why are you riding around in the parking lot of a strip club?" She put a hand on her hip, then pointed toward the well-lit marquee.

"Like I said, I'm not from here." He looked at the hot pink marquee with a woman's silhouette, then shrugged his shoulders.

Shiquanna leaned forward to quote him a price, then stopped herself. She'd just asked God for help, but she knew she had to start by helping herself. The clean-cut man alone in a limousine appeared harmless, so she put the pepper spray back inside her purse. He was dressed casually in a brown silk shirt and black pants. And unlike most athletes, except for a gold hoop in each ear, he wasn't wearing any extravagant jewelry.

"Sir, this club is full of beautiful women who would love to escort you for an evening." She put a hand in each pocket, then looked over her shoulder.

"What if I'm interested in you?"

"I'm flattered, but as you can see, I'm really not dressed for dinner or drinks," she said, then looked down at her faded blue jeans and T-shirt, which she'd slipped on over her outfit.

"It's only eight thirty. I'm sure we can make it to a boutique before they close and buy you a couple of beautiful dresses. You look like a perfect size six, so fitting you shouldn't be a problem."

"Thank you, but I'm not interested." She remembered how she'd frozen onstage and her prayer to God. For whatever reason, he was cruising the parking lot of a strip club in the hood, meaning he was at least ten miles from the nicest hotel.

"Look at me. My name is Ishmael Jamison. I play center for the Miami Hurricanes, and I'm completely harmless." He smiled, then held up both hands. "If you don't believe me, I can show you my driver's license and voter's registration card." He raised his hip to get his wallet out of his back pants pocket. He opened the Gucci bifold, then showed her his Florida driver's license. "I'm not going to ask for your identification, but do you have a name?" He turned on a light above his head, then turned his bifold sideways.

"Shiquanna," she responded after seeing his first and last names on the driver's license. She looked at the mug shot, then looked at him. "Anyone can pay for a fake driver's license."

"You're right. For a man of my status, that would be easy, wouldn't it? But what about my Social Security card and all my credit cards?" One by one he took out at least three credit cards and showed them to her. "Would you like to see a copy of my birth certificate?"

"That ain't necessary." Shiquanna laughed at his suggestion, then watched as he put the cards back into his wallet.

"Shiquanna, I'd still like you to join me for drinks."

Shiquanna looked at him sideways, then pointed toward her car on the other side of the parking lot. "What about my car?"

"If it will make you feel better, I can call someone right now to watch it until we come back." He picked up his cell phone, then touched the screen with his finger.

"No thanks. It's been a long day, and I'm tired." Still doubting, she looked at him, then shook her head from side to side.

"If it's been a long day and you're tired, I'll compromise. We can go back to my hotel and order room service."

"I really appreciate it, but I'm going to call it a night." She smiled, then extended her hand for a handshake. "It was nice talking to you."

"One drink at the bar?" He lifted one finger, then looked at her with puppy dog eyes.

Shiquanna looked into his huge brown eyes, which seemed so innocent, and let out a deep sigh. "One drink at the bar."

"Great." He started to open the door to the limo.

"No thanks. I prefer meeting you there."

"I'm harmless. One phone call is all it will take to have someone watch your car."

"I believe you, but I'd prefer to drive," she said, still being cautious. She didn't want to be stranded at a hotel with a complete stranger.

"Fine with me."

Shiquanna strolled across the parking lot to her car, then got in. Her heart fluttered. She put her hand across her chest, then inhaled. She couldn't count how many times she'd left the club with a stranger, but this time she was nervous. As if to say her final good-byes, she looked toward the club's exit, then followed the limousine out of the parking lot. Not knowing their destination, she followed until they turned into a five-star hotel and drove around the circular drive, stopping at the front entrance. She watched as an attendant wearing a dark suit walked around the front of her car and opened her door.

"Good evening, ma'am. I'll take it from here." The attendant extended his hand to assist her, then got behind the wheel.

Ishmael stood beside his limousine and waited. As if she were a finely dressed raving beauty, he bowed, then extended his hand. Flattered by his chivalry, she accepted his hand, with a smile, and they interlocked their arms.

"Ishmael, I look a mess." She apologized for her frumpy appearance as they walked through the automatic glass doors and entered the elegant lobby.

"Trust me, it's all just a figment of your imagination. Even in jeans, you're the most beautiful woman in this room." With smiles, they walked across the lobby to an open bar that was centrally located.

For the most part, everyone was casually dressed, but Shiquanna felt intimidated after overhearing a conversation about politics. She couldn't remember the last time she'd sat down long enough to watch the evening news.

"Where would you like to sit?" he asked.

"It really doesn't matter."

"There's an empty table on the other side. We can sit there, if that will make you feel more comfortable."

"Yes, that will be fine," she replied.

Arm in arm they walked to the table. He pulled out a chair and waited as she sat down.

"Thank you," she said.

"Good evening, my name is Avant. Can I get the two of you anything from the bar?" asked the bleached-blond waiter, who was wearing a paisley tuxedo vest, a starched white shirt, and black pants.

Ishmael looked at Shiquanna, then nodded his head.

"May I get an apple martini on the rocks?" she said.

"And for you, sir?" Avant folded both hands behind his back and looked at Ishmael.

"Grand Marnier with Coke."

"The main restaurant hasn't closed. Would you like to look at a menu while I get your drinks?" asked Avant.

"That would be fine," Ishmael responded.

"The house special for the day is Alaskan halibut with baby squash perfectly sautéed in organic olive oil and red pepper sauce. Let me tell you, it is to die for." Avant smiled, then blew a kiss into the air. "Take your time to look at the menu. I'll be back with your drinks."

Ishmael nodded his head at the waiter, who then turned and walked away. "Would you like to order dinner?" Ishmael asked Shiquanna, then reached for a menu.

"No thanks. I'm not hungry." She smiled.

"Don't worry about the prices. Dinner and drinks are on me tonight," he said in a tone that sounded slightly offensive.

"Don't get it twisted. I can afford my meal. I said I wasn't hungry," she snapped, not caring who overheard her.

"I'm sorry. I didn't mean to offend you, gorgeous. Please accept my apology. I only wanted to let you know that if you're with me, everything is covered."

"I have an apple martini for the lady and a Grand Marnier with Coke for the gentleman." Avant sat their drinks on the table in front of them. "Have either of you decided on an item from the menu?"

"We're fine," Ishmael said.

"Enjoy your drinks," Avant told them.

"So, Shiquanna, tell me, why was a beautiful lady like you coming out of a strip club?" He picked up his glass, took a drink, then leaned back in his seat.

She folded her arms across her chest, then crossed her legs at the knee. "I'm the damn cleanup lady," she spouted, ready to leave if he insulted her again.

"I was only asking a question. No need to become defensive. It's only innocent conversation." He took another drink, looked at her, then changed positions in his chair. "You're too beautiful to frown. Relax and drink up. Our evening is young, and I'd hate to ruin it with one silly question. If it makes you feel better, ask me a question."

She unfolded her arms and leaned forward to get her drink. She took a few sips, then leaned back.

"If it makes you feel better, ask me anything," he added.

"How tall are you?" she asked, then laughed at herself for asking something trivial like his height.

"At least we've started a conversation. I am six feet five inches tall and have been since the ninth grade. Imagine how I felt being the tallest person in the ninth grade. None of the girls were close to my height, and they wouldn't give me the time of day." He smiled, then drank. "Do you think they would have talked to me if they'd known I was going to get a full scholarship to college and get drafted by the pros my first year?"

Shiquanna parted her lips to speak, but he interrupted.

"I'm sure those chicken heads would die if they knew I was a multimillionaire before the age of thirty. They'd probably drink a gallon of my dirty bathwater now. Wouldn't you?"

"No, I wouldn't." Shiquanna shook her head from side to side, then folded her arms across her chest again.

"Sure you would, gorgeous. If I put fifty thousand dollars on the table right now, you'd do it." He smiled, then pointed at the table.

"Do you think so?" Shiquanna said, then rolled her eyes.

"I know so."

"I don't know what type of women you're used to dealing with, but I'm not impressed," she said, thinking of the countless ballers who'd pay her just as much to perform orally. "Thanks for the drink." She got her purse, then stood.

"Wow, don't be so tense. I was only joking." He reached up and grabbed her by the arm.

"Excuse me, but you don't know me like that." She looked down at his hand, then rolled her eyes. He let go, then held up both hands.

"You're not the type to be played with, huh?" he asked, then motioned for her to sit back down.

"No, I'm not." With an attitude, she sat down and folded her arms across her chest.

"So tell me, what can I do to impress you, then?" he asked, then waved his hand for the waiter to bring them another round of drinks.

The waiter returned and placed their drinks on the table.

In one gulp, half of her drink was gone. Shiquanna looked across the table at Ishmael, who was still bragging about his career. "I've really enjoyed listening to you for the past hour, but it's time for me to leave." Shiquanna stood, then felt her body fall backward into the chair. "Oops," she said and laughed when she had to sit back down. She'd only been drinking apple martinis, but she'd lost count after number two.

"Gorgeous, you're in no condition to drive home. I have a suite. At least come upstairs and sleep it off. I would never forgive myself if I turned on the news and saw you on it."

She looked at him, then closed her eyes when she saw three of him.

"Let's go to my room." He stood, walked to her side of the table, then extended his arm to assist her. She held on to his arm and stood slowly. All she remembered was resting her head against his arm and attempting to take a step forward.

Shiquanna opened her eyes and was on her knees in front of Ishmael. The room was spinning out of control, her head hurt, and her eyes burned when she glanced down at herself. Her T-shirt had been ripped down the middle, and her bra top had been pulled down below her breasts. She could feel her jeans around her ankles. She tried to speak but couldn't. His hardened penis was halfway down her throat. Instead she gagged.

"You ain't through yet." He pushed himself deeper into her mouth.

She used her hands to press against his thighs, but he grabbed her wig and yanked. Her wig and every hairpin she used to secure it flew across the floor. Her scalp burned. For one second, she realized how much power she had and bit down as hard as she could.

"You useless bitch," he screamed, grabbed himself with both hands, then fell backward onto the floor. He moaned, turning from one side to another.

With everything in her, she attempted to stand but fell forward onto her hands and knees. Her head spun as she crawled to the door, reached up for the doorknob, then scrambled to open it. Her body fell forward into the hallway when the door opened. She couldn't see an elevator but began to crawl, hoping she was going in the right direction.

Dear God, please help me. With everything in me, I'm begging you, she pleaded silently on all fours, then stopped when she heard a chime. She dug into the carpet with her nails, then used all her strength to pull herself forward. Thinking he would come after her any second, she became frantic.

When the silver doors parted, an older white lady looked down and saw her on the floor. "Ma'am, are you okay? Somebody call security." The lady removed her jacket and placed it around Shiquanna's shoulders. Before the doors closed, she stepped back inside the elevator and picked up the emergency phone. "I'm on the twenty-third floor. There's a young lady on the floor, bleeding. She needs help immediately," the lady shouted into the phone, then slammed it down.

"Oh my God." Shiquanna tried to move but stopped when she felt a sharp pain in her gut. All she could do was moan.

"It sounds like you're in a lot of pain, so please don't move." The lady, whose name she might never know and whose face she might never see again, rubbed her gently on the shoulders.

Shiquanna gasped for breath, then leaned against her leg.

"Help is on the way."

Chapter 17

India

Thinking it was Reese, India looked into her rearview mirror and smiled when her cell phone started to vibrate. He drove out of the parking lot behind her, and only a few feet separated them. After their conversation, she'd left the coffee shop with a warm feeling inside and was ready to evaluate her relationship with Tracey from a different perspective. Tracey's perspective. How did it feel being comfortable with your own sexuality but taking an emotional risk and approaching someone new? Someone whose sexuality you weren't so sure about. Homosexuality didn't come with a certain face or dress code.

India answered the phone.

"May I speak to India please?"

"This is India," she responded slowly, not at all familiar with the woman's voice on the other end.

"India, this is Shelia Robinson, RN, and I'm calling from the emergency room at County Hospital."

"County Hospital?" India asked, then looked into her rearview mirror and watched Reese's headlights disappear after he turned left.

County Hospital was in the opposite direction, so she pulled into the next drive and started to turn around. She had left Tracey at home, upset. At most Tracey never drank more than two beers, and that was only occasionally. But this day was different. Then she prayed that Tracey hadn't decided to take a drive and had a car accident. If that were the case, India would never forgive herself. With that horrible thought in mind, she sped out of the drive and onto the street.

"I'm sorry to alarm you, but do you know a Shiquanna Jenkins?" the nurse asked calmly.

"Yes, I do. She's my best friend." Grateful the call wasn't about Tracey, India inhaled but panicked, thinking the worst when the nurse said Shiquanna's name.

"She's been admitted through the emergency room. Her cell phone was retrieved at the scene. Your number is the last one she dialed."

"I am on the way." Since high school, that was the phone call she'd never wanted to receive. Shiquanna's biological mother was God knows where, and India knew she was Shiquanna's only real friend, making her the next of kin should anything ever happen.

"You can ask for me when you get here," replied the nurse.

"Thank you." Immediately India called home. She wasn't a fan of hospitals and didn't want to go alone. The term *emergency room* alone almost made her hyperventilate. Her hands trembled as she held the phone to her ear. It rang several times, but Tracey didn't answer. She tried again. Still no answer, so she dialed Tracey's cell phone number, and the call went straight to voice mail. Then she worried about Tracey, who always kept her cell phone on, no matter what.

Shiquanna had been admitted to the emergency room, and India had left Tracey at home, upset. She was still concerned about Tracey's lack of response, and her mind began to race, so she called Reese. Calling Yvonne was never a thought, as India didn't want her in the emergency room, rebuking the devil and praying for Shiquanna's salvation. In India's opinion, there was a time and place for everything, including someone's salvation.

"Hello, beautiful." India could hear the smile in his voice, but it wasn't enough at that point to calm her nerves.

"Reese, I have an emergency."

"Are you okay?"

"County Hospital just called." She paused to take a deep breath. "My best friend is in the emergency room. I'm nervous, and I don't know what to expect. Can you go with me?"

"Of course, I can. If you're too nervous to drive, I can meet you at the coffee shop. We just left there, so I know you're not too far away to turn around."

"No . . . yes," she said, not knowing which statement to affirm first. "No, I'm not too far away from the coffee shop and, yes, I'm too nervous to drive."

"Go back to the coffee shop, and I'll be there in a couple of minutes."

"Thanks."

No sooner than she ended the call, drove up the street, and turned into the coffee shop parking lot, her cell phone vibrated. It was Reese calling to let her know his car was within her sight. She turned to look over her shoulder, and true enough, he was turning into the parking lot. He parked, then hopped out, leaving his car running while he assisted her. She got inside his car, then folded her arms across her chest to hide her hands, which were still trembling. All she could think about was that Shiquanna was in the emergency room and Tracey wasn't answering her cell phone.

"India, I'm sure your friend will be okay." Reese patted her gently on the knee.

"That's all I can hope for." She shook her head from side to side, thinking he didn't know her friend's occupation or clientele. India closed her eyes and leaned her head back.

He rubbed her knee gently when the hospital was within view. "What's your friend's name?" he asked, following the large signs that pointed toward the emergency room.

"Shiquanna."

"India, I'll drop you off here and find a place to park. Don't worry. I'll find you." He stopped in front of the emergency room entrance, then waited as she got out of the car.

India hopped out, made a few steps toward the door, then stopped to look over her shoulder when an ambulance hurled into the parking lot. The lights were flashing, and the sirens were almost deafening.

Seeing her shoulders stiffen and sensing her anxiety, Reese rolled the window down. "India, don't worry. I'm only a few minutes behind you. I'm confident your friend will be okay. County has the best emergency room in our area."

She heard him but was stunned when the ambulance driver jumped out and rushed to open the vehicle's rear door.

"India, I promise it will be okay," Reese confirmed.

With that in mind, she refocused, hurried toward the entrance, and waited as the double doors separated. Her tension didn't ease when she entered a waiting room that seemed filled to capacity. Then she heard a man scream, "Oh Lord, help me!" She dared not look to see who it was or where the plea for help had come from. Immediately to her right was a security guard, seated behind a small desk.

"How may I help you?" the bearded man asked, with a serious facial expression. Before she could respond, he slid a clipboard across the desk and pointed at the sign-in sheet. "Please sign." He looked toward the entrance while handing her a bright orange visitor's pass. "Place this on you, making sure it's visible." Not questioning his authority, she signed in, then took the pass. "There's information," he said coolly, then pointed toward another desk.

India shook her head at his lack of personal skills and walked toward the oval desk. Seated behind it was a heavyset woman, with a friendly smile. She had an all together different attitude as she gave directives to visitors by pointing and speaking into her headset at the same time.

"How may I help you this evening?" she asked, finally looking in India's direction and placing a hand over the mouthpiece of her headset.

"I'm looking for Shelia Robinson, RN," India said after leaning on the edge of the desk for support. She looked back, but Reese wasn't in sight.

"After I buzz you in, the nurses' station is to your right," said the woman.

"Thank you so much."

India walked toward the door, which started to open slowly, then turned to look again. Still no Reese. She approached the nurses' station, then stood. What she saw was a myriad of interactions between staff. She stood for a few moments, waiting for anyone to turn around. Finally, someone looked up from a computer.

"I'm looking for Shelia Robinson, RN," said India.

"Shelia," the young lady occupied with data entry called over her shoulder, never turning to look.

"Be with you in a minute." A woman in her late forties or early fifties looked over her shoulder, then lifted her index finger.

India nodded her head up and down at the woman, who had already refocused on her task at hand.

"I'm Shelia," the woman finally said, taking the multicolored reading glasses off her nose and allowing them to hang loosely on a string around her neck.

"My name is India, and you called me about a patient, Shiquanna Jenkins."

"Yes, I did." Before leaving the nurses' station,

Shelia leaned down to speak to another staff member. "Please follow me." She motioned with her hand as she walked from behind the nurses' station.

India followed her down a hallway that was no calmer than the waiting room and around a corner. She fought to ignore random moans and groans.

Before entering Shiquanna's room, the nurse stopped, then turned to face India.

"Shiquanna was brought in unconscious by ambulance a couple of hours ago."

"Oh my God." India covered her mouth with both hands, then lowered her head.

"Don't worry. We have a great staff, and they worked relentlessly to revive her. She suffered a mild concussion, has several bruises, and is heavily sedated now. Her CAT scan and lab work were normal. Other than a nagging headache, she'll be fine."

"Thank God," India said, then wiped a warm tear as it fell down her cheek.

"The police just left."

"The police?" India asked, stunned by her comment.

"Yes, it was an obvious assault case. Fortunately for your best friend, there was a witness, who had no problem reporting what they'd seen."

"Thank God." Just then India felt a soft tap on her shoulder. It was Reese, and he was holding a cup of coffee. Respecting her conversation with the nurse, he held up his hand, then stepped back.

Shelia went on. "We'll check her stats every thirty minutes, and she'll be free to leave once she has awaken from the medication and is coherent. She has a large bandage on her head and will be sent home with a prescription for pain."

"Thank you so much."

"We can go into the room once you're ready," Shelia said, then stepped closer to Shiquanna's door.

India waved for Reese, then nodded her head up and down for yes. The nurse opened the door; India stepped inside, followed by Reese.

"Shiquanna," India said softly, walked to the bed, and reached underneath the white hospital blanket for her friend's hand. India smiled when she touched her hand, which seemed so frail, then wrapped her fingers around Shiquanna's own. *Thank you, God, for sparing her life this time,* India thought, unable to suppress her tears, which fell on top of Shiquanna's hand. Gently she wiped them off, then looked at the nurse, who was busy checking the monitors at the head of Shiquanna's bed.

There was a white bandage wrapped around Shiquanna's head, and her left eye was bruised and swollen. Her natural hair was matted, and her dark eyeliner was smeared beneath both eyes. Lipstick was on her chin. India shook her head, then gently rubbed the side of Shiquanna's face with her fingers. Then she smiled inside, knowing she'd better have Shiquanna's face clean when she regained consciousness.

"Shelia, may I have a clean face towel before you leave the room?" asked India.

"You most certainly can." Shelia turned, opened a cabinet above her head, and got two towels. Before handing them to India, she soaked them with warm water. "There's more if you need them," she said, then pointed.

"Thank you." Repeating a mantra of thankfulness, India began to gently wipe Shiquanna's face, careful to avoid the swollen areas. She handed the soiled towels to Shelia, who placed them in the proper container.

"There's only one chair in the room," Shelia acknowledged Reese as he entered the room. He moved the chair closer to the bed and motioned for India to sit. "I'll get another one from a vacant room so the two of you can be comfortable while you wait," Shelia said.

"Thank you," said India. Never letting go of Shiquanna's hand, India sat down, then leaned her head on the bed. Reese drank the coffee he'd purchased for her as she drifted to sleep.

"Where in the hell am I?" Shiquanna pulled her hand away, then sat erect in the bed.

"Shiquanna."

"India?" Shiquanna asked, then rubbed the bandage on her forehead. "Where in the hell am I, and how in the hell did I get here?" she asked, with wide eyes, then moved her head from side to side. "Oh, that hurt like hell." She looked behind her, then leaned back onto the pillow. Vaguely she remembered having drinks in a hotel lobby with the ballplayer and only imagined how she could have gotten here. "That low-down son of a bitch did this to me. Oh my God, he must have put something in my drinks." She lifted both hands into the air and looked at them. "You wait until I get through with his ass. He'll never abuse another damn woman again. You just wait." She yanked the blanket off of her body, then attempted to lift her head.

"Shiquanna," India called, "please don't try to talk right now or make any more sudden moves. You need to get some rest." India rubbed the top of Shiquanna's hand. "You're in the emergency room at County Hospital. They brought you here by ambulance several hours ago."

"Several hours ago?" Shiquanna queried, then attempted again to lift her head off of the pillow.

"Yes, you suffered a head injury, so they had you heavily sedated," explained India.

"How did you get here?" Shiquanna asked India, then gripped her fingers when she felt pain. Her eyes closed for a moment. "Oh shit. That hurt like hell."

"You were brought in unconscious, but thank God, my number was one of the last numbers you dialed."

"India, I can step out of the room if the two of you need to talk," Reese said softly.

"Shiquanna, this is Reese." India motioned for him to step closer to the bed.

"Hello, Shiquanna," he said tenderly, then smiled.

"We'd just finished having coffee when I got the phone call, so I had him follow me here," said India. Shiquanna looked at India, then squinted. Knowing Shiquanna's thoughts, India only smiled.

Shiquanna looked at him, then responded, "No, Reese, you're fine."

"Come in," India said in response to a soft knock on the door. It was Shelia.

"Look who's awake." With a warm smile, Shelia

walked toward the bed, checked Shiquanna's vitals, and turned to document them in the computer. "Everything looks good. I'll let the doctor know you're awake, and I'll get his approval for your release."

Shiquanna grabbed India's hand and sat erect.

"Not so fast, young lady." Shelia patted Shiquanna on the shoulder, then looked at India. "Will you be staying with her tonight?" she asked, with a look of concern.

"I most certainly can," replied India.

"Sir, do you mind leaving the room so that I can speak with them privately?" asked Shelia.

"Of course not. I'll get the car and be waiting for the two of you outside," said Reese.

"Ms. Jenkins, when you came into the emergency room, your clothing was already torn, making it easy for our staff to rip what was left. In so many words, your outfit was destroyed, but your life was spared. However, someone from social services did find a pair of jogging pants and a T-shirt that may fit you. I placed them in a bag, and it's underneath your bed."

"Thank you," Shiquanna and India responded at the same time.

"I'll be back in a few minutes with her paperwork and a wheelchair," said Shelia.

The nurse left the room, and India bent down to get the bag from beneath the bed.

"India, you got some explaining to do about Mr. Reese. Where in the hell is Tracey?"

"It's a long story and not what you think." India handed Shiquanna the bag, then leaned against the bed so Shiquanna could use her for support while getting dressed.

"He is a cutie and looks earthy, like you."

"Whatever," India said, never really having looked at Reese that way.

"Don't whatever me, little buddha," Shiquanna joked, as always being sarcastic, no matter what, as she slipped into the clothes.

"I don't have a bandage on my head, either. I'll explain when you've fully recovered. Until then you're under my supervision. It's obvious you can't make it on your own." India laughed and just that fast was overwhelmed by tears. She looked into Shiquanna's eyes, then embraced her best friend.

"You know what?" Shiquanna laughed through her own tears, fighting to make them stop. "Renita taught me to never shed a tear." Tears started to roll down her chin and onto India's shoulder. "I know this looks crazy." She hurried to wipe her face with the back of her hand, then broke the embrace.

"My sister, it's not crazy. It's real." India handed Shiquanna a box of tissues, then took a couple out for herself. Together they wiped tears through laughter as Shiquanna rested on the edge of the bed.

"Knock. Knock," Shelia said, then opened the door slowly.

"I'm dressed," Shiquanna said as they wiped their last tears.

The nurse explained the paperwork, then wished Shiquanna a full recovery. Shiquanna stood and held India's hand as India assisted her into the wheelchair.

"Thanks, sis," Shiquanna whispered gently as

Shelia opened the door and India pushed the wheelchair into the hallway.

"No, thank *you*," India responded, grateful for her best friend's life.

Immune to the hectic atmosphere, India rolled Shiquanna down the hallway, through the waiting room, and to the exit doors, where Reese was visible on the other side. He met India at the doors and assisted them both into the car. India caught a glimpse of Shiquanna in the side-view mirror. Her arms were folded across her chest, her head turned to one side, and she stared into space. Except for the soft hum of the air-conditioning, they rode back to the coffee shop in silence.

There was still silence when they turned into the parking lot and got out of Reese's car.

"Reese, it was nice meeting you, and thank you for being there for my girl. She's like a sister to me, you know. Hell no, she is my sister," Shiquanna said before getting into the car India was driving.

"It was no problem. Take care of yourself," he replied.

"Reese, I can never repay you for your kindness," India said, thanking him once he opened her car door.

"A hug will suffice." He smiled, then spread his arms for a hug.

India waved her hand behind her back at Shiquanna when she playfully cleared her throat. India stepped forward, then yielded to his embrace. He wrapped his arms around her shoulders, then pulled her into him. She held on to his waist. Thankful for all that he'd done, she held him tightly.

"Be careful going home," he cautioned. "As a matter of fact, call me when you get there. It's late, and I want to know you've made it there safely." After a moment he let go.

India leaned her head back and looked into his eyes. She'd never really noticed that they were a deep chestnut, making them seem warm. Yes, they'd spent hours working together, but it was the first time she'd ever looked past his glasses and into his eyes. What she felt was calming. She hopped in her car, and he closed her door, then stepped back when she started the car and drove away.

"My damn eyes may be swollen, but I can still see, girlfriend," Shiquanna teased India.

"He's only a good friend. Don't you remember? He's the one I worked on the project with," India said, wanting to ignore that warm, fuzzy feeling she'd just experienced. She was in love with a woman named Tracey, and Reese was only a colleague turned friend.

"Humph." Shiquanna laughed, then placed a hand on her bandage. "Looks like more than a friend to me. I saw how he stared into your big, pretty brown eyes." Shiquanna laughed again. "Oh shit, that hurt." She rubbed the side of her head.

"Are you hungry?" India asked, wanting to get off the subject of Reese.

"Yeah, I'm hungry for the four-one-one on you and ol' boy."

"There's not a four-one-one."

"Now that my medication is starting to wear off, where in the hell is Tracey?"

"I don't know," India said, then looked at the time on the dashboard, remembering it had been hours since she'd last tried to contact her. She reached inside her bag, pulled out her cell phone, then looked at the display. There were no missed calls or messages, leaving her disappointed.

"Girl, I was just playing. For real, is everything okay between you two?" Shiquanna turned slightly to look at India.

"We need to make sure you're okay. We can talk about me any day. After hours of being asleep, I know you're hungry."

"All I really want now is a hot shower and a shot of tequila."

"No, Shiquanna, you're not drinking, not tonight. Are you really trying to kill yourself?" She snapped her neck at Shiquanna after stopping when the light turned yellow.

"Hell no, but *you* are with this damn reckless driving of yours. Look, girlfriend, take me to my apartment. It seems like you got some issues of your own to take care of." Shiquanna leaned forward and pointed in the direction of her apartment. "All I need you to do is take me to get my car tomorrow."

"We're fine. Making sure you're okay is far more important." India's voice faded at the end of her statement. It was after midnight, and she hadn't talked to Tracey all evening. From the tone of Shiquanna's voice, India assumed she really was okay and didn't need her supervision. But they debated about Shiquanna not spending the night alone during the rest of the drive.

"Girlfriend, I'm fine. I've had headaches far worse than this from a hangover. Why are you trying to act green? You know damn well what I do for a living," Shiquanna said once India turned into her apartment complex. "On a serious note, and please don't start crying like a baby again. You know how much I hate tears." Shiquanna turned her head and looked out of the window. "Thanks for everything, and I mean everything. If it weren't for you, I wouldn't even have a high school diploma." She leaned across the seat, hugged India really fast, then let go.

"Shiquanna, are you going to be okay?" India asked one last time as Shiquanna opened the door and turned to get out of the car.

"I got this. I promise."

India watched as her best friend moved stiffly up the walkway. She wanted to get out of the car and help but knew Shiquanna would only resist, then probably curse her out. "Rest well," India called when Shiquanna unlocked her front door, then waved.

Chapter 18

Yvonne

It never fails that I'm always the first to arrive, Yvonne thought while looking around the well-preserved hotel lobby area, which was elegantly decorated. The hotel had a five-star rating, was 150 years old, and was toured as a historical landmark. Its lavishly decorated rooms were occupied only by the elite and wealthy. Some traveled miles just to say they'd slept in the same room as certain Hollywood icons. She had never spent the night in one, had only seen them in brochures, but had the intention of one day doing so. Until then, she'd relish the hotel's atmosphere at any given opportunity.

She'd made their reservations for five o'clock and spoken to India, making sure they could meet in the lobby at least fifteen minutes early. *Promptness is a virtue that neither of them possesses.* She lifted her nose in the air, walked down the marble steps, and sat in an elegant burgundy upholstered Queen

Anne chair. She crossed her legs, allowing the top one to swing freely, then placed her hand beneath her chin. She exhaled. She was opening her purse to glance at the time on her cell phone when it started to vibrate. It was ten minutes before five.

"Yes, India," she said sternly to convey a slight attitude as she looked toward the entrance. "You're running late and what?" She watched a group of four men dressed in dark suits, crisp white shirts, and dark ties enter. Their conversation seemed intense as one of them motioned with his hands, making a point as they walked by. From the other three, there was an occasional head nod.

"Hello to you to," India said, then laughed. "I'll be there in five minutes."

"And where's Shiquanna?" Yvonne asked, with more attitude than before, again looking toward the entrance.

"She's with me, so we'll see you in a few."

Yvonne ended the call, then looked at the time on her cell phone once more before putting it back into her purse. She picked up a travel magazine and waited on the two, who, she knew, had no sense of urgency. She flipped to the cruise section of the magazine and fantasized about her dream wedding to Reverend Alston and their honeymoon.

"Good evening, girlfriend." That time Shiquanna's heels sounded no different than anyone else's against the fine marble floor.

Yvonne frowned as she closed the magazine and placed it on the table. "Our reservation was for five o'clock." She looked toward the antique clock mounted behind the registration desk. She stood, looked at Shiquanna from head to toe, then placed her purse underneath her arm. Again, Shiquanna was dressed inappropriately. She had on a black sheer top, with a black lace bra underneath, animal print leggings, and three-inch stilettos. Yvonne shook her head in disapproval. It was slightly cloudy outside, and she wondered why Shiquanna was wearing black shades. She assumed it was due to another late night, so she turned sharply, then started to walk away.

"Shiquanna." India stopped Shiquanna with a wave of the hand when Shiquanna's lips parted and she put a hand on her hip. India could tell by Shiquanna's stance and the way her lips moved that she was getting ready to curse.

"Giirrl," Shiquanna said, then rolled her eyes at Yvonne. "Don't make me act a damn fool up in here."

"Yvonne, it's only five minutes after. I'm sure we're still okay. Don't you think?" India asked Yvonne as they followed her to the elevator.

"There's nothing like being on time," snapped Yvonne. She pressed the elevator button, then folded her arms across her chest. Shiquanna only made a face behind her back.

"Time is only a figment of the human's imagination," India said when the bell chimed and the elevator doors separated.

"Floor please?" a gentleman wearing a bright red jacket and dark pants asked once they stepped inside.

"Too fancy for me," Shiquanna mumbled.

"We're going to Chez Lorenz," Yvonne said proudly, loud enough for the couple in the rear to hear.

The gentleman smiled, then pressed the button for the appropriate floor. Yvonne arched her shoulders, then clasped her hands in front of her. India watched the floors light up as they ascended, and Shiquanna leaned against the opposite side.

"Have a good evening," the gentleman said once the elevator stopped on the appropriate floor and the doors parted.

"Thank you," Yvonne responded proudly, taking the lead as they got off the elevator.

"Good evening, ladies, and welcome to Chez Lorenz," said a short, dark-haired white man finely dressed in a tuxedo with tails. He was standing behind a dark cherrywood podium to the right of the entrance.

"I have five o'clock reservations for Yvonne Miller," Yvonne said, then admired a water fountain in the middle of the restaurant. On top was an enormous live floral arrangement, and from it, streams of water flowed, reflecting the beams of natural sunlight.

He smiled, then looked down. "Yes, I see reservations for three." No sooner than he turned his head to look inside, a young woman of maybe eighteen approached the entrance.

"Good evening, ladies. Please follow me," said the young woman.

Shiquanna looked around when the young woman led them to a table in the middle of the room.

"Jasmine will be your server for the evening and will be with you momentarily," the young woman informed them.

"Thank you," Yvonne said, with a smile, then

stared at Shiquanna, who looked wide-eyed, like a fish out of water. Knowing Shiquanna was uncomfortable, Yvonne laughed inside, then sat down.

India's face was expressionless as she pulled out her chair, then sat down. Shiquanna sat down, then placed both elbows on the fine white linen tablecloth.

"Do you have any manners?" Yvonne asked through a fake smile as she leaned forward.

"Hell naw," Shiquanna responded, not caring that a thin white lady with a bouffant hairstyle overheard her comment.

"Jesus." Yvonne maintained that same smile as their waitress approached the table, gave her three-minute spiel, then handed them each a menu. Giving them time to make a decision, she smiled, then walked away.

"What the hell! Where are the damn prices at?" Shiquanna blurted, then waited on Yvonne's response.

Yvonne looked at India, shook her head from side to side, then stared at Shiquanna. She still hadn't removed her shades. "We're inside the restaurant now. Do you mind removing your shades?"

Knowing the real reason Shiquanna wore the shades, India looked at Yvonne, then sank down into her seat. Shiquanna stared at Yvonne, removed her shades, and tilted her head to one side, as if to say, "Now are you satisfied?"

"Oh my God." Yvonne placed both hands over her mouth, then looked around to see how much attention Shiquanna had drawn to their table.

"Oh my God is correct. Would you like to know

exactly how it happened?" Shiquanna snapped as the waitress returned to take their orders.

Yvonne spoke up immediately, placing her order first, followed by India, then Shiquanna, who couldn't wait to finish telling her story.

"I'll be more than happy to share the details. Where do you want me to start? How I met him, the drinks, or the part where he beat my ass?" Shiquanna said as soon as the waitress turned her back to walk away from the table.

India sighed. "Ladies, I'm really not in the mood to mediate while the two of you bicker. Yvonne, you made the reservations, and Shiquanna, you asked me to pick you up. If I've interpreted the signs properly, all of us, including me, wanted to be here."

Yvonne's eyes widened, and Shiquanna smiled, having never seen the feisty side of her best friend.

India went on. "Now, the three of us will sit here, enjoy our overly priced meals, and converse like adults." She rolled her eyes at Yvonne, then looked at Shiquanna, who was still smiling. Yvonne sat back in her seat, crossed her legs, and cupped both hands on her knee. Shiquanna waved her hand to get the waitress's attention.

"May I have a glass of white wine please?" Shiquanna over-enunciated each word, then nodded her head at Yvonne. "Excuse me, but my girlfriends may need a glass also. Especially my good friend Yvonne." Her grin was menacing as she turned to look at India, then Yvonne. They both waved their hands and moved their heads from side to side for no.

"I'll be back with your wine. The first course of your meal will be served momentarily," said the waitress.

"I guess she told you little Ms. Sophisticated, and you thought she was the mellow one in the group." Shiquanna looked at Yvonne, glad the heat had been taken off of her and the bruised eye.

Yvonne threw a hand up at Shiquanna, then turned to India. Not wanting to completely ruin the night out she'd planned, she attempted to change the conversation. "How are your classes going? Shouldn't you be close to graduation by now?" Her facial expression showed true concern. "If you like, I can put you in touch with some reliable contacts at my last job. All you have to do is say the word. They'll have you in the door and climbing the corporate ladder in a few months." After her comment, her eyebrows rose, and she moved closer to the table.

"Working in corporate America isn't my perfect idea of success," India replied.

"How do you define success?" asked Yvonne.

"I don't define it as waking every morning to an annoying buzz, dressing to look successful, as defined by white corporate America, then racing against time to get to the office."

"Humph," Shiquanna interjected.

"As long as I've known you, you've been in college, working toward one degree or another. If you have no intention of complying with the standards set by corporate America, why spend so much time working toward a degree you'll never use?" said Yvonne.

"Believe me, it will be used, just not in corporate America. Let me ask you a question," replied India.

Yvonne shrugged. "Sure, go ahead."

"When you wake up in the morning and look at your reflection in the mirror, are you happy with what you see? At the end of your eight- or ten-hour day, do you feel fulfilled? Other than hitting a time clock, attending a few business meetings, and socializing, what have you accomplished? With all your efforts, have you made a difference in anyone's life? Are you truly happy?"

"Yes." Yvonne paused. "I'm happy."

"Just what I thought," India said, then glanced at Shiquanna. "She's not totally happy. True happiness comes with freedom, not with so many restraints."

"So tell me, how is your love life? How are things going between you and Tracey? Maybe one night we can break the rules and invite him to dinner," Yvonne said, changing the topic of conversation again.

Shiquanna almost choked on her sip of wine.

"Shiquanna, are you okay?" Yvonne asked as Shiquanna covered her mouth with a napkin and patted her chest.

India never looked at Shiquanna. "Actually, I'm glad you mentioned my relationship with Tracey. Right now we're having some relationship issues," she responded sternly, not having the patience to deal with either of them. She and Tracey hadn't spoken or had physical contact in days. Just like anyone else in a relationship, she, too, had needs, and they weren't being met.

"What relationship doesn't have issues? Maybe we can help," offered Yvonne.

"Tracey and I have been in a relationship for two years, and she doesn't understand why I'm not comfortable with the term *lesbian*."

For the first time Shiquanna witnessed Yvonne

without words. "Yvonne, dear, are you all right?" Shiquanna asked, then tapped the table with her fingertips, ready to play the devil's advocate. To make matters worse, she picked up her linen napkin and pretended to fan Yvonne with it.

"Jesus Christ, I need a drink of water." Yvonne placed her hand over her heart and reached for the nearest glass of water. It wasn't hers, but Shiquanna's. She lifted the glass to her lips and drank. She lowered it for a second, then drank again.

"Are you going to Bible study tonight?" Shiquanna leaned forward and asked. By then India had folded her arms across her chest, waiting for Yvonne's response about Tracey. "Now who are you going to pray for, missionary?"

"God help us all," Yvonne said, still holding her chest. "You mean to tell me, all this time you've allowed me to think Tracey was a man?"

"Did you ever ask who Tracey really was?" India retorted.

Yvonne looked up, then looked at India. "No, I didn't. I only assumed it was a man. Plus, if I had known it was a woman, I would have—"

"You would have cursed me to hell, told me it was immoral, and used the Bible to prove your point," India interrupted. "Or would you have remained my best friend regardless of who I'd decided to date?"

"I would have . . ." Yvonne took another sip of water before speaking again. "Honestly, I don't know what I would have said or done. Now I'm astounded, because I thought we had become closer than that."

"Well, now you know." India looked at Yvonne, then held up both hands.

"Maybe you can go to Bible study with me tonight. Take your immorality to the altar and ask God for deliverance. All of us have sinned and fallen short of His glory." Wrinkles formed across Yvonne's forehead as she pleaded with India.

"Now that the door is wide open, let's talk about my immorality," India said, then rolled her neck around.

"Yes, let's talk about it. It's never too late for salvation," replied Yvonne.

"God, let's talk about God," India said convincingly.

"Damn, this is going to be better than Jerry Springer," Shiquanna piped, not caring about the meal in front of her, which she'd only stared at. It was arranged on her plate like an art display, and she didn't know where to start.

"How would you define God?" India asked sincerely.

"He can't be defined." Ready to use the Bible to defend herself, Yvonne placed her hand on her purse, then realized her Bible was in the car.

"If you worship Him, there has to be a comprehendible definition," India insisted.

"God is the creator and ruler of the universe. He spoke and it was. He's omniscient and omnipresent. He's the beginning and the end. He's alpha and omega," explained Yvonne.

"With all that being said, that's your definition of Him, correct?" India leaned her head to one side, then shrugged her shoulders.

Yvonne nodded. "Yes, that's my definition. How would you define Him?"

"Love," said India.

"Love?" Yvonne asked, then stared at India. "Okay. That's only one of His many attributes."

"You say one of many, but I say it encompasses them all. Even my love for another woman, if that is indeed what it really is." India sighed from relief. That admission might be the first step toward solving her problem with Tracey. "Yvonne, that's the problem with humanity today, and it has been for years. Every Sunday morning people like yourself . . . or would you prefer I use the term *Christian*?"

Yvonne's eyes widened.

"Let me rephrase. Every Sunday morning Christians wake up and adorn themselves in their Sunday's best. They go to their preferred place of worship, where they sing, dance, shout, pray, chant, and perform other rituals common to their so-called denomination. This lasts for what? At least two or three hours?" India said, then hunched her shoulders. "After the minister does the benediction, then what? No sooner than he exits the pulpit, chatter groups form. What do they talk about? Do they discuss the content of the sermon or how well the minister performed? Do they concern themselves with the real needs of the community or talk about who's wearing the latest designer suit? Are they ministering to the real needs of the community or gossiping about who Sally Mae Henson had sex with last week? Are they collecting funds to clothe the needy or talking about the teenager that was improperly clothed?"

Yvonne, who'd suddenly lost her appetite, pushed her plate away. "The invitation to attend Bible study with me tonight is still open. Maybe the two of you can come, since you're already together."

"Girlfriend, she still doesn't get it." Shiquanna looked at India and moved her head from side to side.

"Well, ladies, I don't want to be late for Bible study." Yvonne reached inside her purse and pretended to look at her cell phone. India's situation had blown her mind, and she saw only a blur on the display. She reached inside the small pocket of her purse and got the first credit card she touched. "Don't either of you worry about paying. This evening is on me." Yvonne looked restless as she glanced around for their waitress. Impatient, she reached for a waiter who was passing by. He agreed to find their waitress, who returned only a few minutes later with their ticket. Yvonne paid the bill and offered to purchase another glass of wine for Shiquanna. "Girls, you know I hate to be late for Bible study. The first fifteen minutes are the most important. It's not too late for the two of you to join me. You're my best friend, India, and the thought of you perishing in hell is an unsettling thought."

"Perish in hell? If anybody's going to hell, it's you, with your fake ass," Shiquanna blurted, then took a sip of wine.

"Shiquanna, calm down. Please don't embarrass yourself," India said calmly.

"I'm not embarrassed. I ain't gonna never see these faces again, and if I do, so what?" said Shiquanna.

"Shiquanna, believe me it's okay," India said calmly.

"No, it's not okay. She ain't doing nothing but

hiding behind the church, just like everybody else. You're way better than her, even bigger than her, and I've never seen you go to church. Go figure. Believe me, she got some skeletons in her closet, too." Shiquanna bobbed her head.

"India, it's not too late." Yvonne stood, then used the back of her legs to push the chair away.

"Naw, girl, you go ahead. I think you need more prayer than us right now," replied India.

"India, it's your turn to pick our restaurant. Call me and let me know what you decide," said Yvonne. Then, considering the new revelation, she hoped India didn't take them to an eccentric gay venue.

"Peace, my sister," India said, and Shiquanna rolled her eyes.

Without formally saying good-bye, Yvonne walked away. In silence, India and Shiquanna finished their meals and then left.

Chapter 19

India

"I can't do this anymore."

"Excuse me?" Except for the hint of light coming from the kitchen, the room was dark, and soft jazz was playing in the background. The smell of burning incense met her at the door and made her cough. India felt along the wall and flicked on the light. Tracey was sitting on the couch, with the back of her head pressed into an oversize pillow, holding a beer. There were two open cans sitting on the coffee table. India assumed they were empty.

"I can't play these childish games with you anymore." Tracey lifted the can to her mouth and drank.

"Tracey, I'm ready to talk." During her drive home, India had decided she was ready to talk to Tracey about moving their relationship forward. She might not be comfortable with the term *lesbian*, but she knew how she felt. She was in love.

"For the past two years, I've supported you and

your endeavors. You haven't worked a real job since I've known you. When we met, I knew you were a full-time student, and accepted that. I played extra gigs to make everything comfortable for you. I knew you'd never had a female lover before, and I pursued you, anyway. Now, that was my fault."

"Tracey, I've thought about everything. I love you." India walked around the couch and stood in front of Tracey, who sat with her eyes closed. India leaned forward and rubbed Tracey's shoulder to make any type of connection.

Tracey threw a hand up in the air, then sat up. "You love me because your car is God knows where and I'm again helping you out. Will you stop loving me when you finally graduate and possibly get a job?"

"Where is all of this coming from?" India asked as Tracey babbled. "I see you've been drinking, and right now you're not making any sense."

"I'm making plenty of sense. I'm making more sense now than I ever have. I'm seeing everything for what it really is."

"Give me your beer, and let me help you get into bed." India attempted to take the beer can out of her hand. Tracey snatched her hand away.

"I don't need you to help me get into bed. I'm capable of making it on my own."

"Fine." India took a couple of steps back, then looked at Tracey's green eyes, which were bloodshot. They usually glistened, but now they were dull and lifeless. "Sleep it off, and we can talk about everything in the morning."

"There's not going to be an in the morning. I want you to leave tonight."

"You can't mean that." India continued to stare at Tracey's eyes, looking for any sign of emotion. There was none. "Where will I go at this time of the night?"

"I hope you enjoyed your girls' night out. Maybe you can live with one of them."

"Tracey, you've got to be kidding me!" Never had Tracey been so forward or sounded so demanding.

"The other night I guess you thought I was asleep when you came in after midnight. I might not have moved, but I wasn't asleep. As a matter of fact, I couldn't sleep. I tossed and turned all night."

India placed a hand on her forehead. "Tracey, my best friend . . ."

"Your best friend." Tracey took another sip of beer. "Every week it is your best friends and has been for how long now?"

"My best friend had a life-threatening emergency. I called the house and your cell phone. You didn't answer either one."

"I don't remember you calling me."

"Well, I did. Look, Tracey, this conversation isn't going anywhere. I'm going to bed."

"No, I want you to leave tonight."

"You've got to be kidding me."

"No, I'm not kidding you. I want you to get out of my life. I've wasted two years, and for what? Nothing. I can't even show face in front of your friends. I've never met all your family. This isn't a relationship and never has been, now that I think about it."

"Don't do this. Especially now that you've been drinking. Let's go to bed and talk about it in the morning."

"Get out." Tracey sprang up off the couch and

walked toward the bedroom. India watched as she wobbled through the door and returned with two of her suitcases. "You can come and get the rest of your things tomorrow. I'm not going to work. I've taken the rest of the week off."

In disbelief, India looked at Tracey. This was serious. Tracey was a workaholic.

"You can keep the car. That's the least I can do."

India's lips fell apart. She was dumbfounded. Her suitcases were already packed. Whether she was ready to talk or not, the decision had already been made for her to leave. She looked at Tracey, who had become cold as ice, got her suitcases, then left.

For at least an hour, India drove, passing the exit that led to her favorite coffee shop at least three times. Finally, after using up half of her gas, she took the exit and headed to the coffee shop, if for nothing else, to get a hot cup of coffee before finding a hotel room for the next couple of nights. Shiquanna had a two-bedroom apartment, and India never doubted that Shiquanna would let her stay there until she could get her own place. But she didn't feel like talking to anyone. She wanted some time alone to reflect on the past two years.

She parked, then sat still before getting out of the car and going inside. Her heart was broken, and she felt a void without Tracey. How could she blame Tracey, who had given her two years? It was India who had been undecided.

"Hey, girlfriend," Gail said, with a smile.

"Good evening, Gail."

"Where's your partner in crime?"

"I don't know. I'm alone this evening." She looked and saw that their usual booth was occupied by a group of college students who seemed to be having a great time on a budget. There was a large plate of fries in the center of the table, and they all took turns digging into it. No one seemed to mind as they laughed and their conversation continued. India envied their innocence and found a booth on the other side.

"Cup of coffee?" Gail asked once India sat down.

"Yes. Black."

"Coming right up."

India looked out of the window, then covered her face with both hands. She wanted to cry so badly but couldn't, hoping Tracey would sober up and call her tomorrow to apologize. How could their relationship fall apart after two years? Tracey's anger had to be temporary.

Gail placed a cup, along with a fresh pot of coffee, on the table. "Let me know when you're ready to order."

India poured herself a cup of coffee, then stared as the steam rolled off the top. She had lost her appetite for anything but time with Tracey. She looked out the window and across the parking lot, focusing on nothing in particular as a thousand thoughts raced through her mind.

"Can't get enough of this place, huh?"

India looked up when she heard Reese's voice. "What are you doing here?"

"I had a late evening and stopped by to get a patty melt and fries to go."

"What a coincidence." She was drowning in her

thoughts. She thought being alone was the key, but seeing him did make her smile.

"Are you getting ready to leave?" he asked.

"No." India's smile turned into a frown; then she looked down. "Have a seat."

"Tracey?" he asked after sitting down across from her.

"How did you guess?" Certain her facial expression hadn't given her away, she reached for her cup, then drank.

"It's written all over your face."

"What?"

"Pain, disappointment, and confusion."

"Yes, I'm all of the above. There's so much going through my mind right now."

He looked at her, then held up both hands.

"I had dinner with my girls, and my perspective changed. For two years I allowed my best friend to believe Tracey was a man. I did it because I didn't want to be under her religious spotlight. But most of all, I feared losing her as a friend. Then I realized a real friend would love me no matter what."

Reese smiled, then nodded his head up and down.

"My girl Shiquanna lives life on the wild side, so she would have been the last person to question my decision."

"As a friend and as one who has grown to love you, judging you isn't my place. My purpose is to be that strong shoulder for you to lean on." Reese stood, then sat down beside India. All she could do at that point was rest her head on his shoulder. For a few moments they sat in silence.

"I was ready to talk to Tracey. But she'd obviously made her mind up to end the relationship. My bags were packed when I got home. I'm going to get a hotel room for a couple of nights." She sat up, then turned to look at him.

"India, I'm so sorry. Give it a few days. I'm sure the two of you will be able to work it out."

"I don't think so. This time I believe she's serious. The look in her eyes said it all."

"India, you don't have to spend money on a room. I have a two-bedroom condominium downtown. Well, a one-bedroom, after I converted the spare bedroom into my office. You can stay there as long as you need to."

"Reese, thanks, but I can't."

"Why can't you?"

She really didn't have an answer. Tracey had asked her to leave, and both of her girlfriends lived alone, but staying with them wasn't appealing to her at all. Yvonne would throw the Bible at her, and Shiquanna would give her a couple of days, then tell her to get over it. "Only for a couple of nights, until I find somewhere else to stay."

"It's a done deal."

India poured herself another cup of coffee, and Reese ate his meal.

"Mi casa es su casa," Reese said, after unlocking the door and stepping into the foyer.

"Thanks, Reese." India bent over to pick up the suitcase he'd put down to open the door.

"I'll get that."

"Reese, I'm very capable of carrying my own luggage."

"I'm sure, but for the next few days, you're my

guest." He moved to one side as she walked by, then shut the door softly behind them.

India stepped inside and was impressed immediately by his urban contemporary decor.

"Make yourself at home." He led her toward the kitchen area, which had long black cabinetry and stainless-steel appliances. He opened the refrigerator, then pointed inside. There wasn't the usual pitcher of water and beer assortment she expected from a bachelor. His refrigerator was filled with edible items, like eggs, milk, cheese, and fruit juices. "I'll let you decide where you'd like to sleep. You can have my bed or the couch."

His long black leather sectional seemed to be a good option until she saw his king-size bed. She stood in his bedroom door, looked at him, then laughed.

"No problem. I'll sleep on the couch. I'm no stranger to it, anyway," he said.

"My debts are accumulating fast. Before long I will not be able to repay you."

"Who's keeping up?"

Just then their eyes met. He placed a hand on her shoulder and rubbed gently. She leaned her head back, then looked up. It was the first time that India had ever really looked at Reese as anyone other than a friend. He was tall and slender, but not skinny. He wore short dreads and kept the facial hair that framed his mouth and chin neatly trimmed. His lips were full and appeared to be soft. Even though she'd never seen him wear earrings, both ears were pierced. He dressed casually, always wearing jeans, printed T-shirts, and a sports coat. He had his own unique style, which drove the young women on campus insane. Until that moment India had been impressed only by his intellect. Blaming vulnerability on her physical attraction to him, she glanced away.

"Make yourself comfortable. I'll be back with clean linen and towels," he said.

India watched with slight admiration as he turned, strolled down the long hallway, and disappeared into another room.

Chapter 20

Shiquanna

"This shit is for the birds," Shiquanna cursed when her alarm clock buzzed at six o'clock. She rolled forward, wrapping the sheet around her body, and hit the snooze button. Ten minutes later it buzzed again, sounding louder than before. For her, waking up in the early a.m. wasn't the norm. After a good-paying night, it was the time she usually made it home and went to bed. Questioning her decision to search for a job, she pressed her face into the pillow but knew it was the first step toward self-rehabilitation. Plus, her rent, utilities, and cellular phone bill had to be paid. Not to mention, she had to maintain her bimonthly manicure, pedicure, and spa treatments. She didn't have a bank account but had enough in her personal safe to last about two months. After that she'd be broke. The motto of her lifestyle had been "Easy come, easy go." No sooner than she'd made her money, it had been spent on clothes, shoes, jewelry, then the monthly bills. So she had two options: stay in the game longer to save more money or find a normal job with benefits and tax deductions.

With a long moan, she got out of bed and shuffled toward the closet. She stood in the center of it and looked around. From years of dancing, she'd accumulated custom bodysuits, skintight jeans, micro miniskirts, and stilettos. Nothing seemed appropriate. Finally, she glanced at one outfit that might be suitable for a job interview. It was a black double-breasted jacket and a miniskirt with a slit on the left side, which she'd worn as an intro for a bachelor party. "This will have to do." She took the outfit off the hanger, got her lowest pair of black ankle-strap heels and a black leather purse. Ready to experience a new reality, she dressed, then left her apartment.

"Good morning. How may I help you?" Sitting behind the desk was a receptionist who looked like someone's youngest sister trying to play dress up. Her jet-black hair was short and spiked, there was a heavy black line drawn on her eyelids, her fake eyelashes looked heavy, and her shiny lips were dark brown.

"I'm looking for employment." Shiquanna felt confident until she looked around the crowded room. There were rows of chairs filled with people of different age groups, ethnic backgrounds, and levels of experience, as evidenced by their dress and poise.

"We have only five computers, so you'll have to

take a number." Between syllables, the receptionist smacked her gum.

"Computers?" Shiquanna rested both hands on the front of the desk, then leaned forward.

As if she'd said something offensive, the receptionist frowned, then pointed toward the short row of desks with computers on top. Each desk was occupied by a person who seemed to know exactly what they were doing.

Feeling totally out of her element, Shiquanna looked over her shoulder at the other applicants waiting to do the same. "Um, do you have any regular applications?"

"Excuse me?" the young woman asked, as if Shiquanna were speaking Greek.

"Do you have a regular application that I can fill out with an ink pen?" Just then Shiquanna was starting to become impatient.

"First, you have to fill out an electronic application, and then a counselor will speak to you."

Shiquanna rolled her eyes at the sarcastic brat, then took a number and stared at it between her fingers. *To hell with this shit.* She wadded the small piece of paper and tossed it into a garbage can by the desk. With an attitude, she turned to leave, then froze when she saw another dancer seated in the far corner. *Holy shit!* she thought, stunned by what she saw.

The dancer was wearing dark shades, her lips were swollen, and her left arm was in a cast. Shiquanna could only imagine it was another case of assault. They were among the lucky, as she could remember how many girls just never showed up the next night. And how many times they'd been questioned at the club or shown gruesome mug shots of their cohorts' remains. Just when Shiquanna made eye contact, as if ashamed, the dancer looked away quickly. Ignoring any feelings of embarrassment, Shiquanna bent down, retrieved her crumpled number from the garbage can, and sat down in the first empty seat.

Finally, the number sixty-four flashed on the digital display. Shiquanna stood and approached the same receptionist.

"This is a temporary password, and these are your instructions to log in," the receptionist told her.

Shiquanna looked down at the white slip of paper.

"Once you've logged in, you may change the password and set up a personal account."

I ain't seen a damn computer since high school. Shiquanna pretended to comprehend the instructions, took the slip of paper, and sat down in front of a computer. She stared at the screen, took a deep breath, then followed the directions. Completing the first two sections was easy as she had to type in only her name, address, and Social Security number. The rest was a challenge. She had graduated from high school but had no other education or work experience. *What in the hell am I going to put? I can't make this shit up.* She cursed to herself again, feeling frustrated. She left the remaining sections blank, then logged out.

The process continued as she waited to be seen by a counselor, who recommended a job at a fast-food restaurant or college courses to become more marketable. With an attitude, Shiquanna left, refusing to flip anybody's burger after she'd made more money in one night than any of those heffas there had made in six months.

Upset, she drove, stopping by the first liquor store she saw. She got a three-day supply of tequila shots and emptied one before leaving the parking lot.

Damn you, she cursed when her cell phone vibrated. It was the judge. *Damn,* she cursed again, then sped in the direction of her apartment. Not responding to his call made her feel like a heroin addict trying to kick the addiction cold turkey. She reached inside the brown paper bag, twisted off the cap of another shot bottle, and tilted the bottle up. *I can do this. I know I can.* No sooner than she swallowed, her imagination ran wild.

"Now that's what the hell I'm talking about," said the forty-something-year-old man, who was wearing an electric blue polyester suit, matching brimmed hat, and snakeskin shoes, once Renita pushed Shiquanna in front of him. "She fine as hell."

Shiquanna flinched when he sucked air through the gap between his two front teeth and looked at her from head to toe. She noticed his long pinkie nail when he pushed his large gold-rimmed glasses up on his nose.

"Turn around, girl, and let Slim look at you. Ain't I taught you better?" With a push, Renita turned Shiquanna around, allowing him to admire her young, firm ass. Renita grinned, then lifted the glass of golden tonic to her lips. Her breath reeked of alcohol and cigarettes.

"Baby, I got to have it. Name your price," said Slim.

"Motherfucker, you already know the price," Renita spat, then laughed at the man, as if he was expecting some type of deal for her young virgin daughter. "If you want it, you already know the rules of engagement." The smoke from Renita's cigarette burned Shiquanna's eyes, giving

her an excuse to let a lonely tear fall. Before turning Shiquanna around, Renita rubbed Shiquanna's face with the back of her hand. And rubbed it so hard, it burned.

Shiquanna watched as the old pervert reached inside his coat pocket and pulled out a roll of money. He unfolded it, licked his thumb, and began to count, making each bill sound against the table. Shiquanna watched, numbed by the fact that her mother was selling her virgin daughter to the highest bidder. Shiquanna resented Renita, but at that moment she wished her dead. In her mind, no one that evil deserved to live.

Renita picked up the stack of bills, counted, then recounted. "The first bedroom to your right." She pointed, then gave Shiquanna a hard push in the center of her back. "If you fuck this one up, it's me and you. You owe me this for bringing your sorry ass into this world. Do you hear me?" She grabbed Shiquanna by the arm and spoke through clenched teeth. Her breath was hot on the back of Shiquanna's neck, and her words burned, eating to the core of Shiquanna's soul. "Do you hear me?"

Barely able to stand in the red patent stilettos Renita had made her wear with the red suede micro minidress, Shiquanna stumbled in the direction of the bedroom. With a menacing grin, Slim was standing in the door, waiting. He unbuttoned his suit coat, then used a hand to fan it back. His erection showed through his pants. From that point, all Shiquanna remembered was his gold front tooth with the dollar sign in the middle.

"I can do this. I know I can," Shiquanna said when her cell phone started to vibrate again. She picked it up to look, and, yes, it was the judge. She drank the last of her tequila and accelerated, ignoring any urges to turn around and drive toward his condo.

Chapter 21

India

Out of habit India turned onto her left side and arched her back. Before getting out of bed, Tracey would wrap her arm around India's waist to snuggle, then kiss the nape of her neck. Tenderly, she would trace the outline of India's back with her fingertips. Whether they made love or not wasn't as important as the mental connection. India didn't realize how valuable those simple pleasures were and how much they meant until they were gone. India had reciprocated privately but had not given Tracey the one thing she wanted most, public acknowledgment and admission of their relationship. Knowing she was in Reese's bed alone, she kept her eyes closed and imagined Tracey's touch. A touch that she might or might not have again.

Refusing to wallow in self-pity or create negative images, India inhaled, then sat up, allowing her bare feet to touch the floor. Ready to make the best of a new day, she leaned her head back and curled her toes around the carpet fibers. The atmosphere was altogether different as she inhaled the scent of a man. Tracey wore men's cologne, but the aroma that came from her pores was different. She smelled like a woman wearing a man's scent. Reese's room smelled masculine. His linens were fresh but competed with the scent of the natural leather that covered his headboard. In the corner sat a leather recliner, an end table, and a floor lamp. Around the recliner were several neat stacks of books, magazines, and legal pads. It all seemed so typical of him.

India stood and went to the other side of the room, where he'd placed her suitcases. She got down on one knee, unzipped her suitcases, and searched for a change of clothes. Her first class wasn't until ten, so she showered and dressed slowly.

The smell of fresh coffee met her at the kitchen door. Reese was sitting at his small kitchen table, reading the daily newspaper and drinking coffee.

"How did you sleep last night?" With a smile, he leaned his head toward the pot of fresh brew.

"I rested well, and you?" she asked Reese, who looked altogether different in the comfort of his own home. His glasses were on top of his head, and he was slouched down into his seat. Even at the coffee shop, she'd never seen him appear so relaxed. He was wearing a casual shirt, which wasn't tucked, and a pair of jeans, and was barefoot.

"It was rough." He leaned his head forward and rubbed the back of his neck.

"Reese, I'm so sorry. Tonight I'll sleep on the couch. I promise not to inconvenience you more than a few more days."

"Lighten up, kiddo. I was only joking." He looked at her, then laughed. "You can stay here as long as you need to."

India poured herself a cup of coffee, then eyed the fresh fruit on his counter.

"Oh yeah, I thought you would enjoy it. I'm not a big breakfast person. Two cups of coffee and I'm on my way."

"Thanks, but you didn't have to."

"No, I didn't have to. I wanted to."

"What time is your first class?" For a moment, she felt uncomfortable, knowing she'd just spent the night with a professor. She looked at him, then rolled her eyes to the top of her head.

"What did that expression mean?" he asked, then pointed toward an upper cabinet.

"It meant you're a professor and I'm a student." She got a small plate out of his cabinet, put a few pieces of fruit on it, then sat down in front of him. "It meant we've crossed the line of professionalism." She bit into one of her strawberries and chewed.

He folded his paper and placed it on the table in front of him. "What line did we cross? Last night I helped out my friend." He reached across the table and put a hand on top of hers.

"Humph." Quickly she pulled her hand away and ate another piece of fruit.

He detected her uneasiness and folded his arms across his chest. He leaned his head slightly to one side, then looked at her. "Tracey is a fool to ever let you go. May her loss be another man's gain."

"Excuse me?"

He looked down, folded back one edge of the

newspaper, then shook his head from side to side. "Come on, India." He looked into her eyes. "Did you think I lost interest in you because you were in a relationship with Tracey?"

"Well, you . . ."

"Well, I respected it, never asked you out on another date or did anything to make you feel uncomfortable. But don't think I wasn't waiting for another opportunity. India, I've met a lot of women, but no one like you. You're beautiful inside and out. You don't follow the trends, because you're a trendsetter. You're an independent thinker and somewhat defiant. I love it." Like a child, he grinned impishly.

"Reese, if you're trying to make me feel better after Tracey ended our relationship, it isn't working." She stood to refill her coffee.

He stood, stepped out in front of her, and reached for her hand. "India." He held her hand, then placed it on his chest. "This may not be the right time, but it may be my only time. India, I love you, and I was willing to wait for the one perfect opportunity to express myself."

"That's impossible."

"It's very possible."

"Reese, I love Tracey."

"Do you?" He cupped her chin and pulled her face to his. Before she could resist, he kissed her lips gently.

"Reese, you know I . . ." She attempted to speak, but he met her lips with another gentle kiss.

He kissed the tip of her nose, the sensitive spot between her eyes, her forehead, her cheek, making his way back to her lips before she could speak again. He placed a hand on the back of her head; she closed her eyes and leaned her head back. He kissed her chin.

"Reese, this can't be right." As she thought about how much she loved Tracey, something inside of her weakened with every kiss, making her feel more vulnerable.

"Don't fight the inevitable." With the tip of his tongue, he tickled her earlobe, then nibbled it gently. The sensation sent a tingle down her spine, making her knees weak. He placed a hand on each side of her face and looked into her eyes with an intensity she'd never seen before. "Let me love you the way a woman should be loved." Again, he kissed her softly on the lips.

"I . . ."

Just as she began to speak, he placed a finger over her lips and pulled her body closer to his. He held her close, giving her time to either accept or reject his wantonness. For a moment she stood still, then wrapped her arms around his waist. Again, he moved closer, giving her the opportunity to feel his desire for her. Patiently he waited, enjoying their embrace.

Neither of them took note of the time as he allowed her to explore his body with her hand. It started with the rubbing of his face, the running of her fingers through his hair, and ended with her initiating a kiss. A kiss she hoped she wouldn't regret later, as it led to a burning desire she could no longer resist. As if it were her very first time, he led her by the hand into the same room she'd slept in the night before. With another kiss, he assured her everything would be okay. He eased his hand underneath her shirt and pulled it off.

As if they were works of fine and delicate art, he eyed her breasts before taking one in his hand and savoring it with a passionate kiss. The kiss continued as he reached behind her back to unfasten her bra. It fell to the floor, but the kisses continued down the center of her stomach and stopped at her waistline. He looked up and waited for her permission to continue. The answer was yes as she unfastened her pants and placed her hand inside the waistband. She moved her hips from side to side as he used both hands to pull her pants down around her ankles. To step out of them, she placed a hand on his shoulder for balance.

He ran his tongue up her leg and ended where her thighs met. There he took his time. The sensation was unlike any other she'd ever felt before. With mere anticipation, she looked down, then begged him with her eyes to stand. He made a final impression on her delicate flower, then stood to his feet. Before her eyes, he removed one article of clothing at a time, then led her to the bed.

With the same care, he embraced her, giving her time to get used to his essence. Patiently, he waited until she reached for him with a hand and guided him inside. Even then he took his time, allowing her body to satiate his being. He thrust back and forth slowly at first, eventually gaining a momentum that was consensual.

"Reese," she called on the verge of an orgasm, then let out a long sigh.

"India, I love you." His body trembled; then he collapsed behind her.

She reached for his hand, then wrapped it around her waist. Behind her she heard a soft snore. *Oh my God! What have I done?* She held on to a corner of the sheet, then wrapped it around her body.

"Baby, what's the matter?" Gently, Reese rubbed her waist.

"This is all wrong." She stood, still wrapped in the sheet, and walked to his window, which overlooked downtown. Her emotions were mixed as she stared out, looking at nothing in particular. Then her eyes became affixed on the park where she'd met Tracey. Her thoughts ran rapidly.

She loved Tracey but had made love to Reese. And, yes, he possessed every positive characteristic any woman desired in a man. Not to mention his lovemaking was phenomenal. He was handsome, highly respected in his field, strong yet sensitive, serious, but he knew when to lighten up and have a good time. For someone else, she thought, he was perfect.

He walked up behind her and placed his arms around her waist. She stood still, and he leaned down and placed his face against hers.

"India, if I've offended you, please forgive me." His lips tickled the inside of her ear as he spoke.

Realizing she'd done nothing to stop him, she closed her eyes and resisted leaning back into his embrace. Being in his arms felt good. To her, it even felt right, but she had to resolve her situation with Tracey. "Reese, I don't want to lead you on. I've been with Tracey for two years, and those memories can't be erased overnight."

"Please accept my apology. I should have given you time, but I've been in love with you for so long.

From the first conversation we had about your term paper, your intellect and perspective on life have been a magnet that has drawn me closer each time we've talked. In all my years, I've never met anyone like you." He turned her around and kissed her passionately.

"The time," India interjected after glancing at the clock on his nightstand. She'd completely missed her first class, and if he didn't hurry, he would be late.

"Right now the time doesn't matter to me. Knowing that I haven't overstepped my boundaries and ruined a perfect friendship does." He placed his finger on her chin and turned her head toward him. There was a seriousness in his eyes she'd never seen before. "I'm going to love you no matter what decision you make."

"I need to get the rest of my things from Tracey."

"Would you like for me to go with you?"

"I need to deal with this alone." She accepted his soft kiss on the neck. Still covered in the sheet, she picked up her clothes, went into the bathroom, and closed the door behind her. She placed both hands on the counter, leaned forward, and looked at her reflection in the mirror. Now torn between the confession of a man's love and her love for Tracey, she shook her head from side to side. *Where do I go from here?*

Chapter 22

Shiquanna

One last fucking time and this is it, Shiquanna swore to herself as she got into her car, tossed her large black purse onto the passenger's seat, and pulled out of her driveway. For at least two hours, she had tried to ignore the irritating buzz of her cell phone. But the judge wouldn't let her rest and had called her every thirty minutes until she'd answered. He'd told her the wife and children had gone out of town for a family reunion and would be away for three days. He was at his home and wanted her to meet him there instead of at the condo. He'd taken his family to the airport, and he'd promised Shiquanna it would be okay. Even she had some morals and had refused to violate another woman's bed and wouldn't meet him there. He'd made up one million excuses as to why he couldn't leave his home, but she'd reminded him that if he wanted her services, it would be on her terms. Finally, he'd agreed to make the one-hour drive from his home and meet her at the condo.

What in the hell am I doing? Remembering the horror of waking up in a steel hospital bed, from a state of unconsciousness, gave her a chill. The image of him towering over her, with his penis in her mouth, was still real. So was the taste of her blood. Remembering how the side of her face had stung made her wish the memories could be erased. *God, please help me. I can't do this alone, and you know it.* She almost screamed out her plea for help as she continued to drive in the direction of the condo. She hadn't forgotten how many times she'd played Russian roulette and managed to escape alive. The horrible image of her fellow dancer was still vivid in her mind, but she hadn't gotten over the humiliation of her job search, either.

Shiquanna turned into the private community and was glad to see a lonely jogger when she drove by the lake. Seeing the cute little couple again would have made her sick to the stomach and ruined her tequila buzz. "Humph," she grunted when the garage door lifted and she saw the Mrs.'s bright red Cadillac backed into the garage. She parked, got out, and sneered at the visible scratch she'd left the last time. "Low-down dirty bastard," she commented, with a grin, then turned the knob, expecting the door to the kitchen to be unlocked. It was. She walked in, closed the door behind her, then felt her face crumple after seeing him. He was standing in front of the refrigerator, totally naked, with his back facing the door. He had rolls of lumpy back fat, and his flat and flabby buttocks hung down to his knees. She reached inside her purse, making sure she had plenty of tequila.

"Baby, hi." He turned around and extended his arms for a hug.

"Hi." Mesmerized, she stood still as he walked toward her, with his little penis flopping back and forth.

"Can you believe a rookie cop pulled me over? Just for his incompetence, I got his name and badge number. I'm reporting him first thing in the morning. Everyone in this region knows who I am. Isn't that right, baby?"

"That's right, Judge." She frowned when he planted a wet kiss on her forehead, then turned her head, making him miss her lips. "Everybody knows you," she said sarcastically, thinking that before his referral, she'd never heard of his arrogant ass.

"Baby, I wanted you so badly today, I could taste you. I couldn't wait to get my family out of the car so I could call you and make arrangements. Just think, you can spend the next three evenings with me."

"Yeah, I sure can," she said hesitantly, thinking there was no way in hell she would look at his wrinkled ass three days in a row.

"Look, I even thought ahead and had groceries delivered. For the next three days, you don't have to leave the condo for anything."

"I do have other obligations."

"For the next three days, I'm prepared to triple your fees." He looked at her, then pointed at the nightstand in the bedroom.

She turned to look into the bedroom and could see the stack of bills from where she stood.

"Let me pour you a glass of wine."

There were two glasses and an open bottle of white wine already on the counter. Beside them was a platter of shrimp, a plate of oysters, and chocolate-covered strawberries. She looked but had lost her appetite for anything nonalcoholic.

He filled a glass, handed it to her, then lusted as she took her first sip. "You have the most beautiful lips, and I can't wait for you to wrap them around me." He shook his head from side to side, then filled a glass for himself. "The thought alone is giving me an erection. Look." He smiled, then looked down at himself.

This shit is disgusting as hell. She took another drink. She could feel her forehead wrinkle when he walked around the counter and stood in front of her.

"Baby, what's the matter?" he asked, then rubbed her temples with his chubby fingers.

"I have a slight headache." She moved her head away from his hands.

"I've got just the right thing for that headache."

"Humph." She closed her eyes for a second when he reached down and held himself. He took the glass out of her hands, sat it on the counter, and pulled her closer to him.

"She bitched all the way to the airport and in front of my children. I've asked her not to argue or debate with me in front of my children." Just that fast his tone changed, and he turned to walk to the other side of the kitchen.

Glad he'd let her go, but not wanting to hear about his damn wife, she picked up her glass and drank.

"You couldn't take off three days to go with your

family to the reunion," he whined, imitating his wife's voice. "I'm sure you could have taken off three days. You spend more time at the courthouse, working, than you do with your family. The children need you. We all need you. Your time is far more important than anything you could ever buy them." He had started to sound irritated. He turned to look at Shiquanna.

She returned the look, thinking there was no way in hell she was going to listen to him bitch about his wife and children for three days.

"Yeah, I'm the man, and I could have taken off three days or thirty days if I'd chosen to do so. But who wants to be around a nagging wife? You know, she has the best of everything, and all she does is complain. Now she's complaining about sex. Can you believe that?"

"Humph," Shiquanna said, wondering who wanted to have sex with him, anyway. She got paid to do it and, for damn sure, wouldn't do it for free.

"With each child, she gained weight and did nothing to lose it. She could have paid for a personal trainer. Hell, with my income, she could have paid for surgery. You'd think she would have done whatever it took to remain sexually appealing to me. When we met, she was a size four, and I made my expectations perfectly clear to her. I wasn't and never would be sexually attracted to an overweight woman. Who wants to have sex with a fat person?"

Shiquanna's eyes widened as she almost choked on her wine.

"Do you know how many women offer to give me blow jobs on a daily basis?"

"I can't imagine," she responded, wondering

who would want to suck that little thing and why was he bragging about it to her.

"The new court clerk sent two pictures of herself playing with sex toys to my cell phone two days ago."

Shiquanna refilled her glass, then drank until all she could see were his lips moving.

"Come on. Take care of Big Daddy." He grabbed her around the waist and led her into the bedroom. He sat on the edge of the bed and spread his legs. Without undressing, she got down on her knees and put his shame into her mouth. "Oh, baby," he moaned, then used a hand to push her head closer to his body.

No extra effort was made on her part to please him. This time she was there only for the money and couldn't give a damn whether he had an orgasm or not.

"What in the hell was that?" he asked when they both heard the kitchen door open and slam against a wall. Then there was the quick sound of heels against the marble floor. He pushed her head away and stood to his feet.

Shiquanna was stunned and assumed the tall, slender, dark-skinned lady standing in the door, with a hand on each hip, was his mistress. She was alone and had no weapons. Knowing that getting caught was how people got killed, Shiquanna sighed from relief but knew she needed to get the hell out of there.

"I took you to the airport," he squawked. Shiquanna fell backward when he hurried to snatch a sheet off of the bed and cover his body.

Shiquanna's eyes widened. The woman in the

door was his wife and looked nothing like he'd ever described her. She was very attractive, slender, and looked like Vanessa Bell Calloway.

"Baby, it's not what you think," he mumbled.

His wife didn't move but stared as he walked toward her, with both hands in the air.

"This whore tricked me." His words were stern as he pointed back at Shiquanna, but his wife never took her eyes off of him. "Baby, I don't know what I was thinking. She got me drunk and told me to meet her here. You know how much I love you and my children. I would never do anything to jeopardize our relationship. I've never cheated on you and hope you can forgive me for being so foolish."

Shiquanna sobered up quickly, sat up, and watched as he pleaded with his wife. Listening to Mr. Big, who'd just finished bragging about his possibilities, amused her.

"Did she really trick you?" asked his wife.

"Yes, baby, I swear she did." His voice softened, and his facial expression changed.

"So, I guess she tricked you into purchasing this condo in your friend's name. I guess she tricked you into making large cash withdrawals weekly from our joint account," his wife replied.

"I don't know what you're talking about. She brought me here. I've never been here before," he said.

"You're a judge. Will my pictures, videos, and audiotapes of your indiscretions prove to be substantial evidence in court? Pick your sheet up. You look ridiculous." His wife laughed uncontrollably when his arms went limp and his sheet fell to the floor. "Just what I thought. Are you speechless now? Did you think you'd married a fool? Certainly not. You met me in law school. Per your request, I decided not to practice law and agreed to have your family."

"Bitch, get out of here." He reached down, picked up the sheet, and covered his body again. As if she were a complete stranger, he looked at Shiquanna, then pointed toward the door. "I'm not going to let a whore ruin my family."

"I hope you didn't think you were the only one." With a smile, the wife looked around the judge and spoke to Shiquanna, who was blown away by her calmness. "There was someone different in this bed every day. I have pictures and video to prove it."

With nothing to lose, Shiquanna stood and swished to the nightstand where her money was. She looked him up and down, folded the stack in half, and stuck it into her bra. Glad he'd gotten what he deserved, she walked past him and his wife and left, with no intention of ever looking back.

God, that was close. Hell, if she was crazy, she could have killed my ass. God, please excuse my language. You know I'm still a work in progress, Shiquanna thought after she'd backed out of the garage and turned onto the street. Suddenly her heart started to race as she pondered the worst-case scenario . . . death. With both hands, she held on to the steering wheel and continued to drive. Her vision blurred as tears started to form in the wells of her eyes. *Dear God, I know for a fact you're up there now. I really want to thank you for saving my life again. You think I would have learned from my last experience, huh? After his assault, I was glad to be alive and too afraid to press formal charges. But this time I really got it. The message was loud and clear, and I know you're going to give me only so many free passes.*

Look, God, I just want to tell you how sorry I am for having sex with so many men just to make money. I'm sorry for all the families I've broken up. And I'm really sorry for all the wives at home who thought their husbands were in one place when they were with me. Please, if you're still listening, I really need your help one more time. I don't like who I am, and I hate Renita for making me who I am. God, I'm tired of drinking. I'm tired of having sex with strangers just to pay my bills. God, I want to do better, and I want to be a better person, but I can't do it by myself. Just then warm tears flowed uncontrollably down her cheeks. *I'm not perfect, but I'm sorry, and I know with your help, I can do better.* She used the back of her hands to wipe her tears and drove home in silence.

Chapter 23

India

Dealing with mixed emotions, India drove to Tracey's home in silence. She had just had a phenomenal lovemaking session with Reese and was headed to her ex-girlfriend's house to do what? Would she get the rest of her clothes or resolve their issues and possibly make up? Would her encounter with Reese be discussed, or would she keep it a secret forever? If she made up with Tracey, what would she tell Reese, after he'd admitted his love for her? After making love to a man, how did she really feel? Had the essence of his manhood within her secret chambers filled an empty void? Did she feel complete? Had she been drawn to Tracey two years ago because of the security she provided, or was she truly in love with her? Was her attraction to another woman real or a fascination? Could she handle the social pressures of being in a same-sex relationship? Could she handle the hard stares, the ostracism, and the criticism from those who deemed her lifestyle unethical? Like a stampede of raging bulls, those thoughts trampled her mind.

Before turning onto Tracey's street, she debated whether to call, then decided to take her chances and stop by unannounced. Her heart raced when she saw another car parked in the driveway, behind Tracey's SUV. It wasn't a band member's. She knew all of them and what types of cars they all drove. Plus, the tags were from out of state. She stopped at the end of the driveway and called Tracey's cell phone number. Tracey didn't answer, so she dialed her number again. Knowing Tracey was inside the house infuriated her as she listened to the phone ring on the other end. Again she called. Still no answer.

What's going on? Her first thought was to pull into the driveway, blocking both cars in, and knock on the front door until someone answered. But what good would that do? Tracey had asked her to leave, and she'd stopped by unannounced. Even that scenario wasn't calming, and she felt a huge lump form in her throat. Slowly, she swallowed, not knowing what to do. Finally, she drove off.

After two years, this is what I get? If nothing else, I deserve an explanation. I need closure. She owes me that. India drove around the corner, made a right onto Tracey's street, and sped up when she saw the car still parked in her driveway. She turned into the driveway, killed the ignition, and got out of the car. Her steps were long as she strode down the walkway and up the steps. Unsure what to expect, she knocked as hard as she could on the door.

"I'll get it, sweetie."

I'll get it, sweetie. India's heart pounded when she

heard another woman's voice on the other side of the door. Then she could feel her face turn red as her blood pressure started to rise. An exotic-looking woman with hazel brown eyes, scantily dressed in hot pants and a tank top, opened the door. She was of medium height, with a muscular build.

"Sweetie, do you know who this is?" the stranger asked Tracey when she entered the foyer. Tracey stood behind her, wearing pajama pants and a bra top.

"Damn, Tracey. How could you?" India asked, stunned by what she saw. She turned, ran to the car, and slammed the door. Seeing another woman open Tracey's door was the only confirmation she needed. It was more than obvious that Tracey had moved on mentally and physically. So why shouldn't she? Reese had confessed his love for her; now it was her turn to reciprocate.

"India. India." Barefoot, Tracey ran out of the house and down the steps.

India started the ignition, put the car into reverse, and peeled out of the driveway. She watched Tracey as she ran toward the car, waving her hands.

"India!" Tracey yelled as India pulled out into the street and drove away. "This is my half sister Essence," Tracey shouted, flailing her hands in the air.

Through the rearview mirror, all India could see were her lips moving.

"Well, good afternoon," Gail said, with a huge smile, when India entered the coffee shop.

"Hi, Gail."

"Where's that good-looking friend of yours?" As

if expecting Reese to enter any second, Gail looked through the door.

"He's at work." India looked toward their usual booth, which was empty, but decided to have a seat at the bar.

"That's too bad. One cup of black coffee?"

"That would be great."

Gail put a cup on the counter, then poured. "I'm so used to seeing the two of you in here together that you look funny by yourself."

Instead of responding, India lowered her head.

"Did I say something wrong? If so, I do apologize."

"No, you didn't say anything wrong. I have a lot on my mind, that's all," India said, regretting she hadn't sat in the booth on the other side. After her encounter with Tracey, she didn't feel like talking to anyone.

"Honey, I don't mean any harm, but you look like someone just stole your little red tricycle. I've never seen you look sad. You're always so bubbly and full of life."

"Well, I guess everyone's entitled to a bad day."

"Yeah, but even then, it's all in how you deal with it."

India looked up at Gail, who slaved over a hot grill day after day and barely made minimum wage. For a woman in her mid- to late forties, she looked good. Her pupils were bright, and the only signs of aging were the few wrinkles that had formed around her eyes.

"Young lady, the cup is either half empty or half full. I've always said my cup is half full." Gail looked at India, then laughed. "It's obvious that young fellow loves you to death. Honey, Ray Charles could have seen that."

India looked at Gail with wide eyes and wondered where her comment had come from.

"Do you know the best kind of love is when two friends fall in love? There ain't nothing like it." Gail smiled and her eyes sparkled as she walked to the cash register.

India looked at the booth where they'd shared so many good times, then laughed when she remembered one of his corny jokes.

"See there, that's what I'm talking about." Gail waved a finger at India, then refilled her cup with more coffee. "You don't have to say a word. It's written all over your face."

"And what would that be?" India asked, curious to hear Gail's response after she'd just seen another woman open her ex-girlfriend's door. If anything was written on her face, it was pain from a broken heart.

"Love. I ain't trying to get in your business, but you should see the way the two of you look when you're sitting in that booth together. If I were you, I'd embrace it. Real love comes only once in a lifetime, and when it does, it's up to you to run with it and never look back. Do you see this?" Gail stepped closer to India and turned over her identification badge. On the back was a picture of a very handsome man wearing a military uniform. "That's Thomas."

"Wow."

"He was my one true love. My soul mate. We met twenty years ago in this very coffee shop. This place has history, you know? At the time I was in college full-time and working here as a waitress on the weekends. He and some of his buddies were on leave for the weekend. They'd been out partying and came in for a few cups of coffee to sober up before driving back to the base. Even though he could barely walk through the door, it was like love at first sight. Watching them stumble toward that table still makes me laugh."

India looked as Gail pointed to a table on the other side.

"Please forgive me if I'm boring you."

"Gail, don't be silly."

"He flirted with me all night, then asked for my number before he left. I gave it to him, knowing he wouldn't remember anything the next day. Girl, was I wrong. He called me the next evening and wanted to know if I'd go out on a date with him the following weekend. After that we spent hours on the telephone and every free moment together. One year later we got married." India watched as Gail's smile turned into a frown. "Two years later I was a junior in college, and he got called away for duty overseas. He was supposed to come back in six months. Every day we wrote each other letters, until I got a phone call letting me know he'd been killed in the line of duty."

"Gail, I'm so sorry," India said, regretting her love story had such a sad ending.

"I lost it mentally and didn't have the strength to finish college. So I continued working in this coffee shop, praying one day he'd walk through those doors. So listen to one who knows. When real love comes your way, embrace it and treat every day like it's your last." Gail looked at India and patted her gently on top of her hands.

"How will I know it's real?" Torn between two scenarios, India frowned.

"Believe me, baby, you will know and will not have to ask anybody else."

Gail had to assist a party of four, and so India finished her cup of coffee. She paid her ticket and left a tip on the counter. Before exiting the coffee shop, she turned to look at the booth where she'd spent hours with Reese and smiled. *If it's real, I will not have to ask anybody else,* she affirmed silently as she walked to Tracey's car and got in. She turned the key in the ignition and ascribed it to fate when her favorite Chrisette Michele song "Golden" was playing on the radio. India sang as she drove out of the parking lot. Wanting some time alone to digest the events of her day, she drove to the nearest hotel and checked in.

With the words from the love song echoing in her ear, she entered the room, which was only large enough for a bed and dresser. She sat down on the edge of the full-size bed, then stared at her reflection in the dresser mirror. *If it's real, I will not have to ask anybody else,* she affirmed again, leaned back on the bed, and closed her eyes.

Chapter 24

Shiquanna

"Girlfriend, are you sure this is the right place?" Before turning into the small parking lot, Shiquanna looked at India, then frowned.

"Eighty-two-eighty-four Walker Road." India squinted to look at the worn gold foil stickers with faded black numbers above the front entrance. "This is the address she gave me when we talked."

"I'm not believing this shit. This has to be a mistake. I know Miss Thang wouldn't be caught dead in this place. It's an old house." Shiquanna laughed at the white wooden-framed house trimmed in black turned restaurant. On the front lawn was a white wooden sign that read EMMA'S COUNTRY KITCHEN, and it was leaning forward. The windows were covered from top to bottom with black security bars, and an air-conditioning unit extended from one in the rear.

"No, it's an old house that was converted into a

soul-food restaurant, and it's around the corner from her church." India pointed toward the white cross, which could be seen from one street over. "She claimed her pastor requested all members attend a special Bible study session tonight, and she didn't want to be late."

"Well, I'll be damned."

"By the way, we're invited." India laughed.

"This has gotten serious. I'm telling you there's something up with your girl. Ain't no way in hell Miss High-and-Mighty would be caught dead in a place like this." Shiquanna turned into the side yard, which had been paved for a parking lot. Their heads bobbed from side to side as Shiquanna drove across the uneven surface and pulled into the first empty spot. "This shit is going to mess up my damn front-end alignment," Shiquanna cursed when she put the car into park and looked around in disbelief. She'd parked between a black Mercedes-Benz and a Corvette. On the other end of the parking lot was a black Range Rover. "Do you see these cars?"

"Yes, they're very nice," India responded slowly, noticing how out of place the automobiles appeared.

"I can't imagine anyone driving these cars eating inside of this house."

"Maybe the inside has a different atmosphere."

"Ya think?"

"I'm only being optimistic."

"Well, let's go inside and see." Shiquanna turned to get her purse off the backseat, then opened her door gently, careful not to ding the car beside her. "Shit," she cursed when her shoe heel slipped into a small hole outside of her car. "If I break the heel on my Prada pumps, Yvonne is going to buy me a new pair of damn shoes. Hell, now that I'm looking for a real job, there's no telling when I'll be able to buy another pair of designer shoes." To evaluate the damage, she turned her foot to one side.

"It's only a pair of shoes," India commented once she'd gotten out and walked around to the driver's side to see what the fuss was about.

"No, little Miss Gandhi. It's only a pair of Prada pumps." Shiquanna removed her pumps, blew the dust off the heels, then reached behind the passenger's seat. India wasn't surprised when Shiquanna showed her hand and was holding another pair of shoes. "Comes with the job." Shiquanna looked at India, then laughed as she slipped them on.

"This is odd. I don't see Yvonne's car. She's always the first to arrive."

"Maybe that's her Range Rover. You don't believe me, but I think your girl has more secrets than the CIA."

India laughed as they both took their time walking across the broken pavement and up the front steps.

"Damn, somebody's cooking in here." Shiquanna opened the door and was overwhelmed by the scent of fried chicken and steaming collard greens.

"Welcome to Emma's," a heavyset lady holding a silver serving spoon shouted through a small window in the rear. Her chubby face was round, making her age hard to determine. "I've never seen you girls in here before."

"No, ma'am, this is our first time," India responded. About eight square tables covered with mix-and-match tablecloths, with four chairs each, filled the space. A black napkin holder, salt and pepper shakers, and a bottle of hot sauce stood in the center of each table. The interior was painted in a pale yellow, and a television, which no one seemed to be watching, hung from a back wall.

"I'm Emma, and everybody that eats in here calls me Big Mama." Her wide smile illuminated the room. "They say I got the best collard greens on this side of the mighty Mississippi River."

A tall and slender man, with his necktie thrown over his shoulder and a napkin over the front of his shirt, lifted his fork and nodded his head up and down.

"Sit down anywhere you like. My menus are on the table," Big Mama explained.

"Thank you, Big Mama," Shiquanna said, already loving the at-home atmosphere.

They looked around the room, didn't see Yvonne, and decided to sit at a table facing the door. Shiquanna crossed her legs and picked up one of the thin paper menus.

India reached for a menu but frowned when the scent of chicken grease made her nauseated. "I guess Yvonne will be here shortly."

"Where in the hell is she going with that big-ass Bible?" Shiquanna asked India when she looked out of the door and saw Yvonne walking up the steps.

India leaned forward, then shook her head from side to side. Yvonne was dressed like a nun, wearing a tailored black suit with a gold cross on the lapel. Like that of an elderly church mother, her purse dangled from her arm, and she had a Bible pressed against her chest.

"That bitch done lost her damn mind." Shiquanna stood, then looked at India. "I'm leaving. I've had a hard week trying to find a day job, and I'm not in the mood to listen to Miss Saved, Sanctified, and Filled with the Holy Ghost criticize me this evening."

"Well, I spent hours in the library and managed to work up an appetite. So I'm staying," India responded, not at all intimidated by Yvonne's Bible. She wasn't in the mood for Yvonne's holy antics, either. What Shiquanna didn't know was that she had been at odds with Tracey, had made love to Reese, then had gone back to make up with Tracey, and another female had answered the door. "Sit down," India said, motioning with her hand at Shiquanna as Yvonne entered the door and walked toward them.

"Hey, Yvonne." Holding a tray filled with steaming plates, Big Mama exited the kitchen.

"Hello, Big Mama. How have you been?" called Yvonne.

"Blessed by the grace of God." Carefully, Big Mama placed the plates on the table, then wiped her hands on the striped towel that hung out of her floral apron pocket. "Are those pretty little ladies your friends?"

"Yes," Yvonne said sourly, never looking at either of them as she pulled out a chair and sat down.

"You know I'm glad to have them. I'm going back to the kitchen, so let me know when you all are ready," said Big Mama.

"Yes, ma'am." Yvonne sat her Bible and purse on the chair beside her, and looked at India and then at Shiquanna. "Good evening." Her tone was dry.

"Hello," India said, then turned to look at Shiquanna, who stared at the menu.

"Humph. After inviting us here, I'm glad you decided to show up." Shiquanna never looked up.

"You pride yourself in being the first one to arrive every week. This is a first."

"I needed to spend some extra time meditating before I met the two of you for dinner. Your lifestyles have been so heavy on my heart, so I'm interceding in prayer on your behalf." Yvonne placed her hand on her heart.

"Heffa, please," Shiquanna spouted, then placed her menu on the table. "You need to be meditating and interceding for your damn self. How in the hell are you going to pray for me and your shit is messed up?"

"The two of you are my friends, and it saddens me to know if you don't repent and turn from your wicked ways, your souls will perish in hell," Yvonne replied.

"Guess what? We'll be right beside you. Plus, you don't know me like that. India is the only reason I deal with your crazy ass, anyway," snapped Shiquanna.

"No, I don't know you like that. But I do know that unless you repent, hell is waiting," Yvonne proclaimed.

"I'm in hell. For your damn information, I've been looking for a job. Were you praying for me when employers reminded me of a thing called no experience? Since you're praying, have you prayed about sharing that big list of contacts you're always bragging about? Hmmm?" Shiquanna sang. "Don't pray for me. Hook a sister up with a day job. If you want to save me from hell, that's what you need to do. Because if I don't find some work soon, I gotta take it back to the club, girlfriend." Shiquanna grinned mischievously, then rotated her hips in her seat.

"Oh, in the name of Jesus, touch this lost soul

right now, I pray." Yvonne lifted both hands into the air. "I'm always praying for the lost."

"The lost? Who in the hell is she calling the lost?" stormed Shiquanna.

"Are you ladies ready to order some of my fine collard greens?" Big Mama said after walking up behind Shiquanna and placing a hand on her back. Her tone of voice had obviously distracted some older patrons that were eating on the opposite side. Big Mama had hurried to intervene before their conversation got out of control.

"Yes, we're ready to order," India said, then rolled her eyes at Yvonne, who had managed to upset Shiquanna. Big Mama took their orders, then winked her eye at Shiquanna before turning to walk away.

"Where's Tracey?" Yvonne asked softly.

India shrugged. "At her house, I guess."

"I was hoping she would come," said Yvonne.

"What? You mean to tell me, you wouldn't have had a problem eating dinner with India's girlfriend?" Shiquanna said.

"Of course not. She, too, needs love, and after dinner I wanted all of you to follow me to church. After Bible study, we have prayer around the altar. The anointing of God is powerful, and I know each of you could be healed," Yvonne explained.

"Healed?" India blurted, then leaned forward when she saw Big Mama looking through the small window. "Of what?"

"Being in a relationship with another woman is immoral. In the beginning, God created a male and a female. He didn't create two males or two females," Yvonne replied.

"Healed of what?" India asked again as Big Mama returned and placed their hot food in front of them.

"Of your life of sin." As if she were revealing a deep, dark secret, Yvonne looked around, then leaned forward.

"My life of sin?" India looked at Yvonne, pointed at herself, then nodded her head up and down.

"Oh shit," Shiquanna said, knowing Yvonne was getting ready to be browbeaten by the religious scholar.

"Sin. Let's explore the topic," announced India.

Yvonne placed her hand on top of her Bible.

"Since you're so convinced that I am living a life of sin and will go to hell when I die, tell me what is it?" India challenged.

"Aww hell," Shiquanna said before lifting a fork full of collard greens to her mouth.

"Sin, my sister, is not obeying the will of God." As if she'd answered a bonus question on *Jeopardy!* Yvonne nodded her head.

"Oh, is it? So with that simple clarification, are you telling me that you haven't sinned today?" asked India.

"Like I've said before, everyone sins and has fallen short of the grace of God," replied Yvonne.

"Yvonne, answer my question. Have you sinned today? Yes or no?" India pressed her index finger against the table.

Yvonne clutched her Bible.

"What do you need that for? It's a simple question that can be answered with a yes or a no," India declared.

"I told you your girl is full of shit. Why do you

think she rushes out every week for Bible study? Maybe now you'll believe me," Shiquanna said to India, then turned to stare at Yvonne. "Yvonne, now I want to know. Have you sinned today?" Shiquanna asked, with a mischievous grin.

Yvonne stared at India. "Like I said before, everyone has sinned and fallen short of the glory of God. But I'm covered by the blood of His Son, Jesus Christ, who died . . ."

"So you mean to tell me your sin is different from my sin? Are you telling me that because you're saved, it's okay for you to sin? Are there good sins and bad sins? Are there little sins and big sins? That's the veil of illusion that traditional religion has put over your eyes. Honestly, I feel sorry for you if you believe you can do or say what you want and not be held accountable for your own actions. You can hide behind the blood of Jesus all you want to, but I believe that for every action, there is a reaction. Damaging a person's character with harsh words, rumors, and accusations is a sin. Judging our lifestyle is a sin. Turning up your saved and sanctified nose at a beggar is a sin. Thinking a lustful thought is a sin. Would you like for me to continue?" India asked, with wide eyes, anxious for Yvonne's reply.

"Big Mama, may I get some more tea please?" Yvonne asked when she walked by their table.

"You need more than some tea. If we're going to hell, I know for damn sure you're going to hell." Shiquanna looked at India, then laughed. "So drink up, girlfriend. I heard it's hot down there."

Big Mama returned with a pitcher of tea. "Baby, this is fresh." She refilled Yvonne's glass, and before she could sit the pitcher on the table, Yvonne had already drunk half. "Are you thirsty, baby?" Big Mama asked, with a smile.

"She's just hydrating herself. It's hot where she's going." Shiquanna fought to hold back her laugh.

"I'm saved by the blood of Jesus. I only pray that one day the two of you will see the light and give your lives to God." Yvonne turned up her glass and finished her tea.

"What you need is a good, hard dick." Shiquanna hit the small table with her hand, causing their plates to rattle.

"Shiquanna," India sang.

"Well, she does, and you know it. That's why she's always so damn irritable and judgmental," Shiquanna declared.

"I have a man, and his name is Jesus," Yvonne proclaimed.

"Whatever. You can only hide behind Jesus and the church for so long. When was the last time you even had some dick? I bet a hundred dollars, it's drier than the Sahara Desert down there," joked Shiquanna.

"Shiquanna, we're at the dinner table," India said, not at all surprised by her friend's candid comment.

"Satan, I rebuke you in the name of Jesus," Yvonne said, then swept her hand across her chest in the form of a cross. "Unlike you, I have morals and standards. I'm patient enough to wait on God to bless me with a man that will be mine and mine only. I don't want somebody else's husband or boyfriend."

"For your fucking information . . ." Shiquanna

rolled her neck in a circle and pointed her index finger at Yvonne.

"Right now I bind the enemy in Jesus' name." As if she were performing a séance, Yvonne opened her eyes wide and stared at Shiquanna. "Deconada oshata . . ."

"India, call the damn paramedics. This heffa is possessed. She's talking in another language." Shiquanna laughed, almost falling out of her chair.

"It's called speaking in tongues. It's prayer with power." Yvonne placed her hand on her chest and rocked back and forth in her seat.

"Girlfriend, whatever. It sounds like gibberish to me. Pray for me in a language I can understand. I want to hear what in the hell you're saying," Shiquanna retorted.

"Any word from your last job interview?" India asked Yvonne, wanting to change the topic of conversation before Yvonne fell out in the middle of the floor and started to foam at the mouth.

"No, they haven't contacted me." Yvonne rolled her eyes at Shiquanna, picked up a napkin, and began to fan herself. "In the meantime, I'm still volunteering at the church." She took a deep breath, then shook her head from side to side.

As if to say, "I told you so," Shiquanna looked at India.

"Are you still working on the same project at the church?" India asked, ignoring Shiquanna's facial expression.

"As a matter of fact, I am," replied Yvonne.

"Wow, so that means you're at the church how many hours a day?" Just when India asked the question, Yvonne opened her purse and pulled out her cell phone.

"Ladies, I hope you enjoyed Big Mama's cooking, but it's time for me to leave. It's not too late for the two of you to follow me to the house of the Lord. The invitation still stands." Yvonne waved Big Mama over and paid her ticket.

"I'll pass," India said, watching as Yvonne grabbed her purse and Bible, then stood.

"Please send up a prayer for the two of us." Shiquanna laughed as Yvonne hurried out the door and down the steps. "In English please."

"I know. That's my damn friend," India mimicked as Shiquanna looked at her and rolled her eyes.

Chapter 25

Yvonne

Before Yvonne drove out of the restaurant's parking lot, the transgressions of India and Shiquanna had become the least of her concerns. She was five minutes late and had already missed the opportunity for the reverend to see her stroll across the parking lot. Ignoring the speed limit sign, she zoomed down the street, then stopped before turning onto Hestler Street. "He's going to love the way I look tonight." She looked into the rearview mirror, then smoothed her eyebrows with a finger. Her eye shadow was still flawless, but her lips needed some fresh gloss. "Go to hell," Yvonne cursed when an anxious driver pulled up behind her and blew his horn. She lowered the window, then motioned with a wave of the hand for him to drive by. She forced a fake smile when she realized it was one of the deacons from the church.

"Jesus, please forgive me, because only you know

my heart," she prayed, then reached inside of her purse for her make-up bag. She unzipped it, then felt for her lip gloss. She applied the lip gloss, then blew a kiss to herself in the rearview mirror. When another car approached from the rear, she turned onto Hestler Street.

Not wanting to be another minute late, Yvonne drove into the parking lot and parked in the first available space. She killed the ignition, reached for her purse and Bible, then paused before getting out of the car. "This is for you, my love." With a smile, she unbuttoned the first three buttons on her jacket and spread the lapels. She looked down at her breasts and smiled, sure the reverend would be pleased. Almost trotting, she scurried across the parking lot, up the steps, and into the church.

"Sshh . . ." Yvonne frowned when the usher placed a finger over his mouth and closed the door to the sanctuary as she approached it.

"Excuse me?" she said, with an attitude, and tugged on the door. She looked through the small window, then tapped on it when she noticed the deacon hadn't started his prayer. Being seated and poised for the reverend's entrance was a must. The usher didn't give in to her anxiousness and held the door shut with both hands. Impatiently she waited. Several minutes later, when the usher relaxed his firm grip on the door, she jerked it open, then rolled her eyes as she walked by.

Oh, no, she doesn't have her yellow ass in my seat. Everybody, and I mean everybody, knows that is my damn seat, Yvonne thought as she recognized the new secretary from behind. *This heffa is in my seat.* Ignoring the usher's request to sit in another seat, Yvonne walked to the end of her usual row and stood. The new secretary crossed her legs, but never looked up. Yvonne pressed her Bible against her chest and cleared her throat. The new secretary looked up, uncrossed her legs, then turned them to one side for Yvonne to pass by. Refusing to sit anywhere else, Yvonne removed her purse from her shoulder and stepped into the row. With no notice, Yvonne sat down, forcing everyone to shift to the left.

"Jesus Christ," the secretary mumbled beneath her breath, then yanked the edge of her skirt from beneath Yvonne.

"Praise the Lord," Yvonne responded, then lifted her hand just when the reverend entered the sanctuary.

"Let all the people of God say amen," called Reverend Alston.

A chorus of amens, in particular Yvonne's, echoed through the sanctuary.

"I'm grateful to God this evening for your obedience." Reverend Alston smiled and allowed his eyes to scan the audience. "Because I have a special announcement to make, our Bible study will not be long." He opened the large Bible and began to thumb through the thin pages.

For the next hour, Yvonne watched intently as the reverend moved back and forth across the pulpit. She gazed at the way he unbuttoned his top button and loosened his necktie when he got warm. Then her thoughts ran wild when he eased a hand inside of his jacket and placed it on his chest as he pondered a thought. She closed her eyes and imagined it to be one of her firm breasts that he fondled.

"Sister Yvonne Miller." Reverend Alston stood behind the podium, then placed a hand on each side. "Please come to the front."

Shocked when he called her name, Yvonne stood. With a microphone in hand, he walked down three steps as she strolled to the front of the church. With an extended hand, he waited for her. Graciously, she placed a hand into his.

"The spirit of God has been dealing with me on this matter for some time. In obedience, all I could do was ask Him when and how," said Reverend Alston.

Anticipating his next words, Yvonne's hand started to tremble.

"The word of God says that man cannot live by bread alone. Before God and these witnesses, I want to confess my love," he declared.

Yvonne's heart pounded against her chest as she watched the reverend get down on one knee. He reached inside of his pocket, pulled out a red velvet box, and opened it. Behind her, she could hear the members ooh and aah as he removed a diamond ring.

"Will you marry me?" he asked.

"Yes, I will marry you. I want to spend the rest of my life with you." Like a madwoman, Yvonne stirred from her daydream, jumped up out of her seat, and ran toward the front of the church.

"Ushers please," Reverend Alston called from the pulpit as Yvonne ran down the aisle, with her arms outstretched.

"I love you, and I know you love me, too," cried Yvonne. A male usher had her by the arm for only a second before she pulled away and bolted toward the platform.

Immediately Evangelist Alston, Reverend Alston's wife of six years, heeded her husband's hand motion and joined him in the pulpit. She held his hand and shook her head from side to side. Women were disrespectful and flirted with her husband, but Yvonne's tantrum was a first.

"Let the people of God extend their hands toward the pulpit and start to pray." Arms were extended and prayers were murmured throughout the sanctuary. "In the name of Jesus, we bind this spirit of confusion," Reverend Alston began to pray as Yvonne fought with everything in her to reach him.

"In the mighty name of Jesus," Sister Alston echoed.

"No one loves you like me," Yvonne blurted as two men, one on each side, held her by the arms and lifted her. Her legs dangled as she kicked back and forth.

Against her will, she was escorted out a side door, down the steps, and to her car. One of the men opened her car door, and the other stood guard, making sure she got inside. Still in a state of delirium, she started the car, then stared at the church. She placed both hands on the steering wheel, then sped away.

Her thoughts raced, and her hands began to shake uncontrollably. She tightened her grip on the steering wheel and fought to hold back the tears that began to form. *Oh God, I just made a damn fool out of myself in front of the entire congregation. I've never been so embarrassed in all my life. I can never show my face in that place again. Yes, I knew he had a wife and children, but what single woman wouldn't fall in love with such a powerful man? He's every woman's dream, and no one man could fill his shoes. He's God-fearing, educated, financially stable, compassionate, and extremely sexy. Like no man I've ever dated, he made me feel special. In the crowded sanctuary, our eyes would lock, making everyone else's presence insignificant as he ministered only to me. With a smile, he'd shake my hand, then rub it gently. He created a physical desire that became unbearable. I wanted him so bad, it hurt. God, I knew if I prayed hard enough, you would give him to me.*

Now I feel like such a hypocrite, knowing I'm no different than my two girlfriends. India was right. A sin is a sin. How can I ever apologize to them for being such a horrible friend? She fought to see the road through the tears, which continued to fall.

Chapter 26

India

India and Shiquanna stayed at the restaurant for at least an hour after Yvonne left. First, they laughed at Yvonne's self-righteous attitude; then they caught up on things from the past week. Most importantly, India's shocking moment at Tracey's house and Shiquanna's tiring job hunt. India applauded Shiquanna's efforts, gave her interview tips, and shared a few job leads that were posted around campus. Just knowing Shiquanna was giving up dancing pleased India. Seeing Shiquanna in the emergency room, fighting for her life, had been disheartening. But she could only hope the experience was enough to change Shiquanna's perspective on life's value and make her see how quickly life could end. Their conversation continued about nothing in particular as they drove to Shiquanna's house. They bid each other farewell; then India drove to Reese's place in deep thought.

As she drove, she couldn't help but reflect on her relationship with Tracey. The first time they met. The first time they kissed. The first time they made love. She couldn't help but miss the way they'd cuddled in each other's arms at night. Tracey had seemed interested in her goals for higher education and had supported her wholeheartedly. For two years, the good had outweighed the bad. All Tracey had wanted from India was an open commitment. India wondered if she'd ruined a perfect relationship. Then she passed the street she'd normally taken to Tracey's house. At that moment her cloudy thoughts became clear. Real love would have weathered the storm. Tracey would have waited until their issues had been resolved. Instead, she'd found solace in another woman.

Wrinkles formed on India's forehead as her thoughts became more turbulent. Tracey was several years older than her. Had she really been taken advantage of by Tracey? Had Tracey really been looking for a charm bracelet? Had Tracey found someone young and pretty who could be used for bragging rights? Tracey knew the first time they met that India wasn't a lesbian. So why had she pursued her? Then it all became clearer. Tracey had known her every move. She'd known what time her classes started and what time they ended. She'd purchased India's cell phone and paid the bill monthly. On a few occasions she'd appeared on campus just to have lunch. Had India been mentally manipulated for the past two years without realizing it?

She wanted to turn around, go back to Tracey's, and reenact the scenario from earlier. Only this time the outcome would be different. India looked down at the speedometer when she saw a police car parked in the median. She was going fifteen miles over the speed limit. Fortunately, she hit her brakes just before he lifted his radar to clock her speed. She inhaled, then maintained a normal speed for the remainder of her drive.

As she turned onto Reese's street, she felt a warm sensation between her thighs. She was furious with Tracey and wasn't thinking about him. But he'd obviously made a physical impression, with effects beyond her control. To ease the feeling, which she'd welcomed earlier, she rubbed her right thigh. He'd given her one thing Tracey couldn't. Tracey's love could only be exhibited externally. They'd kissed, hugged, and rubbed, but Tracey never satisfied her the way a man did. She hadn't realized until that morning with Reese, how much she missed the intimacy that only a man could provide for her.

Here she was again, dealing with an all-too-familiar scenario: Man meets woman. Man falls in love, but woman doesn't know if she loves man. She turned into his driveway, then sat in the car a few moments before getting out. Just as India lifted her hand to ring Reese's doorbell, the front door opened.

"Sorry if I startled you. I heard your car when you pulled into the driveway." He stepped to one side as India entered. "Do you need help getting your things out of the car?" He glanced down at her empty hands, then looked out the door. The last time they'd spoken, she was on her way to get the rest of her things.

"I didn't get my things," she said sternly. Her cheeks were flushed.

"Okay? How was class?" he asked, thinking something must have gone terribly wrong if she didn't get her things.

"They went well." Really not wanting to go into any details about her day, she turned away from him.

"How was your girls' night out?" He sensed her bad mood and tried to stimulate a cheerful conversation.

"Interesting, as usual."

"India." He reached for her arm, then turned her around. "I love you."

India looked into his eyes, then closed hers. Again, he'd caught her off guard. "How can you love me? What is love? Give me a definition, and I'll tell you if you really love me or not."

"India, if I'm being too forward, let me know." Her response was totally out of character.

"Believe me, it's not you."

"I know you're staying here because you and your girlfriend broke up. In no way am I trying to take advantage of your vulnerability. However long it takes, I'm willing to wait."

"Wait?" she asked, then thought about her own situation. Tracey had proved no one was willing to wait forever.

"Yes, wait."

"For how long?" India asked, then felt a warm tear roll down her cheek. "I thought Tracey would wait, and look what happened. I went over to her house to talk, and another woman opened the front door, wearing hot pants and a tank top. For two years, Tracey waited. But she showed me no one is going to wait forever."

"I'm so sorry." Reese pulled her into him and held her. Then he rubbed the center of her back.

"Please don't." She shook her head from side to side, then pushed away from him. Wanting to feel her pain, he wouldn't let her break the embrace. With the back of her hand, she wiped a lonely tear. Realizing you couldn't keep anyone that didn't want to be kept, she gave in to his embrace. In silence they stood.

"Let me pour you a glass of wine." He held her face between his hands, then kissed her gently on the forehead. It was sweet. He went into the kitchen, and India sat down on the couch. For comfort, she embraced a large throw pillow. She smiled when he returned with two glasses of wine and a bowl of strawberries.

"I'm here if you want to talk," he said as he handed India a glass of wine, then sat down in a chair across from her. She took a sip, then held her glass with both hands. He drank but never took his eyes off of her.

Her heart ached from Tracey. Never in a million years had she thought their relationship would end the way it had. But it was over, and she had to let it go. She opened her mouth to speak but couldn't. How could she confide in a man who was in love with her about a woman she thought she loved? Instead of talking, she put her glass on the coffee table and walked to him. Wanting to be held, she sat on his lap and allowed him to wrap his arms around her waist.

"I love you," he whispered. His lips tickled her

ear making a chill go down the back of her neck. She could feel her nipples harden. "India, don't fight the inevitable," he said when she attempted to stand up. "Let me love you. Real love doesn't hurt. I know you've been in a relationship with a woman, and I face the possibility of you going back. But I love you enough to take that chance."

She thought about his words. She leaned her head on his shoulder, reached for his hand, and guided it underneath her shirt. The rest she left up to him, and he reached inside of her bra and held on to her breast. As if it were the first time he'd touched her, he began to rub slowly. To her, his touch was tender. She turned his face toward hers, then outlined his lips with a finger. The sensual gesture became an aggressive kiss. Unable to stand the ache between his legs, he lifted her into his arms and carried her. He covered her face with kisses as he walked into the bedroom, never stopping until he allowed her to stand. At the same time they undressed.

The room was dark, and the only light shone from the bathroom. From head to toe, India observed his lean but sculpted frame. His brown skin tone was even all over. Since he was nude, his desire for her was more than obvious. Now desperate for each other, they got into bed. India closed her eyes and allowed her body to relax beneath him. He didn't enter her immediately but held her in his arms. Wanting her to feel his manhood, he pressed himself against her. Her body became limp as she gave in to his embrace. Still holding her in his arms, he entered and made her feel like more than a woman. Their song and dance continued as they took turns leading each other into ecstasy.

Chapter 27

Shiquanna

"What the hell?" Shiquanna stopped at the end of her driveway to empty her bulging mailbox. She grabbed the thick bundle and, without looking, tossed it onto the passenger's seat. Everyone hoped for that million-dollar sweepstakes letter, but she knew it was only a stack of bills and useless coupons. With a look of disgust, she parked, then got out. Before unlocking the door, she paused. She was usually leaving home at this time, not going home. For her, normal wasn't normal at all. She used to work all night, then sleep all day. She entered her kitchen and was greeted by stillness. Her place was totally quiet. No one, not even a furry dog, was there to greet her at the door.

"Bill. Bill. Bill," Shiquanna said as she went through the stack of envelopes, smacking them each on the kitchen countertop. "Bill," she said, wanting to toss them all into the garbage can. If nothing else, her rent had been paid up for the next three months. Other than her utilities, everything, including her cell phone, would be a lucky draw until she found a job. Her clients were the only people who called. Just then her cell phone started to ring. Knowing exactly who it was she looked at her purse. All her high-paying clients had unique ring tones. As her phone continued to ring, she got a souvenir shot glass out of the cabinet and a bottle of tequila. No sooner than the phone stopped, it started to ring again. She poured herself a drink, then tossed it back. *Fuck me,* she thought when she looked at the huge stack of bills she'd strewn across her countertop. *This shit ain't gonna be easy.* She consoled herself by fixing another drink.

Again, her phone started to ring. She reached inside of her purse, grabbed her phone, then looked at the display. "Fuck me," she cursed aloud after seeing it was her favorite high-paying client. His name was Johnathon Anderson, and he played professional football. He was six feet tall, weighed 235 pounds, and had more girth than she'd ever seen. He paid her but provided the service. For hours, she'd lie limp as he would kiss her from head to toe, while paying special attention to her clitoris. Orgasm was an understatement for how he made her feel. Her body would tremble like she was having an epileptic seizure. Too bad he was married and had two children. His complaint was that his wife was an evangelist and didn't believe in oral sex. She poured a third shot, tossed it back, and firmly sat the glass on the countertop.

It wasn't often that he called, but she knew he wasn't going to stop calling until she answered.

And then he wouldn't take no for an answer. Like a crackhead, she held on to each side of her wig and paced the floor. She opened up a top cabinet and pulled down the small safe where she kept her stash. She counted, then counted again. There was only nine hundred dollars left. Disappointed, she replaced her stash and put the safe away. She for damn sure could use the money but knew if she did it one time, she'd do it again. Restless, she was looking at the stack of bills when her phone rang again.

"What's your pleasure?" she said sensuously.

"I'm in town for two nights, and Big Daddy really needs to be taken care of. Nobody strokes him like you."

She folded her arms and leaned against the counter. "Really, boo?" She crossed her legs at the ankles and pressed her thighs together. Just hearing his voice reminded her of their last encounter and made her tingle between the legs.

"Really. How soon can you get your fine ass to my hotel room?"

"Where are you staying?"

"I got a suite at the Hyatt. It has a Jacuzzi tub, and I've ordered a bottle of their finest champagne. All I need is your fine ass to top it off."

"I'll call you when I get to the lobby." She got the bottle of tequila off of the counter and went into her bedroom. She took a sip, put the bottle on her nightstand, then went into her closet. He loved her in red, so she looked for her most seductive red outfit. She tossed the outfit on the bed but was held captive by her reflection in the mirror. To fight another flashback, she covered her ears with her hands and shook her head from side to side.

"Hey, precious," her mother's boyfriend said after he opened her bedroom door and peeped inside of her room.

"Hi," Shiquanna said, never looking up from the novel. Reading mystery novels had become an outlet.

"What are you reading?" he asked calmly while taking another step.

"A novel." Shiquanna looked up. He had stepped inside of her room and was closing the door behind him.

"I have a present for you." He had one hand behind his back.

"No thank you," Shiquanna said, then moved farther back on her bed.

"Here. Take it." He stepped toward her and held out a red minidress.

"No thank you." Shiquanna's voice started to tremble as she feared what would happen next. He had a menacing grin, and his shiny shirt was unbuttoned to his navel.

"I picked it out myself."

Shiquanna looked into his eyes, which were bloodshot. It was obvious that he was drunk and high. "Appreciate it, but no thanks. Where's Renita?"

"I gave that bitch five hundred dollars and sent her to the mall."

Shiquanna looked around him at the door, which was closed but not locked. If he took another step toward her, she was going to run like hell.

"I've dated your mother for a while, and I think it's time for me to get to know you a little better."

Shiquanna threw the book down and jumped out of her bed. He held out one arm and stopped her dead in her tracks.

"I said I brought you a gift." He pushed her back down on the bed, then moved his jacket to one side, allowing her to see his gun.

"I'd rather die." Again, Shiquanna jumped off of the bed and bolted toward the door with everything in her. With his body, he blocked the door. In one move he ripped her cotton shirt.

"Put the goddamn dress on right fucking now." He grabbed her by the waist of her pants and pulled her toward him. Hearing Renita's voice, she wanted to cry but couldn't as he unbuttoned her pants and reached inside. In fear her body shivered. He grabbed the side of her face and forced her to kiss him.

Shiquanna pulled away and spat. All she could taste was liquor and smoke. She mumbled something, turning her head from side to side as he held her face again.

"What the fuck is going on?" Renita yelled after she pushed the door open with so much force, the painting on the wall vibrated.

"This little bitch tried to seduce me." He stepped away and pointed at Shiquanna, who was standing there, with her clothes torn. "I came to say hello, and she started to undress in front of me."

"Bitch, get the fuck out of my house. After all I've done for yo' ass, now you tryin' to take my motherfuckin' man!" Renita yelled without questioning him, then pointed toward the door.

"Renita, go to hell. I will not allow you to haunt my thoughts anymore." Like a madwoman, Shiquanna began yanking her clothes off the rack and tossing them in the middle of the floor. "For years I've allowed you to dominate my thoughts," she said, yanking an article of clothing off of a hanger between syllables. "This has to end, and I choose for it to end right now, dammit. There's no law that says I have to be a whore for the rest of my life. I'm not you, and I have never wanted to be like you."

She stormed into the kitchen, got a garbage bag, and went back into her bedroom. With a vengeance, she put all the clothes into the bag, took it outside, and tossed it into the garbage. With the same emotion, she went back inside and looked at her closet, which had nothing but empty hangers and the one outfit she used for her job interviews. She placed a hand on each hip and looked at the outfit with a new sense of pride. "Renita, you were right. I'm not crying anymore. Tonight is the first night of the rest of my life."

Chapter 28

India. Nine weeks later . . .

After Yvonne's last speech about salvation and redemption, no one got as much as a telephone call from her. Initially, India was bothered and decided her and Shiquanna's immorality was too much for the saved and sanctified Yvonne to handle. But after several weeks India decided they'd been friends far too long and it was time for Yvonne to get over her self-righteousness. So India decided on a date and time for their next girls' night out, then made the telephone calls.

"Hola. Cómo está usted?" The dark-haired waiter opened the door for India, then stood to one side as she entered.

"Hola, Jose," India responded, with a smile, not forgetting his lustful stares at Shiquanna.

"Welcome to El Reyes."

"Thank you."

"Will anyone else be joining you today?" he asked.

"Yes, I'll need a table for three." Both Shiquanna and Yvonne had called India when she was en route, letting her know they would be late.

"Would you like to be seated now or wait on your guests here?"

"I'm going to give them a few more minutes." India looked around the small lobby area, then sat down on a wooden bench against a wall.

"Let me know when you're ready." He smiled, then turned away to assist other guests.

"Hello, girlfriend."

"Shiquanna?" India responded, with a look of surprise, then jumped to her feet.

"Remember me?" Shiquanna stood back, then struck several poses for India.

"Oh my God, you look absolutely beautiful." India stepped back, then covered her mouth with both hands.

Shiquanna was wearing a conservative dark brown pantsuit with a cream blouse and brown pumps. Of course, the first two buttons on her blouse were undone, but even that was conservative. Instead of the large black purse, which India knew was filled with tequila shot bottles, Shiquanna carried a small brown clutch. Her natural hair, which India hadn't seen since high school, was cut in an asymmetrical bob. She was wearing make-up, but her palette was natural and complemented her large brown eyes.

"Where's your girl?" Shiquanna frowned, then

looked over her shoulder when she didn't see Yvonne in the lobby.

"She's running late." India smiled at Shiquanna's facial expression, thinking some things, like Shiquanna's dislike for Yvonne, would never change.

"What? Ms. Saved and Sanctified is running late? I bet a hundred dollars she's not going to be late for Bible study." Shiquanna turned up the corners of her mouth, shifted her weight from one foot to the other, then placed her clutch underneath her arm.

"Are you ladies still waiting?" Jose asked, then took a second look at Shiquanna. "Hola, my beautiful queen." He hugged her tight, then stepped back. "I haven't seen you in weeks for happy hour. Where have you been?"

"I've been very busy," Shiquanna said, then smiled at the real reason she hadn't been there.

"I've missed your beautiful face. Please don't stay away so long. Do you promise?" said Jose.

"I promise."

India laughed when Shiquanna arched her back to reveal more cleavage.

India and Shiquanna waited in the small lobby area. After thirty minutes they assumed Yvonne wasn't coming and requested a table.

"This isn't like Yvonne," India said once they were seated. She had a look of concern on her face, but Shiquanna picked up her menu, obviously ignoring India's comment. Yvonne not showing up at all would suit Shiquanna just fine. "I'm going to call her and make sure she's okay."

"What the hell?" Shiquanna spat, then pointed toward the front entrance as India reached into her bag to get her cell phone.

"Oh my God!" India's lips fell apart when she saw Yvonne standing at the front entrance. She was wearing a fringed blue jean miniskirt, a top with a sheer cleavage, and three-inch heels. Her hair, which had been cut, was maybe an inch long and spiked all over. Her make-up was flawless, and it looked like she'd lost at least ten pounds. India gasped at Yvonne's total transformation, which in no way said saved or sanctified.

"I know she's not going to Bible study looking like that," Shiquanna blurted.

India and Shiquanna watched as Yvonne flirted with the waiter, then strolled to their table. Even her walk was brand new, as her hips swung from side to side like a pendulum. Shiquanna laughed as India watched in awe.

"What's up, girlfriends?" Yvonne greeted, then sat down and crossed her legs as if everything were normal.

"You're what's up now, girlfriend." Shiquanna nodded her head up and down, thinking Yvonne did look fabulous. The outfit was out of Yvonne's character, but she wore it well.

"Cat got your tongue?" Yvonne asked India, who still looked like she'd seen a ghost. "Please close your mouth before a fly gets in it." She reached over and touched India's chin. "Have the two of you ordered yet? I'm starving." She arched her back, then looked over her shoulder.

"No, girl, we were waiting on you," said Shiquanna. As if the new and improved Yvonne was someone Shiquanna could relate to, she waved for the waiter.

"You ladies ready to order?" Jose asked flirtatiously,

this time never taking his eyes off of Yvonne's cleavage, which was all in view.

"Let me get a large margarita with an extra shot of tequila," Yvonne said confidently, then rubbed the waiter's arm.

"Will you be having your usual meal?" Jose asked her, with a smile.

"Yes, handsome, you know what I want." Yvonne eyed her two friends, as if to say, "What?" as Jose took their drink and meal orders.

Just then both Shiquanna's and India's lips fell apart.

Working in a strip club, Shiquanna had seen it all, but never in a million years had she expected such a change from Yvonne. "When did you start drinking?" Stunned, Shiquanna rubbed the back of her neck.

"Are you all right?" India asked, with a real look of concern. Yvonne's personality change was like the darkest part of the night and the brightest part of the day. She'd definitely become her polar opposite.

Yvonne nodded. "Girlfriend, I'm fine. I've been set free, that's all."

"Hell, you've been more than set free. What in the hell did you do? Go and rape a twenty-year-old?" Shiquanna asked, really wanting to know the answer. "Nine weeks ago you were a hell, fire, and brimstone–preaching sister who doomed the two of us to the pit of hell. You were a stick-in-the-mud who proposed not to drink, curse, or do anything immoral, for that matter."

Yvonne looked at Shiquanna, then smirked.

Shiquanna shook her head. "Aw, hell. *That's*

what it is. So you *did* take my advice. You've gotten some, and from the way you look, a lot of it."

"Shiquanna," India gasped, then turned her head sharply toward Yvonne. "Well, is it true? What in heaven's name has happened to you? It's only been a few weeks since we last saw you." Even when the waiter returned with their orders, India and Shiquanna never took their eyes off of Yvonne.

"Girl, believe me, it's a long story." Yvonne poured her extra tequila shot into her margarita, stirred, then took a gulp. "And, Shiquanna, for your information, he's twenty-eight years old."

"Damn, Stella," Shiquanna blurted.

"Oh my goodness. Do you think you need to slow it down a little?" India commented, still concerned that she'd never seen this side of Yvonne before. The Yvonne she knew would never drink anything stronger than a cola or have sex out of wedlock.

"Ha! We've got time this evening." Shiquanna folded her arms, placed them on the table, then leaned forward. "Come on, girlfriend. We're all ears for this one. First of all, where did you meet this twenty-eight-year-old stud?"

Before responding, Yvonne laughed. "We met at the gas station. He offered to pump my gas and the rest is—"

"Yeah, we can see the rest," Shiquanna said, then pointed at Yvonne's miniskirt.

"He's shown me another side to life. He's helped me understand that I've been taking it far too seriously," Yvonne confessed. "We've danced, taken walks in the park, and done things for no reason at all. He's so spontaneous, and I love it."

India's eyes widened, and Shiquanna shook her head from side to side.

"Girlfriends, he's taken me to another level." Yvonne rolled her eyes to the top of her head.

"What about church? Are you still attending?" India asked.

Yvonne took another sip of margarita. "Things have changed. I don't attend that church any-more."

Finally, Shiquanna gave India the infamous "I told you so" look as Yvonne entertained them with her past preacher's wife fantasy. She explained how she'd fallen in love with her married pastor. She stunned India with her late-night fantasies. She even told them how she'd made a damn fool out of herself during her last Bible study. With wide eyes, India listened, and Shiquanna interjected an occasional humph and rolled her eyes at India. Shiquanna was actually happy the real Yvonne had finally shown up for dinner.

"What's wrong, India?" Yvonne placed her hand on India's back when she started to look pale.

India placed a napkin over her nose, then shook her head from side to side.

Yvonne went on. "I'm sorry if what I said was too much for you to handle. Maintaining a facade was more important than anything. That's why I kept it bundled up inside. Believe it or not, I really value our friendship. I'm so sorry for all the hateful things I ever said to you and Shiquanna."

"No, it's not your real- life revelation," India said, then fanned herself with another napkin when she started to feel warm.

"What's wrong, India? Do you need me to drive

you home?" Shiquanna asked after looking at India's face, which seemed to be getting paler by the second.

"No, I'll be fine. It's the aroma from your meals," India admitted, then started to smile when no one noticed she hadn't touched her food.

"Wait one damn minute. Ms. Thang, you're smiling. Do you have a public confession?" asked Shiquanna.

Yvonne continued to rub the center of India's back, wondering how she could smile if she was ill. "Well, do you?"

"I'm pregnant." India looked at them both, then rubbed her stomach, which wasn't even a bulge.

"Pregnant," Yvonne and Shiquanna shouted in unison.

"Pregnant? How in the world did that happen? Is there a new technology I don't know anything about?" Yvonne asked, remembering that the last time they met, she was praying for India's deliverance from lesbianism.

"Ha! Yeah, it's a new technology all right, and I bet his name is Reese," Shiquanna interjected, then laughed.

"Reese? What happened to Tracey?" asked Yvonne.

"That's another long story." Still smiling, India shook her head from side to side.

"We haven't seen each other in weeks. Now I really need another margarita. You mean to tell me I'm going to be an aunt?" Yvonne waved her hand for the waiter, who scurried over.

"Yes, the two of you are going to be aunts. Reese and I found out yesterday. According to my last period, the doctor estimated I'm at least six weeks' pregnant, but I remember the night," India explained.

"You sneaky heffa. I can't believe you kept that from me." Shiquanna pointed a finger at India, then smiled. "Was it the night of our last dinner?" She leaned her head to one side and waited on a response.

"Was it?" Yvonne asked, wanting to hear more.

"That was the night. It was a long night, and one I'll never forget," India confessed.

For the next thirty minutes, Shiquanna and Yvonne were all ears as India shared her story. She described how she'd met Reese and the long hours they'd spent working together. She told them about his interest in her and how he'd respected her relationship with Tracey and remained a friend. She gave an account of the night her car wouldn't start and how he'd responded when her girlfriends were nowhere to be found. She even told Yvonne about her last encounter with Tracey.

"This is unbelievable. I'm going to be an aunt." Shiquanna looked shocked when she felt a warm tear roll down her cheek. Her first thought was to wipe it with a napkin, but she let it flow. That one tear was a sign of her freedom from the haunting voice of Renita.

"When do we get to meet your baby's daddy?" Yvonne asked, with a twist of her neck. She had already assumed her role as the overprotective aunt and planned to take it seriously. "Don't forget who I am and who I know. I can always make a few telephone calls. Do we need to check his credit or get a criminal background check? Even though I'm on hiatus from corporate America, I still have a few people that owe me huge favors."

"Again, his name is Reese, and he's not just going to be my baby's daddy," said India.

"What the hell? You mean to tell us there's more?" Shiquanna asked, still stunned India was even pregnant.

"We're talking about getting married in the spring. We've been friends for years. There's no doubt in either of our minds that we are madly in love. I have to admit I've never been happier." India laughed when she had to wipe a tear of her own. "Enough about me," she said, then waved a hand at Shiquanna. "Shiquanna, what's been going on in your world? From the looks of your outfit, things have changed for you, too."

"Yesss . . . some things have changed," Shiquanna sang. "I'm not dancing anymore. I'm taking classes at the junior college three nights a week and working at a law firm as a receptionist during the daytime. A lot has changed in the past few weeks."

"I don't mean to pry. Well, yes, I do. But I noticed you didn't order your usual margarita. The Shiquanna I remember used to drink the average man under the table." Yvonne laughed, then took another sip of her own margarita.

"Well, that is another part of my change. I joined a local AA group three weeks ago, and believe me, it hasn't been easy," Shiquanna confessed. "I've been attending meetings every day after work. Sometimes I attend twice a day. I made a shitload of money dancing. Having to budget to pay bills with a job that pays only slightly over minimum wage is very stressful. So don't think dancing hasn't crossed my mind. Not taking a shot of tequila to numb myself emotionally is difficult."

Without saying another word, both Yvonne and India reached out for Shiquanna's hand.

Shiquanna went on. "Yvonne, what you didn't know was that I was forced into prostitution by my mother at an early age. In order to deal with having sex with men ten or fifteen years older than me, I started drinking whatever I could find around the house. I didn't give a damn what it was as long as it made me high. Thank God I met India in high school. At one point she became my only saving grace. She was patient with me, never judged me, and helped me make it through high school." Remembering the hours they'd spent together, Shiquanna tightened her grip on India's hand as she spoke. No one seemed concerned about the time as Shiquanna continued to share the ups and downs of her childhood and early adult life. Before long all of them were wiping tears.

"Girlfriends, I'm sorry for having my head so far up my ass that I failed to be a real friend. From this point on, I promise, no matter what, to always be there for the two of you," Yvonne said through her tears.

"Girlfriends, I promise to attend my AA meetings, stay in school, and never look back on my past, which I thought was insurmountable. And I'm going to be the best damn auntie ever," said Shiquanna.

"Girlfriends, I thank the creator for this moment in time. He's allowed us to see that three women who thought they were totally different aren't so different at all. We've all endured hurts and pains that we managed, for one reason or another, to harbor inside. For years we've allowed each other to see only what we thought was our perfect self, not realizing it was our imperfections that made us unique."

"Best friends forever," Yvonne said as Shiquanna and India lifted their glasses. Together their glasses chimed sweetly as they made a toast.

ABOUT THE AUTHOR

Recha G. Peay debuted with *Mystery of a Woman.* Her other titles now include *Intimate Betrayal* and *Illusion of Love.* She currently resides on the outskirts of Memphis, Tennessee. When not dividing her time between her primary career and family, she is fulfilling her lifelong passion of writing. Her support system consists of a loving daughter and son. Please visit her Website, www.rechagpeay.com.